A Thousand Tiny Promises

What Reviewers Say About Morgan Lee Miller's Work

The Hues of Me and You

"*The Hues of Me and You* is an enjoyable second chance romance. Miller is known for them and those that like this type of trope will find that she easily nails their nuances. She understands the basics of a good second chance: She gets the main characters right."—*Women Using Words*

"This is a lovely easy to read romance. It's low on the anguish and high on the super cute sweet moments and it was just what I needed to kick off 2023! This book has a great storyline, a brilliant cast of characters, and enough of that sweet, lovely romance to keep you turning the page. I devoured it and loved it."—*Lesbian Review*

The Infinite Summer

"*The Infinite Summer* by Morgan Lee Miller brought back a lot of nostalgic memories of my own youth, especially that summer between high school and college…and that really fun summer after high school. I hope it does the same for you."—*Rainbow Reflections*

"There is something about Morgan Lee Miller's writing that gets me every time…but all in all, Miller delivered yet another enjoyable story that made nerd me happy."—*Hsinju Lit Log*

All the Paths to You

"This book made me, a self-proclaimed hater of sports, care about sports. Even sporting events that were purely fictional. That in and of itself is impressive. ...My god, Kennedy and Quinn are such a cute couple, I love them!! I ship them so much it isn't even funny. Their chemistry is through the roof to be honest."—*Day Dreaming and Book Reading*

"*All the Paths to You* is the kind of romance that makes your heart ache in all the right places."—*Hsinju's Lit Log*

"This book had a lot of feel-good moments and I still have a big smile on my face. ...This was the feel-good and even a little inspirational book that I needed right now."—*Lez Review Books*

"I can strongly say that this is one of my new favourite books (and series) and is definitely a contender for my favourite book of the year so far. ...I'm so happy I had the chance to read it and I don't think I could ever recommend it enough!"—*Althea is Reading*

All the Worlds Between Us

"This book is really sweet and wholesome and also heartbreaking and uplifting. ...I would recommend this book to anyone looking for a cute contemporary."—*Tomes of Our Lives*

"[*All the Worlds Between Us*] deals with friendship, family, sexuality, self-realization, accepting yourself, the harsh reality of high school and the difference between getting to tell your own story and having your own story exposed. Each character plays a vital role...and tells the story of this book perfectly."—*Little Shell's Bookshelf*

"If you're looking for an easy, quick cute f|f read, you should give this a try. ...This was a solid debut and I can't wait to see what else this author publishes in the future!"—*The Black Lit Queen*

"This book took me straight back to all of my gigantic teenage emotions and got right down to the heart of me. I'm not a swimmer and

I wasn't out in high school, but I swear I was right there with Quinn as she navigated her life as a competitive athlete and a queer kid in high school. Experiencing love and betrayal and triumph through her story was bananas. Morgan Lee Miller, you ripped my heart right out with this brilliant book."—Melisa McCarthy, Librarian, Brooklyn Public Library

"I'm always up for fun books about cute girlfriends, and *All the Worlds Between Us* was certainly that: a super cute ex-friends to lovers book about a swimming champion and her ex-best-friend turned girlfriend. ...*All the Worlds Between Us* is a great rom-com and definitely recommended for anyone who's a fan of romance." —*Crowing About Books*

"[*All the Worlds Between Us*] has all the typical drama and typical characters you'd find in high school. It's a tough, yet wonderful journey and transformation. The writing is divine. ...It's a complicated tale involving so much pain, fear, betrayal and humiliation. *All The Worlds Between Us* is a terrific tale of taking what you want."—*Amy's MM Romance Reviews*

"Morgan's novel reiterates the important fact which should be repeated over and over again that coming out should always be done on one's own terms, and how this isn't a thing that any other people, straight or queer, should decide."—*Beyond the Words*

"Finally, a sporty, tropey YA lesbian romance—I've honestly been dreaming about reading something like this for a very long time!" —*Day Dreaming and Book Reading*

Hammers, Strings, and Beautiful Things

"There's more going on than first appears and I was impressed that Ms. Miller won me over with a well written book that deals with some more serious issues."—*C-Spot Reviews*

"*Hammers, Strings, and Beautiful Things* is an emotionally raw read with plenty of drama. The journey Reagan and Blair share is rough in places but there is a beauty that you won't want to miss out on." —*Lesbian Review*

Before. After. Always.

"Miller tackled the tough subject of grief in *Before. After. Always*. It didn't feel too painful reading, but all the emotions were there." —*Hsinju's Lit Log*

By the Author

All the Worlds Between Us

Hammers, Strings, and Beautiful Things

All the Paths to You

Before. After. Always.

The Infinite Summer

The Hues of Me and You

The Memories of Marlie Rose

A Thousand Tiny Promises

A Thousand Tiny Promises

by

Morgan Lee Miller

2025

A THOUSAND TINY PROMISES

ISBN 13: 978-1-63679-630-7

This Trade Paperback Original Is Published By
Bold Strokes Books, Inc.
P.O. Box 249
Valley Falls, NY 12185

First Edition: July 2025

Credits
Editor: Barbara Ann Wright
Production Design: Susan Ramundo
Cover Design By Inkspiral Design

Acknowledgments

I started writing this story in April 2023, an idea I had in the back of my mind for several years. I was excited to finally start writing it and bring the idea to life. Little did I know, a few months into writing, I would lose three family members in four months, a kind of "method writing" I didn't expect, nor did I necessarily want. The idea of writing about grief suddenly became the reality of living *in* grief. The whiplash that followed slowed down my writing process so much, I had to keep asking for extensions. Then, a wave of inspiration finally hit me in May 2024, only to find out a month later that another family member had passed away, making it the fourth death in 11 months. I started to believe the world was playing a cruel joke on me as it was the "perfect time" to douse me with grief while writing about a group of friends navigating grief.

But, somehow, it was shortly after when the story finally formed and blossomed. I couldn't have done it without my amazing support system: Julie, Alex, Arielle, Ana, Kris, Krystina, Erica, Lauren, Kristen, and so many others who make up my found family. A special shout-out to my two fabulous beta readers, Arielle and Stacey, for their invaluable insight and feedback, and who threw me a special surprise party when I FINALLY turned in my manuscript, a celebration I never knew I needed. I will never forget that.

Always a huge thank you to Rad, Sandy, Barbara Ann Wright, and everyone at BSB, for being patient with me while I took my time writing this story so it could live up to its full potential. Having a team that supports not only my writing career but also my personal life makes me feel so incredibly lucky.

Lastly, to the readers, I wish I could personally thank every one of you for reading my books. Your support means the world to me. Thank you.

Dedication

The Muse

PROLOGUE

June 8, 2013—High school graduation night

"I have an idea," Sadie Russo announced with a bottle of Mike's Hard Lemonade in one hand. She hopped off her bed and snatched a journal from her desk drawer. Her long, straight, strawberry blond hair swayed with each step.

Reid Haley couldn't tell if the extra sway in Sadie's long locks was from excitement or her already half-consumed drink. For having a brother four years older than her who provided them Mike's more than once, Sadie didn't have any tolerance. It hit her quickly.

With the journal clutched in her hand, Sadie jumped back onto her bed and opened it to a blank page. "Once we start college, the only time we'll get with each other is Christmas and summer breaks, right? What if we made a bucket list? That way, we can make the most of our limited time together, and then after college, we have a reason to come back to each other."

"Of course we're going to come back to each other. Why wouldn't we?" Emma Lin said. She tucked a strand of her straight black hair behind her ear while nursing her Mike's like it was twelve ounces of Everclear. For someone whose parents owned a winery in Temecula Valley and who grew up on a literal vineyard, Emma didn't know how to appreciate any alcoholic beverage without grapes in it. Reid had no idea how Emma was going to survive her twenty-first birthday…unless she had it at Magnolia Springs Winery with her beloved fruit: the grape.

"We just said how we were worried that college would pull us apart," Sadie said. "We're all leaving home. Hell, Audrey is going to be living abroad."

"Sadie, I'll be in Ohio," Audrey McCann said.

"It's practically the same thing."

"The Midwest is a world away from us," Reid agreed. "You're going back to your homeland. Those cornfields will get you."

"Guys, not all of Ohio is cornfields. I mean, most of it, yes, but not where I'm from. I'm from suburbia. And Reid, you've never been east of Denver. How would you know?" Audrey said teasingly.

This was true. But she had *seen* east of Denver from the airport and had gotten a little peek of the flat, barren lands. They apparently stretched for miles until the Mississippi River.

"Why go east of Denver when everything you need is on the West Coast? Mountains, palm trees, wineries, and most importantly, the ocean."

"They're not going to get me," Audrey continued. "My dad is here, you guys are here, and like Reid said, the mountains and vineyards are here."

"I'm sure you'll find a nice boy at Ohio State," Reid said. "Then you'll graduate and will stay there with him to have that gross white picket fence life in Middle America."

"Is that what you think?" Audrey said through a laugh. "Do I scream traditional, domesticated wife?"

"Just a little," Reid said, holding up an invisible inch.

Audrey rolled her eyes and slugged Reid's arm.

"Yeah, I'm with Reid on this one," Sadie said. "You'll stay to have that 'marry your college sweetheart, three kids within five years, living in the burbs with a golden retriever' kind of life."

"Sadie, *you* want that life," Audrey said.

"I know. But I'm from California. It's less gross when you have Southern California wineries in your backyard."

"Okay, I do see your point," Audrey said. "I promise, I'm coming back, guys. Every school break and then after graduation, I'll be back here for Christmas and summer, and you'll be stuck with me."

Sadie, Reid, and Emma exchanged a look. Reid didn't actually think Audrey wanted all of that, but if she did, it didn't matter. All Reid cared about was if her friends were truly happy. Throughout their four-year friendship, she, Emma, and Sadie—who were all born and raised in Temecula, California—liked teasing Audrey about the fact that she was from Ohio. In their defense, Audrey had started it by constantly making fun of the fact that she had been born in the boring, east Cleveland suburbs. She was the queen of Midwestern jokes. The rest of them just went along with it.

"This is why we should make a bucket list," Sadie said. "A little contract of promises, and we can scratch some off when we're home during the summers and after we graduate."

"I like that idea," Emma said.

"Me too," Audrey said.

"Okay." Reid hesitated. "If we do this, we need to make it realistic. It can't just be a list of ambitious ideas like telling the rest of our classmates we will stay in touch after graduation. We know full well that's not going to happen. Or that Route 66 road trip we've been talking about since sophomore year—"

"Route 66 isn't an ambitious idea," Sadie said. "We just need money…and to be old enough to rent a car. But that's a great idea. I'm adding that to the list." She scribbled it down.

Reid knew Sadie meant business when she clicked her favorite purple gel pen and wrote *ERAS Bucket List* on the header of the lined paper. ERAS was the name of their group text chat, all four of their initials. If she had a dollar for every hallway note covered in purple ink she'd gotten from Sadie throughout middle and high school, she would have had enough to pay her college tuition. Sadie always wrote her juiciest notes in purple ink.

"Now let's start thinking," Sadie said, tapping the end of the pen against her cheek. "Once it's on the paper, it's set in stone."

"You certainly mean business," Reid said. "You *are* using a purple pen." She paused and thought about what they could possibly put on the list. "I think we need a blood oath. Really commit to this list since I have doubts that we will actually finish it."

"Oh, we're going to finish it," Sadie said, her tone firm and adamant. "I'm serious."

"I'm serious too," Emma said.

"Me three," Audrey added.

Everyone looked at Reid. "Hey, I just suggested a blood oath. Once there's been a blood oath, you can't go back."

Emma gave her a look of mild disgust. "Maybe something slightly more sanitary."

"I'm thinking more like matching tattoos, Ems. And it can be a nice reminder of all of us when we're apart at school."

"Before I officially add anything to the list, we all have to consent," Sadie said. "If we agree and think we can actually do it, I'll mark it in stone." She wiggled her pen. "Tattoos scare me, but I'd get one with the four of you. Do we all consent?"

The other three went around in agreement, one item on the list. Audrey said they needed to set some ground rules. *Leave it to Audrey being her usual rule-following self.* It was no wonder why she was going to Ohio State for education. Teachers were always the rule followers.

The rules were pretty simple. They all had to agree. Since Sadie was anal about certain things like even numbers, they were going to have eighteen things on the list.

"While you guys think, I have another one," Sadie said. "Remember the fireflies I talk about, like, every summer?"

"Of course," Reid said.

When they were still alive, Sadie's grandparents lived in the Great Smoky Mountains, and the Russos had visited them every summer. Sadie had stopped going by the time she and Reid met in sixth grade, but that hadn't stopped Sadie from talking about the fireflies. Apparently, in the Smoky Mountains, there were synchronous fireflies, a specific species that glowed at the same time. Sadie had always described them as being magical, as if she was in an enchanted forest, and how she wished California had more fireflies.

Reid had never really understood how a bug could be magical. She hated bugs, loathed them, and that included the ones other people thought were cute like ladybugs, bumblebees, or caterpillars. She also wouldn't ever be caught in a butterfly house. If it had more than four legs, she got the instant ick.

But this mattered a lot to Sadie, so of course, Reid and the rest of the group agreed to add seeing the synchronous fireflies to their bucket list.

For the next hour, they sipped Mike's and rattled off a bunch of ideas. By midnight, the bucket list was set in stone by the touch of Sadie's purple pen.

Sadie held out the list like it was her life's masterpiece. "She's all grown-up now." She laid the piece of paper in the middle of the bed so they could sit around and admire what they spent the whole night working on:

The ERAS Bucket List
Route 66 road trip
Get matching tattoos
See synchronous fireflies in the Smoky Mountains
Make a time capsule and open together as adults
Go to a music festival
Skinny dip!
Go camping the real way…in actual tents
Volunteer at an animal shelter
Napa Valley wine tasting
Vegas, baby!
Go to a spa resort
See Disneyland at Christmas
Have dinner at a Michelin Star restaurant
Finally ride in a hot-air balloon over Temecula like the tourists
Fly first class
Celebrate someone's twenty-first birthday at Magnolia Springs
Stay in a log cabin
Go scuba diving

"You know what would be a cool idea?" Emma said. "If we make the time capsule this summer. That way, fifteen or twenty years from now when we open it, we can think back on the night we created the list and the memories of our summer before college."

"This is why you just graduated in the top ten percent of the class and are going to Berkeley," Sadie said. "Genius idea."

"It's a good thing you're trying to make disposable cameras happen again," Reid said, hopping off the bed to Sadie's dresser where she knew her disposable camera sat. She'd been carrying it round all day, snapping pictures at every opportunity. She checked how many photos they had remaining. "We have six pictures left."

"We can take pictures of us with the list," Sadie said and held the piece of paper up to her face and smiled. Reid snapped a picture.

"That's a waste of a picture," Emma said. "Audrey and I weren't even ready."

"Then hush and pose," Reid said.

When the three of them smiled, she pressed the button. "I would show you how it looks but…again, Sadie's trying to bring Kodak back so we won't know how great the picture is until she gets it developed the old-fashioned way."

"Oh, shut up. Disposable cameras are cool," Sadie said, rolling her sapphire blue eyes. "Now let's save the other four pictures."

"We should take one of us getting our tattoos," Audrey said.

And that was exactly what they did. Two days later, they brought the disposable camera to the tattoo parlor and asked the artist to take a picture of them with their new ink: four overlapping triangles in a line on their inner wrists. Each of them had a different triangle filled in with black ink. Emma got the first filled in, Reid the second, Audrey the third, and Sadie the last to match the sequence of their ERAS acronym.

The promise to complete the list was sealed then and there.

CHAPTER ONE

Eleven years later

Audrey had never expected that the first time her childhood friend group reunited after six, long years would be at one of their funerals.

She stared at the TV, watching what seemed to be an infinite amount of pictures of Sadie Russo's life scrolling by. There were pictures she'd never seen before from Sadie's childhood, awkward preteen years, and even some of her as an adult. Her English rose beauty was evident in each image.

Watching each picture swiping across the funeral home's TV, accompanied by somber instrumental music, made it feel even more real that Sadie was gone. It felt way too familiar. Fifteen years ago, she had been sitting in what felt like the same scenario but at her mother's funeral. As the memories surfaced, reality struck searing pain into her chest.

No matter how many times she tried to blink—or how hard—she couldn't get herself out of this world that didn't have Sadie.

A picture of the four of them appeared on the TV. They had to have been on a break from college, their arms slung around each other with the rolling vineyards of the Lins' winery in the background. Her stomach bottomed out as she took in the memory that seemed like eight lifetimes ago. Back when the fearsome foursome were all together and before life severed their friend group.

She had no control over her eyes leaking continuously. She couldn't keep watching. She peeled her stare off the TV and looked at the front of the room where several large bouquets of flowers stood next to a blown-up picture of Sadie with her beloved a black-and-white border collie mix, Charlie. Audrey smiled at the memory of meeting Charlie when the four of them had volunteered at the animal shelter. For Sadie, it had been love at first poop scoop.

Right in front of the collection of flowers was a small, mahogany box with *Sadie Russo-Barnes* engraved on a gold plaque with a gold paw on top of the box. Audrey figured it was because Sadie had become a vet, started her own practice with her husband, Jeremy, and had always been a loud and proud animal lover all of her life.

Just then, Audrey felt a warm hand on her shoulder. She looked over and found Emma blotting her eyes with a tissue. She handed Audrey one too.

"It's so unfair," Emma said through her sniffles. Her boyfriend, Matt, stood next to her and flashed Audrey a smile that didn't reach his eyes.

"I know." Audrey said and dabbed the tears from her face.

"No, I mean, that's unfair," she continued and pointed to the mahogany box. "Sadie told me a few weeks ago that she was going to be put into a dog urn to save money…she said human urns were too much. She thought it would be hysterical to be put in a paw box, and she actually really did it. She's in a paw box."

Audrey blinked back the eye roll. That was Sadie, always finding a way to slip in a joke no matter how serious the subject. Her terminal acute myelogenous leukemia cancer diagnosis had brought out her dark humor even more. Therapist Emma had reassured Audrey it was Sadie's coping skill and that they should just laugh along with her.

"At least she got what she wanted," Audrey said, trying to channel Sadie's dark humor. She knew that if there was an afterlife and Sadie was actually with them at that moment, she would have been so proud.

Emma let out a small laugh and blotted her eyes. "I'm so glad she dreamed big."

Audrey heard the sadness saturating her voice, as if leaning into Sadie's dark humor was too painful for her.

"What are the chances we're stuck in an awful nightmare?" Emma said.

The question hit Audrey in the stomach. This was Emma's first major loss, and Audrey resented life for putting her in the position to "mentor" Emma through the battle that was grief. She wished she didn't have experience in that department, and she wished she didn't have to be the bearer of bad news: the feeling like they were stuck in a nightmare was going to last for a while.

"I've already pinched my arm about ten times, and I can't seem to wake up," Audrey said.

Emma buzzed her lips as she blew out a heavy breath. "I guess we should sit."

When they turned and took in the funeral home, Audrey spotted Emma's parents talking to Audrey's dad. Sadie's parents and her older brother Bryan spoke to Reid's parents and her younger brother, Cameron. Audrey was pretty shocked to see Mr. And Mrs. Haley standing next to each other after their terrible divorce ten years ago when they were all in college. Audrey hadn't spoken to Reid in six years, so she assumed that her parents were either holding in their disdain for one another or they'd somehow mended things. She highly doubted that.

Her heart sank when she saw Reid's brother Cameron wipe his face with a tissue. His eyes were swollen and red. She wished she could go up to him and hug him. Sadie Russo had been his biggest crush ever since meeting her during his freshman year of high school.

She continued looking around. Everyone was accounted for. Except for Reid. "Where's Reid?" she said as she and Emma took an empty seat in the third row.

Emma and Matt scanned the room. "Is she not here?" Emma said.

"Her entire family is here, but it doesn't look like she is. I would have definitely noticed."

"She'll be here."

"She has to be," Matt said.

"You're underestimating the power of Reid time," Audrey said, crossing her arms.

Soon, everyone made their way to their seats. The Russos forced out friendly smiles to Audrey and Emma as they walked to the front row. The Lins took a seat on the other side of Emma and Matt, Audrey's dad sitting right next to her. The Haleys sat behind them, and Mrs. Haley handed Cameron a fresh batch of tissues.

But still, no Reid. Apparently, nothing had changed in the last six years.

It was their best friend's funeral, and still, Reid couldn't show up on time. Audrey added it to the list of the many times Reid had let her down. It was like the time she had bailed early on Audrey's twenty-first birthday to hang out with some girl and how she'd spent their summers in college more interested in her flings than her best friends. Reid Haley was always on her own time, and quite literally, nothing could sync her up to actual Earth time.

That answered the question Audrey had always asked herself: would Reid pull that shit at one of their funerals? She finally got her answer, and as it settled in her, she fought to tame the anger that mixed with immense grief and sadness.

The funeral director stepped on the podium and said that while he'd only known Sadie for a short amount of time, he could easily see how funny and kind she was. Audrey tuned it out. She hated this part of a funeral where the director tried to talk about the dead as if they knew them. It was something that had bothered her when she'd had to sit through some empty spiel at her mother's funeral, and now she had to hear it again at her best friend's.

Luckily, the director didn't say much. Instead, he said others who knew Sadie much better should come to the front and share a few words.

Sadie's college sweetheart and husband, Jeremy, stood and went to the podium. His dark eyes were red, and it tore through Audrey. One of the many things she loved about Jeremy Barnes was that he was a sensitive soul and not afraid to show his emotions, which complemented Sadie because she was all jokes, keeping everyone happy and entertained, and very rarely showed any negative emotion. However, ever since being with Jeremy, Sadie had seemed a little more comfortable showing others the emotions she'd previously buried.

"First, I want to thank you all for being here," Jeremy said. The shake in his voice caused Audrey's eyes to well up again. "We're all here because you meant something really special to my wife, Sadie. She didn't want a funeral at first. She said they were 'too depressing,' and we all know Sadie wanted to laugh as much as possible. She finally decided on having a very small private service for her family and closest friends. So all of you are here because you meant so much to her…and me." He cleared his throat. "Sadie did a lot of writing during chemo. She wrote so many letters, and she wrote one she wanted me to read to you all today. We all know Sadie had a unique sense of humor, and this letter I'm about to read is filled with it, so just be prepared."

There were a few knowing chuckles while others continued to wipe their eyes. Audrey and Emma exchanged a glance. Audrey wanted to know if Emma knew anything about all these supposed letters, but Emma's confused expression told her everything she needed to know.

Jeremy unfolded the piece of paper, exhaled a breath, and read the letter out loud:

To all my family and my closest friends,

I'm really sorry I died. I totally didn't mean to. Is there anyone mad at me? No? Yes?—insert a dramatic pause here, Jeremy—I would say I'm open to feedback but…I hightailed it out of there to avoid any accountability. Sorry.

I hope you don't focus on the sadness. I really hate it when people are sad. It makes me uncomfortable. You know how uncomfortable you get at those damn ASPCA Sarah McLachlan commercials? That's how I feel when I see one of you sad.

Instead of focusing on my very sad outro to life, PLEASE—note to Jeremy to emphasize that the "please" is in all caps—focus on all the good. I had so many good things in my life that overshadow how awful and unfair my AML diagnosis was. You're not convinced yet? Okay, let me try to sway you:

1. I got married to my college sweetheart. Jeremy Barnes is the reason why I never had to go through the turbulent world of dating, and for that, I'm forever grateful. He's been my best friend since we were nineteen, we eloped in paradise, and we built an amazing life together. I've never felt as loved as I did in my last ten years of life. Thank you, Jeremy, for loving me the way that you did.

2. I had my dream job. I wanted to be a vet since I was a kid, and somehow, I got so lucky that my soulmate and my best friend also had the same dream as me. We opened our own veterinary clinic, and I got to pet all the dogs and cats every single day. I had the best coworkers who were just as passionate as Jeremy and I were. Going to work every single day brought me so much joy. How many people can say that?

3. My other best friend and my son, Charlie. He's my soul dog.

4. My childhood best friends: Emma, Reid, and Audrey. We've been best friends since we were fourteen, and Reid and I have been best friends since we were eleven. I know just how lucky I am that we grew up together and that you all are still in my life.

5. My family. My parents, my brother, who married an amazing woman and finally gave me the sister I always wanted.

So to say my heart is absolutely full is an understatement.

There's a part of me that feels grateful for the limited time I had on Earth because it forced me to make the rest of the time I had left mean something. We can't control what happens to us, but we can control how we live. Of course, getting an aggressive cancer wasn't on my bingo card, and as devastating as that news was, I chose not to mourn the life I was losing but instead chose to celebrate the moments I had left, and honestly, the last ten weeks have been some of my most rewarding days.

Thank you for bringing so much happiness and love into my life. I hope you all know that I do know how loved I was. The feeling of your love never wavered. In fact, I felt it getting stronger even as I was getting weaker, and I hope you know that I loved all of you just as much.

Now go out there and enjoy your life. And please, enjoy all of life's little moments. I want you all to smile and remember all the wonderful memories we shared. I promise you I'm thinking about those memories as I write this.

Love you all,
Sadie

By the time he folded up the paper, there wasn't a dry eye in the room. Audrey had no idea how Jeremy had gotten through that letter, especially the part where Sadie had gushed about him.

He quickly ran a finger under his eye. "So we will do exactly that today," he said through a rattling voice. "We're going to share all those wonderful Sadie stories, and we're going to laugh a lot because crying made Sadie uncomfortable, hence this letter. She worded it so much better than what I can say right now. Just…thank you all for loving her and making her feel it until the very end. Because of that, I'm forever grateful to each and every one of you. She was an incredible human, and I'm going to miss her terribly. I already do. She was my best friend, my soulmate, and being her husband was the biggest honor of my life."

By the time the service ended, the laughter that filled the room when others came to the podium and shared their Sadie stories died down and turned back into a heavy silence. Audrey's dad squeezed her wrist as the music started playing to Sadie's slideshow. Even though she had already watched it before the service, she knew that with the stories of her best friend fresh in her mind, she was going to absolutely lose it. Her dad wrapped his arm around her shoulders and held her as the slideshow showcased Sadie's entire life.

When it ended, all the emotions she'd tried swallowing collected in a brick in her throat. Everyone stood, and she scanned the room yet again for Reid.

Nowhere in the room was the familiar head of wavy, sandy blond hair.

This was the new normal now, Audrey thought. Their fearsome foursome was barely a threesome. More like two different couples. Reid and Emma, and Audrey and Emma.

For the last six years, she'd thought it was ironic how all four of them had matching friend tattoos. The "blood oath" they'd made back when they were eighteen wasn't as permanent as the triangles on the inside of their wrists.

Now that the funeral was over, her anger simmered. Anger from losing Sadie, anger for going through the grieving process all over again before she turned thirty, anger that she and Reid hadn't patched things up in time for Sadie, and anger over Reid not showing up when she needed to.

She honestly couldn't believe it.

But somehow, she wasn't surprised. She'd stopped being surprised six years ago.

Jeremy found them in the crowd and waved the three of them over.

"You did a really great job," Emma said, giving him a tight hug.

"Thank you. I just read her letter. The rest was all Sadie."

Matt and Jeremy shared a hug before Jeremy embraced Audrey. She closed her eyes, feeling the immense sadness emanating from him. She could tell by his long expression and the bags under his eyes that he was exhausted. Planning a funeral was exhausting, especially when you were so depressed and lost that getting out of bed seemed impossible. The funeral itself was a whole other feat, trying to get through the service without falling into a millions pieces in front of everyone.

"You know that we're here for you. Seriously," Emma said. "You have our numbers. We aren't going anywhere."

He offered a half-smile. "I know, and I appreciate that so much. I might hold you to it."

"Might?" Audrey said. "You better."

"I have something for you." He reached into his suit pocket, pulled out an envelope, and handed it to Emma. As she observed it, Audrey caught, *Emma, Reid, and Audrey* in Sadie's handwriting, and for a moment, she felt Sadie again. A simple piece of paper was now the closest thing she had to her best friend.

"What is it?" Emma said.

"If I tell you what all this is, it defeats the purpose," Jeremy said.

"The purpose of what?"

"It's something Sadie's been working on. I wasn't joking when I said she wrote a bunch of letters during chemo. She said she was working on some big project and didn't tell me what it was until it was finished."

"So there are more of these?" Audrey said.

"There are a lot more. I have the rest of them at home."

"Why are they at home?" Emma said.

He put up his hands in surrender. "I was given very explicit instructions from Sadie, and she said if I didn't follow her instructions to a T, she'd, quote, 'haunt the shit out of me,' and I was a little bit terrified by her enthusiasm."

Audrey felt the smallest smile form. "I don't know if there's an afterlife," she said, "but if anyone is capable of haunting us, it's Sadie."

Jeremy let out a chuckle. "I'm with you on that, which is why I'm not saying anything. Trust me, everything is in that letter. It's addressed to the three of you, so you should sit down together and read it."

"Easier said than done when Reid is nowhere to be found," Audrey scolded.

"She was here," he said. "She stood in the back the entire time."

"What? Reid was here?" Emma said.

"You didn't see her? Once it ended, she ran out. She looked pretty distraught."

Audrey was a little relieved that Reid had at least showed up, but the fact that she'd walked in late and bolted right when it was done dug up the resentment that she'd thought she had buried long ago.

"You three really meant a lot to Sadie," Jeremy said. "You were her chosen family. All I can say is that she worked really hard on this, and it shows just how much the three of you meant to her."

Emma placed a comforting hand on his shoulder. "She meant the world to us too."

"I know she did." He blew out a heavy exhale. "All right, I need to go mingle with everyone. Please read the letter together. I know that's easier said than done given everything that's happened but…I know that's what Sadie wanted, and given what's in the letter, it's important that the three of you do it together. Anyway, don't hesitate to reach out. You're my family too, you know."

"I'm just a text away, man," Matt said. "If you need to escape, just let me know. We can always watch baseball on the projector outside anytime you want. Dodgers home game next weekend if you're feeling it."

Jeremy smiled. "I might hold you to that, bud."

He said his good-byes and joined in a conversation with Sadie's parents.

"I'll hunt Reid down," Emma said, pulling her phone out of her purse. "And if she doesn't pick up, I'll talk to her parents. I don't see Cameron either. She might be with him."

"We shouldn't have to hunt her down," Audrey said after an eye roll.

"Yeah, well, that's Reid, isn't it?"

Reid had always been flighty, even in high school, but there was an excuse for being a flighty teenager. Being twenty-nine and still flighty? That was just never growing out of bad behavior.

Audrey was glad that it wasn't her problem to deal with anymore. "Are we just going to excuse her behavior?" she said.

"What is there to do? Lecture her right after her best friend's funeral?"

"Uh, a nice lecture, yeah."

Emma shook her head. "No. But I am going to use my stern voice and get her to meet us."

Audrey's pulse quickened. "Oh, we're reading this now?"

"Don't you want to? This is the last thing we have from Sadie. We can all grab a beer." When Audrey gave her a look, Emma said, "It's *one* beer. We'll be in and out in an hour." She held the phone up to her ear. Audrey heard the rings on the other end, the first, the second, the third—*oh my God, was she really not going to pick up*—the fourth—*and this is why we stopped being friends six years ago. This was one of the reasons—*

"Hey, where are you?" Emma said. "Oh...okay. You're meeting up with us for a drink. Jeremy gave me something for all of us...I don't know. It's an envelope addressed to the three of us. He said we need to read it together...Yeah, well, Sadie requested we read it together, so I think we can all suck it for a bit. It will be just for a drink. Meet us downtown in twenty? See you soon."

"This is not going to go over well," Audrey said.

Emma pinched the bridge of her nose. "Auds, Sadie is gone. Today was her service, and Jeremy said she spent most of her last two and a half months working on some project for us. We're going to see what this is all about. Together."

She hated how right Emma was. Just because Audrey knew that she had about ten minutes to temporarily quash all her history with Reid didn't mean that the sense of dread didn't wash over her. Processing the fact that her best friend was gone was hard enough. Now she had to process her death right next to her ex-best friend who she hadn't spoken to in six years.

Audrey followed Emma and Matt to a beer garden in Old Town Temecula. It was a beer garden they had gone to a handful of times before the summer after all of them had turned twenty-one. Emma kissed Matt good-bye and led Audrey to the outside patio where she spotted that familiar head of wavy blond hair at a table. Reid fixed her stare on the mountains in the distance.

Audrey hadn't seen Reid in six years. So much of her looked the same as her twenty-three-year-old self. She'd heard through Emma and Sadie that she lived in Oceanside, a few blocks from the ocean, where she worked as a scuba instructor. All the hours she must have spent outside had tinted her skin in a soft bronze, and a few new freckles dotted her nose and cheeks.

When Reid's eyes met hers, her heart rate sped up as nerves coiled in her stomach. She knew that even though they'd all agreed on one drink, it was going to be one of the most awkward rounds she'd ever had. The tension already budded in the warm air within a few seconds of them standing next to each other.

The server needed to come by their table quick because Audrey required a beer to get through the next hour.

"There you are," Emma said, giving Reid a tight hug. "Where were you? We didn't see you at all."

"Yeah, um, I came in late," Reid said and scratched the back of her head. "I stood in the back. I didn't want to draw attention from Jeremy."

Audrey fought the urge to roll her eyes. Of course Reid had come in late. Getting Reid to show up to things on time was just as impossible as Audrey trying to get her sixth graders to settle down during the last weeks of the school year. Even if she only had seven years of teaching experience and still considered herself a relatively "new" teacher, she was more confident in getting her students to settle than getting Reid to show up to something on time.

"Your family was right behind us," Emma said as she took a seat next to Reid.

Reid glanced at Audrey again and forced out a thin smile. "Hey," she said and quickly sat back down, which Audrey was grateful for because she was definitely not in a place to give Reid a hug. Not when she was fuming.

She took the seat opposite of Emma.

Reid pushed the beer menus over to them and reached for her glass. Clearly, she'd wasted no time ordering herself a pint, but Audrey didn't fault her for that, given the heaviness of the day; hell, the last two and a half months.

Emma carried the small talk about beer until the server took their orders and promptly returned with their drinks. Once she left, Reid blew out a heavy sigh and said, "So what's this envelope thing about?"

"Right," Emma said, reaching for her purse. She pulled out the envelope. "We're supposed to read this together."

"Oh, we're doing this now? Okay." Reid gulped down more beer.

Emma frowned. "Of course we are. Why else are we here?"

"Because her funeral was just, like, ten minutes ago?"

"If you need more time—"

"I don't need more time," Reid said flatly, and Audrey couldn't help but take it a little personally, although she agreed with her. She didn't want any more time. She wanted to find out what was in the letter, head back to her dad's, and not be around Reid for longer than she had to.

"Let's just see what's in the letter," Audrey said.

"Okay, fine," Emma said and opened the envelope.

Audrey's stomach sank when she saw the purple ink all over the lined notebook paper. She'd never thought purple gel pen would send pangs all over her body, but it did. She drank her beer, attempting to loosen the brick still lodged in her throat. If she had been by herself and not in public-—or in front of Reid—she would have allowed herself to cry.

"Share with the class," Reid said.

Emma cleared her throat. "Right. Sorry." She inhaled and read the letter out loud:

Hi friends,

If you're reading this, that means I died.

I know what you're thinking: a world without me is going to suck for a bit, and you're right because I was a fucking hoot.

But in all seriousness, I know you must be feeling like absolute shit right now, and I'm so sorry. I hope you all know that being your friend for the last fifteen years has been one of the best things that's happened to me.

So you're probably wondering why I forced you all together. Remember that time we made a bucket list and were so serious about it that we made a "blood oath" with matching tattoos that we would complete it? Well, obviously, I won't be completing it, but I think you should try.

And before you roll your eyes at me, yes, I'm well aware that Audrey and Reid haven't talked since our attempt at the Route 66 road trip. You two can be upset with me for using my death as an excuse for you guys to work on the bucket list. That's all fair, but also, I need some kind of silver lining, and my three best friends back together is the silver lining…in addition to my haunting capabilities.

But here's the thing I've learned in the last two and a half months: life is incredibly short. You don't realize how short until you're on your deathbed and replay your entire life over and over again, and you realize that some of the things that you spent so much time worrying about seem so small compared to an entire lifetime.

That's why I'm kindly asking you to continue on with the bucket list. See attached. I added a nineteenth item. GASP! I know. I broke the rules, and part of me is irritated that there are now nineteen items instead of a solid, even eighteen. But I'm dying, so I feel like I can do whatever I want with the rules. So fuck the rules. There is now a new item, and you can't give me shit about it.

We never finished Route 66. It would be amazing if you could finish it. Start in San Diego this time, drive into the now infamous Springfield, Missouri and veer off east because guess what? Remember how I stopped trying to get firefly tickets when Audrey and Reid had a friend breakup? Well, I entered the lottery…using three different emails, Jeremy used three different emails, Bryan used his personal and work email, and together, we finally got tickets! CAN YOU BELIEVE? We finally got tickets!

So if all three of you consent to completing the bucket list, then you will receive the next steps from Jeremy. Emma, you are in charge because Excel spreadsheets and vacation planning excites you to no end. Go wild, girl.

If you do decide to finish it, know that I'll be with you. Not because I'm in heaven or anything biblical like that, but because I have a master plan for if you do go on this grand bucket list adventure. You'll be reading a lot more of me. And while you're on the adventure and feel a heavy presence, that's me. I finally hooked up to the afterlife Wi-Fi and figured out how to, kindly, haunt you. Say hi.

I'm so very sorry I have to leave you all so soon. I love you, Emma, Reid, and Audrey. Thank you for giving me fifteen years' worth of wonderful memories and friendship. I couldn't have asked for better friends.

I'll forever be your fourth triangle.

XOXO Sadie

Audrey swatted the thick tears from her eyes. She looked at her right inner wrist, and the outline of the last triangle that Sadie had colored in on her own wrist. It was at that moment that their tattoos had gone from friendship tattoos to a memorial one. That last triangle would forever be empty, forever incomplete.

"Wow, okay," Emma said softly and stared at her pint.

"We're not actually going to do that, right?" Reid said.

Audrey's eyebrows furrowed. "Did you not hear what Sadie wrote in the letter?"

Reid directed a glare at her. "Of course I heard it, but she said if we consented. We haven't all been together in six years, and now we're just going to go on the very trip that ended everything?"

"I mean, we wouldn't be going right into the trip," Emma said. "We'll have to plan and book everything, but summer is right around the corner. Audrey's off for summer break, and I can easily take time off. Sadie finally won the lottery tickets to see the fireflies. We've been trying to get those since we were eighteen, and we finally have them. We have to at least go see them for her."

Audrey couldn't blame Reid for the nerves ringing through her voice. She wasn't sure if she could emotionally deal with another road trip on top of losing Sadie. And not just any road trip: a goddamn cross-country road trip.

The last road trip hadn't even lasted for three days before everything had blown up. The four of them had flown to Chicago and had made it down to Springfield, Missouri when Audrey had finally had enough of Reid, and Reid had finally had enough of her. It was a year's worth of tension and growing apart that had built up and exploded.

Looking back, she was well aware of the mistakes she'd made during the whole ordeal. She wondered if Reid still remained adamant about the things she had said during the heated exchange or if, like Audrey, she wished she could take some of it back.

Whether she was uncomfortable or not, only one person could convince Audrey to be stuck on a cross-country road trip with Reid Haley, and it was Sadie. She knew how much Sadie wanted them to see the fireflies.

On top of all the anger, hurt, and regret from her argument and friend breakup with Reid, Audrey had felt immense guilt for being the reason they'd never finished their Route 66 trip. When she'd found out Sadie had stopped trying for tickets afterward, another boulder had stacked on top of her. She'd worried that she and Reid had killed Sadie's dream of seeing the fireflies as a group. Now that Sadie was gone, the guilt swelled in her chest like a balloon, ready to burst at any wrong moment.

She had to make it right. For Sadie and for herself.

"We should do it," Audrey said softly.

"Okay, but the last time didn't really go as planned," Reid said and directed another glare at her, as if the entire failed road trip was her fault.

"No, it really didn't," she responded with a bite.

"Redoing the road trip wasn't part of the original eighteen. That wasn't part of the blood oath."

"Oh, now you care about the blood oath?" Audrey muttered under her breath.

"The blood oath was a joke."

"Oh really? Is that why all four of us got matching tattoos? Sadie didn't even want to get tattoos but she did it for us, for *you*."

"She apparently wanted it if she consented to it and put it on the list."

"You were the one who made it a huge point that if we were going to make the bucket list, we needed to finish it. Now it's time to finish it, and you don't care about it anymore?"

"Wow, that's a huge assumption," Reid said, her voice rising. "I do care about it, but do we really think right now—just two weeks after she died and the first time the three of us have been together in six years—is the wisest time to go on a cross-country road trip when we didn't survive the last one?"

"We have firefly tickets," Emma said. "That's why we should go. Sadie won those tickets. She waited years for them, and now we have them. It's a perfect time to go. We all lost the same person, and I think it would be good for all of us."

"If we couldn't do it back then, do we really think we can now?" Reid said.

"I'd hope so," Audrey said. "It's quite literally Sadie's dying wish."

Reid narrowed her eyes, but Audrey really didn't care. Reid was notoriously selfish. Always had been really, and this time, there was zero room for that. Reid had been Sadie's longest friend. The two had met in sixth grade while Emma was at the other middle school in Temecula and before Audrey had even moved to California. Out of the three of them, Reid should have been the person to truly understand how much the synchronous fireflies had meant to her.

"How about this?" Emma said. While Emma probably thought she hid the sound of her annoyance, it was loud and clear to Audrey. "Why don't we take time to process? Maybe next weekend, the three of us could meet up at the winery and decide what we want to do. We'll need to start booking things now if we want to make it out to Tennessee by mid-June. Deal?"

"Deal," Audrey said and looked at Reid.

"Deal," Reid said, hesitantly and way less than enthused.

Chapter Two

Finally, Reid felt weightless.

She didn't realize how much she needed her job to cope with losing Sadie until she fully descended into an entirely different world.

Literally.

Seventy feet below the water's surface, she found absolute peace. The cold, deep water cradled her. Below her were beds of kelp forests gently swaying, and schools of fish swam all around her and her class. She was greeted by garibaldi fish, a moray eel, and she even spotted a sea lion swimming a few meters away, chasing after a school of mackerel.

The best part about this world was that it was untouched by all the chaos on land. In this world, her chest hurt less, and she didn't feel the knots in her shoulders as much. There was so much ethereal beauty surrounding her that there was simply no room for her brain to take in anything else.

Diving was her safe place. Some people read, listened to music, or played video games to escape their current reality, but the ocean was hers. Once she'd found out that Sadie wasn't likely to live until summer, she'd decided that she would spend her summer in a different world completely. She considered doing some of her favorite nearby dives like Catalina Island, the Channel Islands, and the oil rigs. Or she thought about crossing off one of the dives on her diving bucket list like the Galapagos, the Manta night dive in Hawaii, or finally taking the ultimate "pipe dream" trip to the Tuamotu Atolls in French Polynesia.

What wasn't the ultimate escape was a road trip with Audrey. That was just confinement, the exact opposite of what she needed.

As she monitored her diving class swimming through the surfgrass and admiring all the fish, she remembered when the four of them had scratched off scuba diving the summer after their freshman year of college, and Reid had absolutely fallen in love with it and decided that she wanted to be an instructor. They'd gone to La Jolla Cove, and she'd watched as Sadie had embraced the mermaid that had apparently lived inside her and swam across the beds of surfgrass. She'd enthusiastically freaked out any time she'd seen marine life, especially sea lions. When Reid had checked in by signaling to Sadie to give her a thumbs-up or down, Sadie flipped her off in return. If it had been anyone else, Reid would have had to stress the importance of giving the thumbs-up or down underwater—since a thumbs down could indicate a serious problem—but since it was Sadie, she'd let the middle finger replace the thumbs-up.

Once Reid returned to the surface and herded her entire class back onto the boat, the warm air hit her skin, relieving her just a bit from the cold water. She was back to real life again. She could feel reality starting to suction around her body like the seven millimeter wet suit she wore, except at least she got to peel the wet suit off and feel relief.

The grief constricted her as she made her way back to her condo in Oceanside where her younger brother, Cameron, waited. She had given him a key back when she'd moved into her apartment, and he'd decided to drive to spend the night with her. They were best friends, and Cameron didn't want Reid to be on her own. It was nice to know that she had him waiting for her after work and that her night would be just a little easier with him there.

She found him out on her balcony sipping on a Corona as he stared at the view. A sliver of sparkling ocean was off in the distance, just a few blocks away. Indie folk music played from the Bluetooth speaker that sat next to his feet.

She pulled a Corona from the fridge and joined him. "You look like you're pondering life," she said as she stepped onto the balcony and sat in the lounge chair next to him.

"I guess you can say that." He seemed to notice the beer in her hands and lifted his. "Cheers."

She hadn't seen him since the funeral five days before. After her drink with Emma and Audrey, she'd spent her days out on the boat for classes and immersed in the underwater world. But after five days on her own, she'd needed someone, and not just anyone; she'd needed Cam.

The five year difference had nothing on them.

"So are you going to tell me why you stayed in the back during the funeral?"

She kept her gaze on the streak of ocean. As the sun dipped closer to the horizon, the ocean soaked up the orange and yellows forming in the sky. She exhaled heavily. "I had a panic attack."

"You did?"

She nodded and drank her beer. When she had pulled into the parking lot and stared at the funeral home sign, she'd absolutely lost it. She'd lost control of herself, her emotions, and sobbed and gasped for air in her car. It had taken her twenty minutes to calm down enough to go inside, and by that time, she was a few minutes late, and Jeremy had taken the podium.

The panic attack had taken her by surprise and claimed her completely, as if she was a piece of debris in the path of a tumultuous wave. She'd felt drained for the rest of the day, her mind foggy during drinks with Emma and Audrey.

"I've never had a panic attack before," she said. "I had no idea what was happening, but once I parked, something in me broke. I didn't go inside until I was able to get out of the car."

He frowned. "I'm so sorry. You could have texted me, you know."

She shook her head. "I didn't want to draw attention."

"How are you feeling now?"

"Like shit but a little better now that you're here."

He forced a thin smile and looked back out at the view. "I don't know how many times we've driven by the funeral home, seen the entire parking lot filled, and wondered who died. I thought about it when Dad and I pulled up, how the lot was packed, and—" He shook his head as his voice cracked. "I couldn't believe it was for Sadie. I just can't believe she's gone. It just happened so quickly that she died before I could even fully process the news that she had cancer."

She squeezed his shoulder. "Yeah, me too."

God, she hated the pain in his voice. Sadie had been Cameron's first and biggest crush. He'd spent most of his teen years pining for her. It was one thing for Reid to feel that kind of pain, but she *hated* when Cameron—or any other loved one—sounded that hurt. She wanted to fix it, but she knew she couldn't.

"So, um, Sadie wrote us a letter," she said, attempting to clear the lump forming in her throat.

He faced her. "Wait, what?"

"She wrote us a letter: me, Emma, and Audrey. Emma said Jeremy gave it to her after the funeral and that Sadie spent most of chemo writing these letters for some big 'project,' I guess. We read it together—"

"Whoa, wait," he said and pinched the bridge of his nose. "This is a lot to digest at once. Sadie wrote you letters?"

"Yes, but we've only read one."

"Are there more?"

"Cam, I don't know. I don't even know what the next letter is all about. We're meeting at Magnolia Springs on Friday. Emma already got the second letter from Jeremy."

"What did the first say?"

She exhaled a ragged breath. "She wants us to complete the bucket list."

His blond eyebrows rose. "Seriously?"

"Seriously."

"Are you going to?"

She shrugged. "I don't know how I feel about it. I mean, the last time we tried to cross something off the bucket list was when the four of us did the Route 66 trip, and we only lasted three days."

"You and Audrey read the letter together?"

"Well, Emma read the letter, but Audrey was there."

"Wow. I didn't think you two could be around each other again."

"Me neither, but alas, Sadie died right after she got firefly tickets."

His eyes widened. "She got firefly tickets?" She nodded, and he looked back at the ocean, shaking his head. "Of course she did." He paused, took a long sip, and let out a deep breath. "You need to go on that road trip."

Reid grunted. He was supposed to tell her that being around Audrey for at least ten days was a terrible idea. "I don't want to be around Audrey. That's the last thing the three of us need, two people who are grieving and don't like each other."

He shrugged. "Isn't it a small price to pay after losing Sadie? She's been waiting for those tickets for years."

God, not Cameron too. He might have been five years younger than her, but he was at least ten years older emotionally. She wasn't sure when he'd become so wise, but she always valued his opinion.

"You don't think that's a terrible idea? The only times we got together after that trip was Sadie's engagement party and wedding reception at Magnolia Springs, and it was awkward as fuck. I swear, Sadie and Jeremy just eloped because of how bad the tension was at the engagement party. Audrey and I spent the entire time on opposite sides of the patio and acted like the other person didn't exist, and it really sucked."

"Or they eloped because, you know, weddings are expensive as fuck, and Sadie hated spending money, hence why she put herself in a dog urn."

She rolled her eyes. "I know she wanted to save money. Even from the back of the room, I noticed that ridiculous urn."

He chuckled. "You have to admit, that's kind of funny. Typical Sadie-humor funny."

"It was. It's very…Sadie," she said. "Back to the point. Completing the bucket list is a terrible idea. Audrey and I will spend the whole time arguing."

"You don't have to."

She let out a hollow laugh. "Please. Audrey loves a little dig. It's what caused the whole argument to happen last time."

"Well, last time, you two were trying to be friends. This time around, you're just trying to complete the list for Sadie."

She paused and took a better look at him. The more they had these deep conversations, the more she realized that he really wasn't a little kid anymore. "How did you get to be so wise?"

"Therapy."

They shared a small laugh.

Both of them had been in and out of therapy for various reasons, but Cameron had started that trend. When Reid was eighteen, her parents had started their long, drawn out divorce process. Luckily for her, it happened right around when she left for college at USC. She reaped the "ignorance is bliss" benefits. Cameron, however, was only in eighth grade and was stuck in the divorce trenches, witnessing every battle in person or on the phone. She was just proud of him for deciding to go to therapy to work through it all. It encouraged her to get therapy after her first heartbreak.

"But really, Reid," he said, his voice low and stern. "You need to do it. I know that you know, deep down, under all that anxiety, it's the right thing to do too."

Damn it. She hated how well he knew her. She couldn't keep a secret even if she had one.

"I know it's the right thing to do…for Sadie. But what about us? Audrey doesn't need to be worrying about me right now just as much as I shouldn't have to worry about her. And Emma doesn't deserve to mother us the entire road trip. We're all fragile right now and can only handle so much. If we had the firefly tickets a year from now, it would be an entirely different story."

"That might be true, but that's not the reality. Sadie got those tickets for this summer, and I'm sure she was really excited about it."

Reid looked at her beer bottle. "She was. At least, she seemed like it in the letter."

"Plus, weren't you the one who was worried about not finishing it? Isn't that why all four of you got matching tattoos?"

She flitted her gaze over her wrist. The second triangle was shaded in black on hers. "I mean, I always wanted a tattoo."

"But that specific tattoo represents your friendship. Your promise to each other."

Reid buzzed her lips. "Therapy made you way too mature for this conversation. Your girlfriend is lucky that she's dating such an emotionally intelligent twenty-four-year-old dude."

He smiled. "She knows she's lucky."

As the conversation ended, Reid couldn't believe how her whole world had crumbled in a matter of ten weeks, leaving a giant, Sadie-sized hole in the middle of her heart.

They spent the rest of the evening sipping beer in contemplative and comfortable silence, watching the sun slowly set while the speaker played soothing music.

Her diving trip to French Polynesia was going to have to wait because she had a very strong feeling she was going to embark on a cross-country road trip.

With her ex-best friend.

Chapter Three

Magnolia Springs Winery was right in the heart of Temecula Valley's wine country, owned and run by Emma's parents, Daniel and Marian Lin. Mr. Lin's family owned a winery in Shangri-La County, China, and when he'd come over to California to go to college, he'd met Mrs. Lin on a wine tour on his twenty-first birthday. The two had built Magnolia Springs from the ground up. When they'd first told Reid their story in middle school, she was in awe, and since then, the winery was where they'd celebrated life's biggest milestones: sweet sixteens, high school graduation, twenty-first birthdays, and Sadie and Jeremy's engagement party and post-elopement reception. It was even the last place Reid and Audrey had seen each other six years before Sadie's funeral.

Reid was actually quite impressed how well she and Audrey had successfully avoided each other all these years.

She speed-walked up to the main building that always made her feel like she had been transported to Tuscany with its stucco walls and clay terracotta roof. She made her way through the tasting room and out onto the back patio that had the most incredible view of the rolling vineyards and the Santa Ana Mountains in the background.

She found Emma, Audrey, and Jeremy at a table, an umbrella popped open to protect them from the Southern California sun. She didn't realize she was that late until she noticed that the three of them each had their own glass of red wine.

Ah, great, she internally sighed. She was ten minutes late. She started mentally preparing to get chastised by Audrey. It was one of the biggest pieces of "constructive feedback" Audrey tossed at her like a dart. Apparently, she was "notoriously late" and on "Reid time," which Audrey considered incredibly rude.

She hadn't forgotten those words as she'd navigated through the typical Southern California traffic. She'd purposefully left early because her goal had been to make a point to Audrey that she could be the first one to get to Magnolia Springs, even though she was the only one who didn't still live in Temecula. She knew that Audrey, the clock's biggest fan, would be counting the seconds. But of course, the damn traffic had delayed her.

Maybe Audrey had been on to something. Even when Reid tried arriving on time, she still managed to be late.

"There you are," Emma said, greeting her with a friendly smile, seemingly unfazed that she was late.

Reid purposely avoided eye contact with Audrey. She smiled at Emma and went over to hug Jeremy. He had the best hugs, and she really needed one of them.

"I had no idea you were going to be here," she said as she broke the hug and took the empty chair between him and Emma, the safest spot at the table.

"Surprise," he said with a trace of a grin.

"I'm sorry I'm late. Traffic was a mess."

"All good," Emma said. "We just ordered some wine. Here." She handed Reid the unused wineglass next to her, and Jeremy filled it from the bottle of red in the middle of the table. She accidentally caught a glimpse of Audrey. She couldn't see her glare underneath her dark sunglasses, but she could tell by the thin expression that touched her lips that she was not impressed.

Yup, she was definitely pissed about "Reid time."

"This is the new cabernet sauvignon of the season," Emma said, swirling the wine in her glass.

Reid sampled the smallest sip. Even though Emma had been her best friend since they were fourteen and she had visited the Lin's winery a million times, she still knew very little about wine. The Lins could go on about how the cab had hints of dark berries and oak, but to her, it tasted like red wine, and that was good enough.

"Tastes like a cab," she said. "I'm glad it's not Riesling, though. Still can't do that after your twenty-first birthday."

The four of them might have gone a little overboard on Emma's twenty-first birthday. The con of Emma's parents owning the winery was that they got to take advantage of free drinks, and when they were freshly twenty-one, it felt like being a kid in a candy store. They'd pounded back the most digestible wine for twenty-one year olds—Riesling—and had the whole thirty acre property to drunkenly roam around well into the night and early morning. Reid had definitely thrown up somewhere in the vineyard. Luckily, the Lin house was also on the property, so all she'd had to do was stumble back into the house and put herself to sleep afterward.

Eight years later, she still couldn't even allow herself to think about Riesling. Sweet white wine was forever ruined.

"Oh my God, is the gang back together?" Reid looked up to find Mr. Lin walking over with a big smile. "I must be dreaming."

Embarrassment crawled up Emma's face. Reid was positive Mr. Lin didn't know any details about Reid's friend breakup with Audrey, or if he did, he'd probably assumed they had reconciled. He was just another sweet but clueless dad who couldn't keep up with constantly changing dynamics. He was too preoccupied with the winery, now more than ever since all three of his daughters, Eva, Emma, and Elaine, had moved out, and he was officially an empty nester.

He opened his arms for a hug, and Reid accepted it. "Hi, Mr. Lin," she said. "It's good to see you."

He placed his hands on his hips and looked at the four of them. "This is a rare sight," he continued. The red on Emma's face deepened. She eyed him with a tight jaw, as if trying to tell him to shut up telepathically. "I think this might call for a special bottle of Riesling." He cackled at his own joke.

"I'm sure the Riesling is delicious, but I did a really great job ruining it for myself," Reid said.

Mr. Lin patted her shoulder. "No puking in the vineyards, that's all I ask."

Now it was her turn to feel embarrassment heat her face. She turned to Emma, who shrugged. Reid had no idea Mr. Lin knew about the puking. She thought that had gone into the vault of secrets.

"I have something special for all four of you," he said. "I need to go find it, but don't leave until I give it to you. Something you can enjoy now or on your road trip, all right?"

"Thanks, Dad," Emma said through her clenched jaw.

Apparently, Daniel Lin knew more than Reid thought he did, between the puking in the vineyards and the supposed road trip that, according to him, sounded like a done deal.

Once he headed back inside, Emma shook her head.

"How does your dad know I puked in the vineyard?" Reid said. "I thought that was in the vault."

"Well, it was," Emma said. "Until I was reminiscing about all of us with my parents a few days ago. Don't worry. He just laughed."

"What's this special gift he's talking about?" Audrey said.

"I have no idea. Twenty-nine years of knowing him, and I still don't know what's up his sleeves. Anyway, before we get too tipsy, we should probably discuss the road trip. One of the reasons why Jeremy is here."

He waved. "Hi, that's me. I have a special delivery for you guys." He pulled an envelope from his back pocket and handed it to Emma. She flashed the letter to Reid and Audrey, and in the same purple gel pen, Sadie had written, *So you've decided to finish the bucket list…*

"Should we read it?" Emma said. "See what we're in store before we agree or disagree to do the road trip?"

"Do you know what's in this letter?" Reid asked Jeremy.

"I know all about her plan, but I don't know what's specifically in each letter. I'm just the mailman. She only let me read the first one, and the rest were already written and sealed by the time she told me the plan."

Reid gulped down a couple sips of cab. She hated how quickly her chest tightened, knowing Sadie's words were going to plow right through her.

"Let's open it," Audrey said.

"Okay." Emma exhaled as she opened the envelope and pulled the letter out. When she unfolded it, the bucket list fell out. It was haunting them. Reid hadn't seen it in well over six years.

Hi friends!

If you're reading this, you decided to embark on a wonderful almost-cross-country road trip. Not only are you finally going to be experiencing the heart and soul of Route 66, but you're going to end with the most magical firefly show in the entire US. Trust me, it will be worth the trip.

I have everything planned out for you so you don't have to stress about researching everything—looking at you, Emma. It's my way to live vicariously through you guys. I know Audrey gets cranky when she's forced in the car for longer than four hours, so I've planned each day with that in mind, with the exception of one day. Don't worry, you'll thank me later. It will take eleven days. Emma, Jeremy knows to give you a binder, so hopefully, he gave you that with this letter. All the hotels are listed, itineraries, suggested pit stops, and all that fun stuff. All you will need to do—Emma—is book everything.

As for Audrey and Reid, bring your good-looking selves, and before you get mad at me for forcing the two of you to do another road trip together, please remember that once upon a time, the four of us were all friends. We all made this list together. We all took the "blood oath," and it was painful. I know I'm a baby with pain, but I got that tattoo for all of you. We promised we would finish this...together.

I know our first attempt at a road trip didn't go as planned, but if you're reading this letter, and you consented to the trip, I hope you all make the most of it and enjoy it. I'm sure there will be tough times, but don't forget, there was one point in time we all trusted each other. I have faith that you can finish. Just leave the past in the past and start with a fresh slate because I guess in some way, this is a fresh a new chapter without the most perfect friend in your lives, aka, me.

I know it's a huge ask that comes with complications, but it's just another reason why the three of you were always the brightest lights in my life. We can't undo the past, but who knows? Maybe this trip is what's needed to patch up the friend group? And if that happens, imagine how happy my ghost-self will be? I'd be the happiest ghost.

I love you all. I'll see you in my next letter.

XOXO Sadie

"I have the binder in my car," Jeremy said, his voice a few notches softer than before the letter. "The rest of the letters are in there as well."

This was the second letter, and it still found a way to tilt Reid's entire world on its axis. If there was a whole binder of letters, was she going to feel choked by Sadie's absence every time they read them on their bucket list adventure? She hoped that eventually, she would learn to breathe through the pain. She just wished she had already found a way.

She imagined Sadie spending all her chemotherapy hooked up to machines, writing away with her purple pen. Sadie must have believed that the three of them would agree to go on the adventure if she spent all of her energy writing and planning the trip details.

"Look, the entire trip is basically all planned," Emma said. "That takes care of most of the stressful part."

Reid grunted. "Speak for yourself."

"Clearly, the bucket list really meant something to Sadie if she spent her last two and a half months planning all this, and I think at one point, it meant something to all of us because why else would we have gotten matching tattoos?" Emma lifted her right arm and showed off her tattoo as if Reid and Audrey had forgotten.

"She was really excited about this plan," Jeremy said. "If you can believe someone would have an ounce of excitement while they're dying. It really did mean a lot to her. All three of you did. She knew it was a big ask. I know it's a big ask, but God, she'd be so happy if you guys agreed to do it."

"Okay, how many things do we have left, and what did she add?" Reid said begrudgingly and reached across the table to grab the bucket list.

Seeing the piece of paper covered in Sadie's messy handwriting brought back a wave of memories from graduation night, the adventures they'd had crossed off, and the eventual breakdown of their group.

The ERAS Bucket List
Route 66 road trip
~~Get matching tattoos~~
See synchronous fireflies in the Smoky Mountains
Make a time capsule and open together as adults

~~Go to a music festival~~
~~Skinny dip!~~
~~Go camping the real way…in actual tents~~
~~Volunteer at an animal shelter~~
~~Napa Valley wine tasting~~
~~Vegas, baby!~~
Go to a spa resort
~~See Disneyland at Christmas~~
Have dinner at a Michelin Star restaurant
~~Finally ride in a hot-air balloon over Temecula like the tourists~~
Fly first class
~~Celebrate someone's twenty-first birthday at Magnolia Springs~~
Stay in a log cabin
~~Go scuba diving~~
**Start a tradition!*

"Start a tradition?" Reid asked. "We can't even have one beer without arguing, and she wants us to start a tradition?"

"I'll do it," Audrey said. "I want to…for Sadie."

All eyes landed on Reid. She felt like three giant spotlights shone on her, and the warm early May temperatures encouraged sweat to bead around her hairline. As much as it stressed her out to imagine her and Audrey trapped in a car together from Santa Monica to Gatlinburg, Tennessee, her gut knew it was the right thing to do. She would always choose Sadie, no matter how uncomfortable things could possibly get.

"Fine," she said through a grunt.

"Don't sound too enthused," Audrey said.

Sadie's death had torn open fresh wounds and reopened some old ones. Ever since they'd found out about her terminal illness, Reid's guilt over her rift with Audrey had grown bigger and cut deeper as Sadie's cancer progressed. At any moment, Reid felt like she could burst at the seams and lose it. The last thing she wanted was to be put in an extremely uncomfortable and stressful situation after her whole world had fallen apart in a matter of ten weeks.

Right as Reid opened her mouth to rebut, Emma jumped in. "We're not doing this here, guys."

Sure, it had been Reid's idea to scratch the bucket list items every summer, and it had also been her idea to get tattoos to seal the promise of finishing the list. But that was eleven years ago. So much had transpired since then. She'd honestly thought the plan had died when her friendship with Audrey died.

"See, this is a little preview about what to expect if we complete this list." Reid downed the rest of her wine. As much as she wanted to give Sadie exactly what she wanted, it was all easier said than done. The hurtful exchange during their first attempt at the Route 66 road trip might have been six years ago, but the words still stung. Just thinking about putting herself in a position where it could happen again made her skin crawl.

"Why are you so against it?" Audrey said.

"Because I don't want to deal with this for however long it takes to finish it," Reid said, gesturing to the empty space between them.

Audrey rolled her eyes again. The prickling on Reid's skin intensified. She could feel the anger in her blood. She hadn't experienced that feeling in a while; it was almost foreign. But it quickly reminded her how being around Audrey had made her feel during their last trip. How every movement and word had felt like walking on eggshells. She'd been in a mood the entire time. But only with Reid, of course.

"I don't know," Jeremy said. "I think Sadie's right. This could be good for the three of you. You all lost your best friend, and instead of dealing with that grief on your own, you can lean on each other. You don't have to be alone right now."

She wouldn't be leaning on Audrey for anything. If she was going to lean on anyone, it was going to be Emma…or she would do what she usually did and just kept her thoughts and feelings to herself.

"Here it is," Mr. Lin said.

His bold, enthusiastic voice pulled all four of them out of the discussion. He walked toward them with Syrah bottles in each hand. Once she saw the labels, her heart sank.

Those were the custom wine bottles from Sadie and Jeremy's wedding.

Jeremy's expression fell as Mr. Min handed him two bottles, and he stared at the black label and gold text as if lost in a bittersweet memory.

"I saved a few bottles from the reception," Mr. Lin said. "I was really proud of this wine. Maybe because the bride was like a fourth daughter to me. I wanted you to have them, Jeremy."

"Daniel, this is very sweet of you," Jeremy said hoarsely. He stood up and gave Mr. Lin a hug.

Mr. Lin patted his back before breaking up. "Sadie was a very special woman. All of you are, really. The three of you girls are like my own children. I just wanted you to have a piece of your special day to hold on to, for whatever reason."

"Thank you. Seriously," Jeremy said.

"I'll let the four of you get back to your wine," he said with a faded smile. Reid knew how much Mr. Lin cared about them not only in how he'd always treated them over the years, but also how he currently stared at each of them with love and sympathy.

When Mr. Lin headed back inside, Jeremy returned to his seat and scratched the corner of his eye. "Well, damn. I had no idea any of these existed."

"I didn't either, to be honest," Emma said.

He studied the bottles for a few more silent moments and handed Emma one of them. "I want you to take one."

"What? Jeremy, no."

He held up a hand. "I'm serious. She would have wanted you three to have a bottle. Maybe you could open it when you make it to the Smoky Mountains. Have a glass before you see the fireflies."

"It feels too important to accept," Reid said.

"It has my name on it, doesn't it? I want you three to have it. I have my bottle right here. The other is for you."

Seeing the bottle of Sadie's wedding wine right in front of her brought her back to the present. Bickering with Audrey about the past seemed so small.

The realization swelled in her gut.

They needed to take this road trip to the fireflies.

"Okay, I'm officially in," Reid said.

"Really?" Emma said with hope in her tone.

"Really."

She hoped her reluctance didn't saturate too much of her response. It had nothing to do with Sadie. In fact, if Sadie was alive, she would have felt much more comfortable about completing the list with Audrey. She and Sadie had known each other the longest, since sixth grade. She always felt like they were soul friends.

Jeremy squeezed her shoulder and smiled.

"Great. I'll text you guys as we get closer," Emma said and let out a sigh of relief. "I'm really glad we all agreed to do this. I know things haven't been ideal for quite some time, but…I don't know. I don't really want to be alone during all this."

The stiffness in Reid's chest deflated as Emma's eyes welled up. Being considered the mom of the group also meant that Emma always tried so hard to be the rock, like she did in her professional life as a therapist. The few times Reid had seen her parents cry, it was like taking a punch to the stomach, and that was exactly how she felt as Emma wiped her watery eyes.

In that moment, Reid realized that completing the bucket list had nothing to do with her feud with Audrey. It had everything to do with honoring her best friend and being there for Emma.

"You're not going to be alone," Reid said and squeezed Emma's hand. "We're going to do this for all of us."

CHAPTER FOUR

Summer vacation as a teacher was even more liberating than summer vacation as a student. Audrey's middle school was finally cleared. The hallways were blissfully quiet after the last two rambunctious weeks of the school year.

She'd never needed a summer vacation more than she needed this one. Since Sadie's death six weeks prior and the group deciding to finish the bucket list three weeks prior, teaching had been extremely difficult. She was down on herself for having less patience with her sixth graders; and middle schoolers needed a lot of patience. Her brain had been in a constant state of fog. The energy to teach her students new lessons on the precipice of the end of the school year had sucked the motivation from her. She needed to recharge. She needed to escape home for a bit. She needed zero responsibilities as she learned to stand on her two feet again.

Thank God for her girlfriend, Becca. Since Sadie had gotten her cancer diagnosis back in early February, life had been extremely difficult and stressful. Audrey knew she hadn't been present in their relationship since she'd gotten the news. Even though she'd spent too many nights crying and too many weekends curled up in bed, Becca had been by her side the entire time. Her overwhelming grief had tested their relationship, and if they could get through this hurdle just a few weeks shy of their one-year anniversary, Audrey was optimistic that their relationship was strong enough for the long run.

Part of her felt guilty for leaving Becca for eleven days right as her summer break started. She invited Becca over that night, not wanting to spend her first evening of summer vacation with anyone except her girlfriend. She opened a bottle of Magnolia Springs Sangiovese and arranged a charcuterie board. Nothing cured the sads like an array of cheese, crackers, and meats. She was a sucker for a charcuterie board and didn't care how basic that made her.

There was a knock on the front door. She swallowed her bite of smoked gouda and a rosemary cracker and headed over to the front door. Becca wore a black T-shirt and black track pants with her dark brown hair thrown up in a messy bun, her usual attire after spending the morning training for her first marathon in September.

"Hey, baby," Audrey said and went in for a hug and a kiss. She was so glad to be celebrating the start of summer—and much needed relaxation time—with Becca. She really needed a night wrapped up in Becca's arms.

What she wasn't expecting was such a frail hug or short peck on the lips in greeting. She didn't think too much of it. Becca had spent the morning training for her first marathon. She was probably exhausted. Audrey would have been. It was a good thing she had cheese and wine, the magical fix for everything.

Audrey poured a glass of wine as Becca took a seat in one of the barstools at the kitchen island. Over the eleven and a half months of their relationship, crafting the perfect charcuterie board had been their "thing," at least in the early stages before life had gotten in the way. They'd had debates over the best cheese and meat combinations to include and enjoyed the results during movie nights.

But now, Becca stared at the board blankly and didn't go for her favorite pairing: goat cheese on a rosemary cracker topped with prosciutto. Audrey didn't even like goat cheese. Actually, she loathed it. She thought it tasted like a farm. Goat and blue cheese were forbidden on her charcuterie boards, with the exception of the ones with Becca. It was the main topic of their cheese debates, and she only bought goat cheese because she knew that it was one of Becca's favorites.

"Okay, something is off," Audrey said.

Becca looked up, and for the first time since walking through her front door, she made eye contact. "What? Why do you think that?"

"Because you're acting off, and you're staring at the board like you don't know what to do with it."

"I'm not hungry."

"Didn't you run, like, ten miles today?"

"More like sixteen."

Audrey's eyes widened. "Sixteen? I didn't think you were there yet in your training." She didn't understand how anyone could run more than a mile and enjoy it.

Becca gave a one-shoulder shrug. "I had a lot on my mind."

Ah, there it was. Something was bothering her. "Do you want to talk about it?"

It wasn't until the unusually long pause that she started getting worried. Becca's dark brown eyes still struggled to meet hers, as if she or Audrey had done something wrong. Audrey combed through her memory, trying to figure out if she could have possibly have done anything to upset her. The only thing she could come up with was that she was going to spend the first eleven days of her summer vacation on a road trip. But Becca had seemed supportive when Audrey had told her, so she didn't understand why she would be upset about it now.

Unless it wasn't that at all.

"Becca?"

Becca closed her eyes, sucked in her lips, and exhaled. The ground felt unstable, and an ache in Audrey's chest expanded with each second that Becca struggled to get out her next words.

This wasn't good. The moment Becca had walked had in, she'd brought in an uncomfortable energy. Audrey's chest hadn't loosened once since February. It only tightened as she settled into her new reality without Sadie. She wasn't sure if she could handle another knot. What more was coming her way?

She needed to sit. She had a feeling it was in her best interest.

"Becca," Audrey said, her authoritative teacher voice slipping out. "What's going on? Please tell me."

Becca rubbed her eyes and pinched her nose. "I don't know if I can do this anymore."

She said it so softly, Audrey thought she must have misheard her.

"What?"

Becca lowered her head and finally met her gaze. "I can't do this anymore."

Despair stole her breath. "What?"

"I'm sorry, Audrey."

"You're breaking up with me?"

Becca nodded.

It was a good thing Audrey had decided to sit because the little knots of pain that had collected in her chest for the last couple months fused into one massive throbbing ache.

Becca pried her eyes away; her inability to even look Audrey in the eye was a very telltale sign that she was, indeed, breaking up with her. She felt absolutely blindsided.

"I'm sorry," Becca mumbled.

"Why? We can talk about whatever is bothering you—"

"Audrey, we haven't really had much of a relationship in the last few months."

Audrey laughed hollowly. "Because my best friend was dying."

"I know that, and I'm really sorry about the timing of all of this but…it's been hard. I haven't felt connected to you. I try to do things with you, and you don't want to. I come over to hang out, and it feels like you're not mentally here—"

"Then talk to me about it. Why am I just hearing about all this now?" She hated how easily her eyes leaked.

She hated even more how easily Becca's remained dry. "I didn't know how to tell you," Becca said. "I've thought about it a lot and—"

"You thought about it a lot, yet didn't tell me?" She wiped the moisture off her face.

Becca's stare softened. "I'm really sorry, Audrey. I just don't think we're in the same place right now."

No matter how hard Audrey tried keeping her composure, the tears wouldn't stop. She didn't want Becca to see the breakup crack through the armor she tried putting on in that moment. She really just needed her to leave so she could fall apart.

"Okay," Audrey said, her voice breaking as if accepting the defeat had cracked something inside her.

"That's it?" Becca said. "Just okay?"

"You don't want to be with me anymore. I'm not going to beg you to do something you don't want to, so if that's that and there's no conversation to be had, I honestly don't want to hear any more. Not right now."

Becca stood. She opened her arms as she took a step closer, but Audrey shook her head.

"I think you should leave."

Becca lowered her arms. "Okay, if that's what you really want—"

"That's what I want."

"Okay," she said, also sounding like she had accepted defeat. "I'm really sorry, Audrey."

After that, everything blurred together. She couldn't tell if it was from the continuous flow of tears or the realization that in what felt like a blink of an eye, she'd lost her best friend and her girlfriend. It was a painful irony that the person she'd been leaning on the entire time wasn't strong enough to support her weight and that leaning on her was actually crumbling their very relationship.

She didn't even hear Becca leave. When she finally gasped a breath of air and looked up, she was gone.

And now Audrey was stuck with the fucking goat cheese stinking up her perfect charcuterie board.

Audrey always loved how the air smelled on the first morning of summer vacation.

Even as a student, she'd loved waking up that first morning, stepping outside, and letting the summer air and fresh dew greet her. The smell of summer hinted at three months of absolute freedom.

This summer break started very differently. She hadn't stepped foot outside since Becca had broken up with her. She'd spent her first three days of her summer break in bed, paralyzed by heartbreak and betrayal. Her dad and Emma had both come over to check on her at various points of the weekend, but none of those checkups included breathing in the summer air.

It was only the impending start of their road trip that forced Audrey up and outside. She waited on her front porch for Emma to pick her up in their rental car, rocking back and forth on her wicker rocking chair, closing her eyes, and taking in the smell of the warm morning. She tried focusing on the birds chirping, the lightness in the air, and how, in just a couple of hours, the Pacific Ocean would be in front of her as they started their road trip at the end of Route 66 in Santa Monica. She hoped that by focusing on those small things, there wouldn't be room in her mind to dwell on the breakup, the fact that she'd be stuck in a car with Reid for the next eleven days, or how much she missed Sadie.

She just needed a small moment to breathe through that boulder in her chest.

She opened her eyes when she heard a humming from the Honda CR-V pulling up in her driveway. Emma hopped out of the car with her black sunglasses perched on her head. Audrey grabbed her suitcase and book bag and hauled it over to the car.

Emma held out her arms, and Audrey fell into her embrace. Emma held her tightly. "How are you doing?"

Audrey shrugged as she broke the hug. "As good as one can be."

"I think getting away will help. Change of scenery, outta sight, outta mind—"

"And instead, my mind can focus on how obnoxious Reid is."

Emma gave her a stern look. "Audrey…let's assume positive intent. That's all we can really do."

"What? I've got about an hour to get it all out of my system before we get to her place. If I let it out now, maybe I'll be less annoyed and bitter."

"She's not even here, and you're already annoyed and bitter."

"You can blame Becca for my joyful mood."

"Have you two talked at all?"

"No. Not at all. She seems pretty done."

Emma placed a comforting hand on her shoulder. "We'll take good care of you. I promise."

She didn't get to take advantage of the hour drive over to Oceanside. She was too busy having an impromptu therapy session with Emma. How she should stop rereading their old texts, how she should stay no contact for a while, and how she shouldn't obsessively look at Becca's social media, which would be her biggest hurdle. She knew herself. She still wanted to know everything going on in Becca's life. What she was doing, how she was feeling, where she was, and who she was with.

If her conversation with Emma did anything, it made her wonder more about why this breakup had happened. What exactly promoted this blindside breakup? It didn't seem like Becca had randomly woken up and thought, "This isn't working anymore." With the amount of struggle Becca had getting the words out, hindsight finally became twenty-twenty. As Audrey raked through all her moments with Becca since life had come to a standstill after Sadie's diagnosis, she finally saw the breadcrumbs of Becca pulling away. They had been texting less, with more time between her responses. She was somehow always busy, even though Audrey knew her schedule hadn't changed, with the exception of her adding a few miles to her marathon training plan.

Audrey needed to investigate, and she knew there was a large possibility she could find clues on Becca's social media.

The first hour of their adventure went by fast. Before she knew it, they'd pulled into Reid's three-story condo building, two palm trees on either side. Emma texted that they were there, and a minute later, Reid hauled her suitcase and a book bag down the stairs.

"You know, we could have helped," Emma said as she and Audrey got out of the car.

Reid grunted when she got on the ground. "I'm a strong, independent woman," she said, wheeling the suitcase over to the car. "A CR-V? You could have picked any car for our one-way drive across the country, and you picked a mom car? That's not really a cool, road trip movie car."

Emma unlocked the truck, and Audrey popped open the passenger door. She assumed Reid would want the passenger seat since she "always got motion sick" in cars, which Audrey thought was bullshit because Reid was a scuba instructor. She got paid to be on boats every single day. She just figured Reid was lying to get the front. Audrey didn't care enough to argue, though. Having the back to herself meant she could stretch out.

"What were you expecting? A Lexus?" Emma said.

"No, more like a vintage convertible," Reid said and threw her stuff in the trunk. "Every great road trip movie has a vintage convertible. *Thelma and Louise. Crossroads*—"

"Was *Crossroads* a good movie?" Emma protested.

Reid directed a point at her. "I'm not here for *Crossroads* slander. Here, I'm envisioning a Thunderbird from the sixties, and instead, we get a mom car. Are you driving us to soccer practice?" She snickered on her way to the passenger seat.

Audrey was annoyed that Reid walked straight to the front, almost as if it was just a given that she'd get that seat. Her bad mood made her regret not being a little petty. At least she had the snack seat, the most important seat.

Reid strapped herself in. "*Crossroads: Honda Mom Edition.*"

Emma started up the car. "I thought we had a no-*Crossroads*-slander rule? Also, should we revive the rules like last time?"

Before their first attempt, the four of them had agreed on "rules" for the road trip since somehow, all of them had different ways of going about long drives.

Rule One: pee breaks outside of gas and food stops only occurred when it was a DEFCON 1 situation. Of course, that was Reid's first proposed rule. It was the first little jab that had started their disastrous first attempt. Audrey was the most hydrated one out of the four of them, which meant she needed to use the bathroom more often.

"Time to train your bladder. You need to consume way more cranberry. How do you already have to pee?" Reid would always say, and it always pissed her off. DEFCON 1 was when someone could no longer handle the bumps without worrying about their bladder exploding. And when pee stops happened, everyone had to go.

Which led into Audrey countering with Rule Two: Reid got the front so the rest of them didn't have to hear her complaining about motion sickness that, "only happens in the car but not on a scuba boat."

And then, Rule Three: the driver chose the music, Audrey's second proposed rule because she couldn't stand it when Reid criticized her country music. She never complained about Reid's weird electronic music, so why couldn't Reid shut up about her music?

"Yes," she and Reid both said adamantly. They turned to each other, and at the eye contact, Audrey looked away.

"Okay, cool. Now it's *my* turn to add a rule. Rule Four: when you two are driving, I'm taking the back because…well…we all know what moving vehicles do to me when I'm just riding."

"Make you narcoleptic?" Reid said.

"I'm like a baby. I don't get it, either," Emma said. "I can never stay awake for long periods of time in a planes, trains—"

"And automobiles," Reid said. "We know. I'm fine with that as long as I can enforce Rule Five," she said, holding up her hand. "I can listen to my own music while Audrey drives."

"Absolutely fine by me," Audrey said flatly.

Twist her arm, for God's sake.

Reid rolled her eyes. "Wow, guys. Isn't this going to be fun?" she said, her voice dripping with sarcasm.

"Rule Six," Emma said. "No more passive aggressive comments, or we will all have a group therapy session." When Audrey and Reid didn't answer, Emma continued. "Great. Glad that's all clear. Ah, there's nothing like a CR-V full of sad girls. Watch out, America!" She turned to look at both of them while backing out of the driveway. "Now, we have an hour and a half drive to Santa Monica. Everyone behave."

"Yes, Mom," Reid said.

CHAPTER FIVE

Reid stood silently before the *Route 66 End of the Trail* sign posted at the start of the Santa Monica Pier. She stared up at the sign, engulfed in a riptide of grief. It felt like she was below the surface of the water without an oxygen tank, desperately trying to breathe. She'd always envisioned Sadie standing next to her when they finally made it to the Santa Monica sign.

The summer after they all graduated college, they'd flown to Chicago to start their Route 66 adventure. They'd spent the day wandering the city, walking off the many slices of deep dish pizza they'd indulged in, and snapped a group photo in front of the *Route 66 Begin* sign on the corner of Adams Street and Michigan Avenue.

Emma snapped Reid out of her memory by asking a stranger on the pier to take a picture. As she stood between Audrey and Reid and put her arms around each of them, Reid tacked on a smile, fighting through the emotion rising in her throat like bile.

When Emma got her phone back, they looked at the picture. There they were, arms around each other, with very convincing fake smiles plastered on their faces, as if a six-year hole hadn't been punched in their timeline. Even though the background of the image was filled with the Memorial Day crowd, the top of the West Coaster that hovered above the shops lining the pier, and a sliver of the ocean off to the right, the picture looked so empty. Sadie's absence haunted them yet again. Reid knew once she saw the two Route 66 photos side-by-side, the twisting knot in her stomach would take over, and she would be debilitated in bed.

For Reid, the original group photo was a reminder of what they'd failed to accomplish six years ago. It was a reminder of how she and Audrey had turned Sadie's Route 66 bucket list item into a fantasy.

The more she thought about Sadie dying, the more anger she felt. Everything about it was so unfair. Sadie had such an idyllic life. Her parents were still together and actually loved each other. She was close with her brother, Bryan, despite their four year age difference. She'd met the love of her life in college and didn't have to go through a series of horrible dates or breakups in order to find that love. Sadie Russo had the parents, partner, dog, job, house, and life everyone would have envied.

So why the hell had it suddenly changed, and why the hell had she left this world so fast? Ten weeks from her diagnosis to her death. That was a blink of an eye.

Nothing about it was fair. No one deserved to be taken at twenty-nine but especially not Sadie. She was the glue of their friend group, and without her, all of them could shatter and crumble at any given moment.

She found it hard to believe that she would ever get used to Sadie's absence. She didn't want to. She refused to, and she knew that was a problem within itself because she had no control over the universe. She couldn't bring Sadie back or go back in time. This was her new normal now: life without her best friend. She never could fathom how much Audrey missed her mom and how hard life must have been, especially for a kid, to grow up without a mother. She didn't expect Sadie to take so much of Reid when she died, as if part of her had died too.

Maybe in some ways, a part of her had.

Their Airbnb for a night was a studio guest house in Silver Lake. When they lugged all of their bags in, the first thing Reid noticed was the one queen bed and a couch off to the left that she hoped contained a pullout mattress because there was no way she was going to share a bed with Audrey. If that was the case, she'd rather sleep out on the hammock on the deck. At least the hammock came with views of downtown LA in the distance.

She lifted the couch cushions and let out a sigh of relief when she found a mattress. She plopped her suitcase down. "I'll take the couch," she said.

"Are you sure?" Emma said. "I don't mind—"

Reid accidentally met Audrey's gaze and quickly flitted her stare away. "I do mind, and that's why I'm claiming the couch."

"I think it's for the best," Audrey mumbled to Emma as she put her things on the opposite side of the bed from Reid.

"Dinner is at six," Emma said, completely ignoring the dig, and placed her suitcase on the opposite side of the bed from Audrey.

An hour and a half later, they had napped, showered, and gotten ready for their first road trip bucket list item, dinner at a Michelin Star restaurant.

Reid wore the nicest thing she'd brought onto the trip: a white blouse tucked into her skinny black ankle pants. She finally rinsed the salt out of her hair after distracting herself with diving. Her wavy blond hair tousled down to the tops of her breasts.

When she walked out of the bathroom, she flinched when she saw Emma and Audrey had already changed. Audrey wore a black jumpsuit and red heels. She stared at herself in the mirror, putting gold earrings in. Her straight, dark brown hair fell to her shoulders, and her rich brown eyes were darkened with mascara. Reid wasn't expecting for her to look so, well, beautiful, a beautiful thorn in her side.

"Emma, can I steal some of your lipstick?" Audrey said, glancing inside Emma's makeup bag.

"Of course. I have a red one in there that would match your shoes."

Reid stared way too long as Audrey traced the scarlet across her lips. When she rubbed her lips and smacked them, she turned to place the lipstick back in Emma's toiletry bag. She glanced up, catching Reid's stare. Reid flitted her eyes away as her entire body flushed with prickly warmth.

She couldn't let herself stare for that long again.

While Reid couldn't remember the last time she'd dressed up for a dinner, she definitely remembered the last time she'd eaten and enjoyed a pizza Lunchables. It was a week ago out on the boat at work. She didn't care how childish it made her seem. It was quick and easy, and sometimes, she just didn't have the energy to cook, especially after spending all day outside.

Her palate was too trashy for her first Michelin restaurant: Axis LA.

Emma didn't seem to care about the awkward tension that had been following Reid and Audrey around like a shadow because her excitement was palpable as their elevator climbed to the fifty-third floor of a building in the heart of downtown Los Angeles.

As they waited for the hostess to take them to their table, she noticed the wall to the left held framed pictures of the celebrities who had dined there. The collection ranged from A-list movie stars to directors, musicians like Reagan Moore and Blair Bennett, and even Broadway stars like the legendary Marlie Rose. Reid took a step closer. Marlie Rose had two that spanned ten years apart, both signed in black permanent marker. One that was labeled, *Marlie Rose's 60th birthday. March 26, 2014*, and right next to it was a recent picture of Marlie Rose and her wife: *Marlie Rose's 70th birthday, March 26, 2024*.

"We're going to dine just like the greats," Emma said, pointing to the photos. "You know this place rotates, right?"

"It rotates?" Audrey said.

"I guess that's why it's called Axis, huh?" Reid said.

"The one in New York City rotates too," Emma said. "I've always wanted to come here but had no one to go with."

"It might make up for the caviar on the menu."

They followed the hostess into the restaurant. White tablecloths adorned each table. Their table was right next to a floor-to-ceiling window that offered a panoramic view of downtown. Reid was absolutely in awe of the view. The surrounding skyscrapers created a kaleidoscope of lights that stretched for miles until they dissolved into the horizon and the Hollywood Hills.

Reid could have sworn that everyone inside the restaurant knew she had a pizza Lunchables the week before. It was just a matter of time before they escorted her out for having taste buds like a twelve year old boy.

"This is stunning," Audrey said, taking the empty seat across the table from Reid and Emma.

"The food is going to be just as amazing," Emma said and opened the menu.

"We'll be the judge of that," Reid said.

"You still eat Lunchables. I don't think you get a say."

She caught Audrey biting back a smile.

See, everyone knows. I'm an imposter.

Apparently, Michelin restaurants had their own language because there were so many words she had never seen before. What the hell was a smoked Linzer potato? What was maitake? What the hell was celeriac? And pickled walnuts were a thing? "I had no idea you could pickle a walnut, but the more you know," Reid said.

"I'm pretty sure you can pickle anything," Emma responded.

"Can you pickle celeriac?"

Audrey looked up from her menu and made a confused face. "What the hell is celeriac?"

"A new word I just learned," Reid said. "Somehow, Michelin restaurants make potatoes confusing and complicated."

"It's celery root," Emma said and flipped the menu page casually, as if Reid should have known the answer.

"Okay, why can't they just say that?"

"It's to elevate the experience. This is a Michelin Star restaurant."

Reid held up her hands in surrender. "I'm sorry I don't have a sophisticated palate. Whose bucket list item was this?"

"It was mine," Emma said. Mr. and Mrs. Lin might have been experts in wine, but they were also foodies. When Emma had hosted the group sleepovers, her parents had made them the best homemade food. She, Sadie, and Audrey had never left hungry. "If you can't move off the couch, you're not eating enough," Mrs. Lin would joke as she handed them more plates of food.

"I'm a bit shocked Sadie consented to this," Reid said. "Our chicken tender friend would have been very disappointed that the closest thing to that is…duck."

"They have fancy tater tots, Reid," Emma said and pointed to the item. "Plenty to eat."

"The tots are ruined by the broccolini crema. Don't put vegetables on my starch."

"I don't know," Audrey said skeptically. "In-and-Out sounds incredibly good right now."

"You two are being the chicken tender friend right now," Emma said. "Come on, guys. I've never been to a Michelin restaurant before. I want to enjoy it with my best friends."

Emma's hurt tone filtered through Reid. In their friend group, all four of them had used teasing as a way to show the others how much they loved them, but sometimes, there was a fine line between teasing and hurting. Her friendship with Audrey was a prime example of that. What Reid had thought was a playful comment, Audrey processed as an attack.

"You're right," Reid said. "I'm sorry. Tell us what you're going to get."

"The Wagyu steak. I've never had one before. And they have Lambrusco. We're getting a bottle."

"Isn't that, like, cheap sparkling wine?"

Apparently, she had just said the wrong thing because Emma lowered her menu and directed a glare at her. "Yeah, if you buy the cheap stuff."

"What the hell is Lambrusco?" Audrey said.

"It's delicious sparkling red wine from Italy," Emma said, the human equivalent of Wine Wikipedia. "Some people think it's cheap because wine brands, like Riunite, mass produced them and made them cheap. But there are good quality Lambruscos out there, and this is a great quality. We're getting it."

All of Reid's Lambrusco experience was from drinking Riunite that had resulted in massive headaches the next morning. But she wasn't going to stop Emma from living out her Michelin restaurant dream. After the server poured their Lambrusco, Emma pulled out the third envelope.

Reid, feeling the impending twist in her stomach, braced herself and drank a large gulp. She paused and savored the taste. Okay, this Lambrusco was on a totally different playing field than Riunite. She took another sip and smacked her lips. She needed to stop doubting

Emma's wine knowledge because she had yet to steer them in the wrong direction.

"Should we read this?" Emma wiggled the letter back and forth.

"Did she write a letter for every bucket list item?" Audrey said.

"She did. They're all in the binder."

Reid wondered if any of these letters would get easier to digest. They were so full of Sadie. It was hard to believe she had been dying as she was writing them because her humor and spunk saturated the paper so much that Reid could feel it feed into her denial that Sadie was actually gone.

"Do one of you want to read it, or should I?" Emma said.

There was no way Reid was going to read it. She could barely listen to Sadie's words without feeling her throat closing in.

"I'll read it," Audrey said, taking the envelope.

Hi friends,

Are you guys ready for a FEAST? I know Emma is.

I got Jeremy to help me with this one since he's also a foodie like Emma. According to the internet, this place in LA is supposed to be amazing. It's owned by the host of Home Kitchen Masters, *the show that Emma forced us to watch when she was all high on pain meds after her wisdom tooth surgery. The food is supposed to be delicious, and you get to enjoy it with gorgeous 360 views of LA. Sadly, I don't see any chicken tenders on the menu, but if I was to get anything, it would be that Wagyu steak. I hope you eat all the delicious food, drink all of the delicious wine, and enjoy the views. Dinner is on us, see the gift card.*

And just an FYI for Reid and Auds, there's a burger spot two blocks away from the Airbnb if it's too fancy for you. You're welcome. Savor a burger for me please. I doubt the afterlife has many burger options. Maybe I'll be pleasantly surprised.

And Emma, if you ever need someone to keep you company while you appreciate fine cuisine, Jeremy says he'll gladly be your date. He's never been to a Michelin restaurant, and now I really want you to take him sometime.

Love you all!

XOXO Sadie

"Look at that, you have a date for your next Michelin adventure," Reid said. All the gulps of wine she'd had during that letter had loosened the ball in her throat.

"I should take him up on that so I don't have to hear so much complaining," Emma said. "Even Sadie found something. If she could find something on the menu, so can both of you."

Audrey silently folded the letter and passed it back to Emma. Reid sensed that reading it had packed another punch to Audrey's probably sore heart. She had been extra quiet today, which would have usually been nice because that meant Reid didn't have to brace for a passive aggressive comment. But she felt awful that it was because of a breakup. They had their long history, but as someone who had been through two rough heartbreaks, she empathized.

She just hoped that she wouldn't be the punching bag.

She had a feeling Emma sensed the dying conversation. She looked at Reid, then Audrey, and then the wine. She topped herself off, took a sip, and said, "I brought something else for us." She reached in her bag and presented their *ERAs Bucket List* and a brand-new purple gel pen. "For us to cross off the items as we go," she explained. "Since Audrey read the letter, she can do the honors." Emma handed Audrey the pen, and they sat in ceremonious silence as she drew a purple line over *Dinner at a Michelin restaurant.*

"A toast to Sadie." Reid raised her glass.

"To Sadie," they said together.

"I was trying to pick my favorite memory with her," Emma said, a faint smile touching her lips. "I was thinking about it when we all met up at Magnolia Springs, and I just love that so many of our big moments were there. I know my parents loved watching us grow up too. I loved my twenty-first birthday and how we closed the place down."

"It helped that we had a really cute waiter," Audrey said.

"Ah, Dean. He was so hot."

"I think that's what probably made me puke in the vineyard," Reid said teasingly. She had been the group's token lesbian the entire time, being subjected to the three of them gushing about cute boys at almost every hangout. She was a bit bummed when she heard about Audrey dating a woman years after their friend breakup. Growing up, she'd really needed another queer friend in that group to counteract Emma and Sadie's constant boy talk.

"The boy talk?" Emma said with a laugh.

"You guys went on and on about it. He was mid at best."

"You're also really gay."

"I am. That really affirmed it." She looked at Audrey. "It's a shame I didn't know you were bi until years after that."

"I think it's a shame too," Audrey said, and Reid noted it was the first time they'd agreed on something in six years. She chalked that up as a little victory.

"Your turn, Auds," Emma said. "What's your favorite Sadie memory?"

Audrey hesitated for a moment as she looked at her wineglass. "I mean, I have a lot of them, but I think the one that I keep coming back to is when I had a breakdown in the bathroom during gym class."

Reid had first met Audrey in that freshman year gym class, but it had taken until that following summer for Audrey to open up to them and tell them she and her dad had moved because her mom had died from breast cancer. Reid was a little shocked at the time that it had taken Audrey so long to tell them, but based on Audrey's story, Sadie had already known for a while.

"It was my mom's birthday, so it was a hard day," Audrey continued, her voice becoming more delicate as she spoke. "I went into the locker room to hide in one of the bathroom stalls and cry, but she found me in there, and I lost it when she hugged me. I cried for, like, ten minutes, and she held me the entire time and asked me sweet questions about my mom. Then, Mr. Loomis was upset that we'd missed ten minutes of gym class and didn't give us full credit for that day, which I was also upset about. But at least on that really shitty day, I knew I had just made a lifelong friend. I think that was the first time I'd felt safe in my new town and school. It was all Sadie's doing."

Sadie was similar to Reid in that they didn't like talking about hard feelings, listening to sad music, or watching sad movies. But just because Sadie didn't like talking about sad things involving herself, it didn't deter her from being someone's emotional rock when they needed it. In fact, she was always the first one to catch someone when they were falling, and because of her, no one ever really landed hard on the ground until now, when they had to carry on without her.

She was so glad that Sadie had been there for Audrey.

"Anyway," Audrey said, quickly wiped her eyes, and looked at Reid. "I'm passing the baton to you." She downed the last drink before topping herself up.

Ried tried to avoid the inevitable by glancing over her shoulder and looking to see if the server was arriving with their food. What was taking forever? She pursed her lips and stared out at the large windows overlooking downtown.

She had been friends with Sadie three years before the rest of them had met. While they'd became the "fearsome foursome" during freshman year of high school, she and Sadie had met in sixth grade at one of the two middle schools in town. Emma had gone to the other one. Reid had three crucial years of navigating the tumultuous terrain that was middle school, which served as ample time for collecting a bunch of core memories with her best friend.

"Well, I have a lot," she said, exhaling from the pits of her knotted stomach. "A very early favorite was when Sadie and I went to the eighth grade dance. Travis O'Malley had just broken up with her via Facebook, like, two days before the dance, and he had already moved on to Stephanie King. But Sadie still wanted to go to the dance, and when the *one* slow song of the night played, we danced together and laughed the entire time. She didn't even notice that Travis and Stephanie were dancing just a few people away from us. We were having our own best friend moment to 'Chasing Cars' and that was all that mattered."

Reid felt the memory swelling in her chest. Anytime she'd heard "Chasing Cars" by Snow Patrol, she thought of Sadie, and it always came with a pleasant wave of nostalgia. Now, she worried about how the next time she heard the song would turn the wave of nostalgia into a riptide of immense grief.

She wanted to know when memories stopped hurting so much as they resurfaced. She wanted to get through the stages of grief as fast as possible, but apparently, one couldn't dictate the process, according to her own personal therapist, Emma Lin.

Of course, right after Reid felt the grief flooding inside her, the server came out with their entrees. She had to give the chefs credit. The plate not only looked delicious, but it smelled absolutely divine. One whiff of the Wagyu steak and the delicious aromas woke up her hunger. Her stomach growled.

Okay, maybe Emma was really on to something here.

She watched Emma slice her first bite and dunk it in the celeriac purée. Reid copied her, and goddamn, did it taste like something angels grilled in heaven. She was now a believer. She felt foolish for giving the Michelin restaurant idea—and celeriac—a hard time.

"Oh, Jesus Christ," Reid said, closing her eyes and enjoying all the flavors on her tongue.

"Oh, I'm sorry. Was that a little moan?" Emma said.

"This is delicious."

"I'm sorry, can you please say that a little louder for me?"

"This. Is. Delicious."

"Even with the celeriac purée and pickled walnut?"

"The pickled walnut is suspicious, but the celeriac purée is much better than it sounded."

"Our deepest apologies," Audrey said to Emma and took a bite of her seared scallops.

For all the shit talking leading up to dinner, Reid polished off her plate. Audrey too. They ordered another bottle of wine and chocolate cake for dessert while keeping the conversation on a safe—yet heavy—topic that was Sadie.

By the time they got in their Uber and headed back to their Airbnb, they were all extremely full…and tipsy. Emma plopped right out the couch. "Everything was so good," she muttered into the couch pillow.

"Is someone a little tipsy on Lambrusco?" Reid said. "Have you been Lambrusced?"

Emma grinned. "I have been Lambrusced and have no regrets about it."

"How about you make it through the night without throwing it up, and then maybe you can celebrate being Lambrusced."

As Emma rambled about how much she loved Lambrusco, Reid went to the kitchen to pour her a large glass of ice water. Audrey situated herself on the bed and dove right into her phone, which was ironic because their argument all those years ago had started when Audrey had brought up how Reid was always on her phone while the four of them hung out. Reid could have used some help with a drunk Emma currently flopped on the couch.

She resisted the urge to make a snarky comment. She could tell by the somber look that had been flickering in Audrey's dark brown eyes all night that she must have been fighting some battles in her mind. If she needed that time to decompress, Reid would begrudgingly give it to her if that meant keeping the peace.

She could handle a drunk Emma. "Drink water," she said, handing Emma the glass as if handing it to an uncoordinated toddler.

Emma made a face. "I'm fine."

"Then humor me and drink it."

"Ugh, fine." She guzzled a couple liberal sips before setting it on the farthest edge of the table.

Reid practically dove to save the glass from falling onto the ground. "Don't get too comfortable. Your bed is over there."

"I'm just resting my eyes," Emma grumbled.

Reid looked up at Audrey, who sat crossed-legged on the bed, hunched forward and lost in the world of her phone. "Can you make sure she doesn't pass out on the couch?" When Audrey didn't look up, Reid pressed, "Audrey?"

Audrey glanced up with furrowed brows. "What?"

"Make sure she doesn't pass out. We all know once she's out, she's dead to the world. I'm going to get ready for bed."

"Yeah, okay."

Audrey didn't seem as drunk as Emma, but she certainly wasn't mentally in the studio.

"Oh my God, just kiss and make up already," Emma slurred, her words sounding like they were written in cursive. "Reid's been wanting to since we were teens anyway."

Reid's mouth fell open. Audrey snapped her gaze up, and Reid's entire body heated as if Emma had positioned the interrogation lamp directly on her. "Make sure she doesn't sleep," Reid barked and bolted into the bathroom.

She noted in the bathroom mirror just how beet red the embarrassment had slammed onto her face and neck. She couldn't believe Emma had just blurted out her fifteen year old secret, one so old that she often forgot about the crush she'd had on Audrey their freshman year of high school.

She stalled, taking as long as possible to get ready for bed before it became noticeable she was trying to avoid the aftermath of the truth bomb Emma had dropped. She walked back out, keeping her stare away from Audrey. All she wanted to do was bury herself under a blanket on the couch—

The sound of Emma's heavy breathing filled the studio. *Fuck.* Reid shook Emma's shoulder to no avail. "You let her fall asleep," she snapped at Audrey. Okay, now she was pissed. Moving the log that was a sleeping Emma was going to be the night's version of climbing Everest.

Audrey lowered her phone. "Have you tried waking her up?"

"No, that hadn't crossed my mind," she said acrimoniously. "Of course I tried."

"Okay, you don't need to be a dick about it."

"I asked you to watch her, and you were on your phone instead. But God forbid, I'm on my phone—"

Audrey shot a glare at her. "Me being on my phone right now is entirely different than you constantly being on your phone during the few times we hung out throughout the summer."

"Ah, yes, that's right. It's different because it's you."

Audrey finally abandoned her phone and got off the bed to assist, but her help was a little too late. Emma had chosen the couch as her bed for the night, which meant on their very first night of the trip, she and Audrey had to share a bed.

"Great, fucking great," Reid said. But just like Emma, when Reid was exhausted, she had no problem falling asleep. She'd spent plenty of nights camping with her family with nothing but a sleeping bag and Cameron snoring away next to her in their tent. Even when Emma and Sadie had hogged the air mattresses at their sleepovers and she'd ended up on the carpet with her blanket and pillow, she still was able to fall asleep. She had no reason to take the bed when she could make do with the accent chair for one night. She snatched a pillow and headed over to the chair, where she threw the pillow and curled up into it.

"You're not actually sleeping there, are you?" Audrey said, resentment laced through her voice.

"I am because you failed to make sure she didn't fall asleep on my bed."

"Reid, this is a queen bed—"

Reid cackled. "We couldn't survive being in a car with each other last time. You think we can survive sleeping in the same bed?"

"Okay, you're being a real dick. I think we can suck it up for a night and share a bed without killing each other."

"You don't know where my mind's at," Reid said dryly.

"Does anyone?"

"Who's being a dick now?"

Audrey rolled her eyes. "You're driving tomorrow, and you want to sleep curled up on a chair?"

"I don't want to sleep on the chair. I want to sleep on the couch, but a wrench got thrown into those plans."

"There's plenty of space here, Reid. I'm not going to spend any more time telling you that. You can sleep on that chair and be miserable on the drive tomorrow, or you can swallow your pride and sleep on the bed. Take your pick."

Audrey turned off the lights, only the glow of the phone lighting up her face. Reid was already uncomfortable, and she hated how her discomfort overtook her pride. She grunted as she snatched up the pillow and took the walk of shame back to the empty side of the bed. She slid into the crisp linen sheets and attempted to get comfortable on the farthest edge of the bed.

Now it was too quiet. Even Emma's heavy breathing had quieted. She stiffened as she tried cementing herself in place on the mattress, afraid to move just an inch and accidentally touch the person she hadn't spoken to in six years.

At one point in time, she and Audrey could talk about anything. They'd gone from being the last ones awake at sleepovers, whispering until they both fell asleep, to the silence blanketing them like a comforter, tucking them into the queen-size bed that felt too big and too small all at once.

They were strangers with memories, and Reid didn't like it one bit.

"So…what's this about you wanting to kiss me in high school?" Audrey said, slicing through the silence. Reid could hear the smile in her tone.

She grunted and flopped over on her side, her back facing Audrey. "Emma's drunk."

"A drunk person's words are a sober woman's thoughts."

"Go to sleep, Audrey," Reid said sternly.

Audrey laughed. "No, not until you elaborate."

Reid tossed her extra pillow over the top of her head. Emma owed her a very stiff drink the next day, that was for sure.

Chapter Six

"Oh, so surprise, I booked us a cave hotel tonight," Emma said casually as she nursed a lemon lime Gatorade in the passenger seat, as if staying in a cave was something a person did on a normal Tuesday.

"You're joking, right?" Audrey said, feeling the claustrophobia slowly squeezing around her chest.

Emma poked her head around the passenger seat. "No. Did I not tell you guys that?"

"I can't tell if you're joking or not."

"I don't think she's joking," Reid said, catching Audrey's gaze in the rearview mirror.

There was Emma again, casually firing off truth bombs. What a thing to drop on them while they battled the LA traffic first thing in the morning. She and Reid hadn't spoken all morning following Emma's big reveal last night, and now she barely had time to think about that as she needed to start mentally preparing herself to sleep in a cave like a bear going into hibernation. Her questions about Reid were shoved to the back of her mind when fear of being buried alive overtook her.

"I'm not joking," Emma said. She typed away on her phone and showed Audrey a picture of a hotel room in a literal cave. "It seemed cool. We need to get the most out of this road trip, and come on, a cave beats your very average hotel room."

"I think that sounds awesome," Reid said.

Audrey wasn't surprised that Reid was excited for it. She loved weird places like that, and so did Audrey, to an extent. Sleeping in a cave sounded…incredibly creepy, and she didn't do well with creepy things. She was the only one out of the four of them who loathed scary movies and haunted houses, but she'd sucked it up during October back in their youth when they had scary movie marathons and haunted house hangouts. She'd focused more on the snacks and watched the movie through the gaps in her fingers.

"How deep is this cave?" Audrey said.

Emma checked her phone. "Two hundred and twenty feet."

Her lungs tightened, and she didn't even have claustrophobia. She didn't know which was worse: a cave two hundred and twenty feet below the surface or LA traffic.

At least she had a five and a half hour car ride to mentally prepare.

Thanks to Emma's ability to fall asleep in any moving vehicle, she soon zonked out, leaving Audrey in the back with nothing but Reid and the Mojave Desert stretched out for miles.

It got painfully quiet in the car once Emma passed out. Audrey had no idea what to do with herself, but making small talk with Reid was not on her list. She pulled out her AirPods and played her newly created Spotify playlist of sad breakup songs.

If Sadie had been in the car, she would have said it was very Pisces thing to do. When Sadie's and Reid's hearts ached, they always tried drowning their sadness out with distractions and upbeat music. When Emma's and Audrey's hearts ached, they engulfed their ears in the sounds of melancholy. She and Emma even had a shared playlist of sad songs, and some of those recommendations were perfect for her new breakup playlist. In some strange way, listening to the devastating melodies and lyrics helped stitch her back together. At least when she listened to those songs, she felt significantly less alone.

God, she was so lonely. Who sang a song about losing their best friend and then getting dumped shortly after? Because she really needed that song on her playlist.

She let the music cleanse her mind for about an hour until her brain needed something new to fixate on. She leaned over to check the remaining time on the car's map display. Two hours until they reached Peach Springs, Arizona.

Plenty of time to cyberstalk Becca.

Since meeting the summer before on a dating app, this was the longest she and Becca had gone without talking. Day four of zero contact. What the hell was Becca up to? Was she just as sad? Was she able to get out of her house? Or was it only Audrey who was suffering?

The only window into Becca's life was social media, so Audrey opened up Instagram on her phone. There Becca was in her sports bra and spandex running shorts, flaunting her sexy stomach that was definitely more toned than when she'd first started training for the marathon.

Audrey hated how traitorous her body was in that moment, reacting to Becca looking hot in her running attire. The small hints of abs poking through, how good her biceps and chest looked in that sports bra. For a second, she forgot that they were no longer together because an urge to comment with the fire emoji ran rampant through her mind.

Until she remembered she couldn't do that anymore.

Of course, the picture had gotten almost a hundred likes. Becca didn't post too much, so the fact that she'd posted a low-key thirst trap kickstarted the worry in Audrey's already scrambled brain. There was a voice in her that told her to go check out the fifteen comments while another voice told her to put her phone down and keep listening to music, knowing full well that something hiding in those comments would give her the answer she didn't want to know.

So why her thumb went against her mind's wishes, she wasn't sure. But the comments were right in front of her, and her eyes hooked around each one, fishing for the very thing to validate her worries that there was someone else.

Then, she found a comment from Maya, one of Becca's new friends from her marathon training group.

Maya: *Well damn...I think I need some water. It's hot in here.*

Becca: *I have plenty of water at my place if you wanted to stop by.*

Maya: *I think I'm going to need more than just water...*

Becca: *I'm a fabulous host. Just ask and you shall receive.*

Maya: *Don't worry. I'm not shy.*

Each comment punched Audrey as if her stomach was a speed bag. What the hell had she just read?

She read it again…and again…and again…and again until she felt the hot tears running down her cheeks.

Was this real flirting? It couldn't have been. Becca had hardly flirted with *Audrey* on socials. It couldn't have been real.

But what if it was? Wouldn't that explain why Becca had pulled the rug out from under them?

Just a week ago, she'd told Audrey she loved her. Now, she was flirting with someone in her comment section, something Audrey had never seen her do. That was enough for the worry to grow into a lavish field. She'd known about Becca's new friend Maya but hadn't thought anything of it. She was glad Becca was making new friends who were encouraging her to continue to train for something she'd always wanted to accomplish. She'd loved that Becca had found an "accountability partner," loved that she'd gone out and grabbed drinks with her on occasion. She'd had no reason to question or worry about their relationship.

Until now, when the comments made her feel like an old sweater tossed in the donation bin.

A sob rose in her chest, blossomed, and escaped down her cheeks.

"Are you going to vom?"

She looked up at the rearview mirror to find Reid's sapphire eyes fixed on hers. It was the first thing she had said to Audrey since the night before. Audrey had almost thought she'd turned invisible. "No," she said, her throat swollen with rising emotion.

Reid's blond eyebrows furrowed. "If you need to vom, I can just pull over—"

"I don't need to vom."

"Then why do you look like that?" Reid's voice was thick with more worry about possible throw-up than it was of annoyance or resentment, but the comment was just one more push over the edge for the tears to burst from her eyes.

A cry escaped Audrey, and she covered her mouth to hold the rest in. Breaking down with only Reid was not what she wanted to happen while stranded in the middle of the Mojave Desert. She felt safer hugging a cactus than she did relying on Reid emotionally.

Maybe if she cried loud enough, Emma would wake up, but that would show more vulnerability to Reid than Audrey was comfortable with. She didn't need any advice or feigned support. She hadn't considered Reid part of her support system since college, and it sure as hell wasn't going to change in the middle of a desert.

"Becca. She's…she's flirting with someone in her comments."

"Okay, that might not mean anything—"

"It's a friend who she got really close with recently."

"It could be friendly banter."

Something in Audrey's gut told her that wasn't the case, and she had a pretty good intuition. Whenever she felt it, she was usually right. That was something else Sadie would have said was very Pisces of her.

But she didn't want to share all that with Reid, at least, not when Emma was deep in REM sleep based on how wide her mouth hung open.

She read the exchange over and over until her leaking eyes told her that was enough. She tossed her phone to the side and let the music cradle her broken heart.

They pulled up into the Cavern Inn parking lot. The outdated yellow sign simply read *avern Inn*, and Reid hoped that the lack of upkeep had nothing to do with the conditions of the room down in the cave.

A tall, lanky, middle-aged man with gray hair and a mustache introduced himself as Lawrence, their attendant for the evening. He led them into the elevator and on their way down to the cave, explained that he would be on duty to help them for anything they needed: room service or emergencies.

"The only connection to the outside is via elevator…and me," he said proudly. "But don't worry. I know these caves like the back of my hand. You'll be fine."

"Sounds amazing," Reid said. "I'm in."

"There's probably no Wi-Fi," Audrey muttered.

"I think a break from Wi-Fi might be good for you," Reid said.

"I can assure you there is, indeed, no Wi-Fi down there," Lawrence said.

"Are you social media stalking?" Emma said.

"She is," Reid answered.

Audrey glared. "Thanks, Reid."

"What? You're not going to listen to me when I say you need to stop. Maybe you'll listen to Emma." She turned to Emma. "While you were passed out in the car, Audrey found Becca flirting with some girl on an Instagram post."

"Oh no," Emma said, her tone deflating.

"Wow, Reid. Snitch much?" Audrey said.

"Who's the girl?"

"One of her marathon training friends," Audrey muttered.

"Okay, well," Emma said and let out a heavy sigh. "Reid is right. You don't need Wi-Fi right now—"

"But—"

"But nothing. There's nothing you can do right now. Keeping tabs on her social media is just going to drive you crazy."

"Which will then drive us crazy," Reid added for good measure.

"Thanks, Reid," Audrey said sarcastically. Her eyebrows furrowed. "Great to have your support."

"I'm giving you support by telling you to stop engaging in things that aren't going to help you."

"Yeah, while being a dick about it—"

"I'm so happy the three of us are going to be staying in a literal cave for the evening," Emma said, her voice dripping with sarcasm. She turned to Lawrence. "Sorry about that, Lawrence. Breakups are hard this day and age."

"Look, I don't know much outside of what's in these caves," Lawrence said. "But it sounds like just the place you need to decompress for a night. Breakups are hard. I can't imagine going through a breakup these days with the internet and all that. I see my granddaughter struggling with it. Makes me glad that I was born a hundred years ago," he said with a wink.

"Listen to Lawrence," Emma said to Audrey. "He's wiser than all of us."

"Not sure about that, but I can distract you with a little tour of the caves if you would like."

Reid noticed Audrey tacking on a forced smile. "That would be great, Lawrence. Anything will help."

After the elevator rumbled as it descended two hundred and twenty feet, the doors opened with blackness on the other side, the cool, damp air greeting them. Lawrence turned on an LED flashlight, the beams revealing craggy limestone walls that towered above them. Dim light illuminated the cement pathway to a sectioned off area, the "room" they were going to stay in for the evening. Lawerence filled them in on everything they needed to know. The caves were formed over sixty-five million years ago and were the largest dry caverns in the US. The extremely dry conditions created an ideal environment for preservation, Lawrence explained right as they approached a mummified bobcat on the other side of the metal guardrail.

Reid tried holding in her laughter when Audrey flinched at the bobcat with its mouth open, body twisted and nestled in the rocks. A sign hung right next to it that said, *Mummified Bobcat, Died Approx. 1850.*

In addition to mummified animals, the caves also included a restaurant, a hotel room, and plenty of ghosts.

"Ghosts?" Audrey said in a panic. "How are there ghosts in a cave?"

"Well, in the last fifty years, eight people have died on the property, and legend has it, these caves were used as a Native American burial ground."

"Fascinating," Reid said. She loved stuff like this, but Audrey did not. She hated scary movies and always watched them through her fingers.

"Have you seen a ghost?" Audrey said.

"No," Lawrence said. "But I've heard things. Just some whispers."

"*Just* some whispers?"

"Some people say they saw a man appear by the elevator shaft—"

"Oh God," Audrey said and shivered.

"Too bad we don't have 'see a ghost' on the bucket list," Reid said.

"Is it weird that I kind of want to see something?" Emma said.

"Yes, it's very weird," Audrey said. "If I see something, I'm coming up."

Lawrence chuckled. "If it makes you feel any better, they won't harm you."

"No, that doesn't make me feel better."

Finally, they reached their "suite," nestled on top of a wooden platform in what Lawrence said was the biggest room in the cave. Their room had two queen beds, two couches, and a TV nestled in a wooden entertainment system stacked with books, coloring books, board games, and even a collection of records. It looked like a regular hotel room besides having no walls and being in the middle of a dark cave.

"A TV, books, games, a fallout shelter, and a mummified bobcat," Reid said once Lawrence departed up the elevator. "Everything you need for a sleepover. Also, this would be an awesome place to have sex in." She examined the space and wished—just for a moment—that she could cross that off her own personal bucket list.

"I really regret watching that Chilean coal miner movie," Audrey said. "It's all I can think about."

"At least it's distracting you from Becca, so…silver lining?"

"We're going to be fine," Emma said. "We have Lawrence just a short elevator away. And he's bringing us wine."

"I think you should probably take a little break from wine," Reid said flatly. "You were super drunk last night and spilling secrets."

Emma frowned. "What?"

"We'll talk later," Reid said, lowering her voice so Audrey couldn't hear from the bed.

"I'd like to think Sadie would be bummed if I don't drink wine in this cave," Emma said, carrying on.

"She would be drinking the wine next to the mummified bobcat, let's be real."

"Would this be a bad time to bring back the ghost stories?" Emma said, exchanging a glance at both Reid and Audrey.

"Um, yes," Audrey shouted from the bed. Her voice echoed.

Telling ghost stories was something that Reid and Sadie had started back in middle school. What had started out as a funny way to scare each other right before bed had followed them into high school, when they'd met Emma and Audrey. It had soon became part of their sleepovers. They would always have great food, the best snacks, gossip sessions, and right before bed, Reid and Sadie would make up some ridiculous story for shits and giggles. Emma had always seemed to enjoy them. Audrey would either plug her ears or "go to the bathroom."

"I can tell you about Frankie Christianson, who died in these caves during the turn of the century," Reid said as her fictional story popped up in her head.

"Can we save the story for the car ride tomorrow? Please?" Audrey said.

"Okay, fine," Reid said. "But it's a great tale. Don't let me forget."

"I can't believe she's flirting with her. Right in the open," Audrey said, hugging the pillow tighter.

Emma stopped looking around the books and games in the entertainment system and glanced over. "Are we *sure* it wasn't just, like, friendly banter?"

"That's what I said," Reid said.

"My gut says no, and my gut is always right."

Emma sighed and walked over to the bed with an *Uno* deck. "It's probably a good thing we're down here for the night. You need to stop looking. Nothing good is going to come from looking."

"I don't understand what she's doing," Audrey said with a soft crack in her throat. "I have no idea what our relationship even meant if she can move on that quickly. Four days, to be exact. This just feels so cruel, doing it right in front of me."

"You're not going to get those answers looking at her Instagram," Emma said as she patted Audrey's back. "She's distracting herself from the breakup. Plain and simple. It has nothing to do with you and more to do with her and her coping skills."

"It doesn't feel plain and simple," Audrey said, swatting her watery eyes.

No matter what had come between them in the last six years, Reid hated seeing Audrey this upset. She knew heartbreak all too well. It was what made her stay clear of seriously dating again. When a person opened their heart for someone to trample on, it was debilitating. She questioned her own worth, if the relationship or feelings for her were even real. She wished she had something helpful to say to Audrey, but even with her experience in heartbreak, her words paled in comparison to Emma's.

Audrey didn't trust her, and honestly, Reid didn't blame her. If roles were reversed, she wouldn't have trusted Audrey with her brittle heart either.

Emma wiggled the *Uno* deck. "How about we play a little game? Try to clear our minds of the ghosts and ex-girlfriends?"

Emma to the rescue. For the next hour, they sat around the coffee table and played *Uno*. Reid controlled the record player, playing Neil Diamond, Bennett and Sons, and in honor of Sadie and her love for musicals, the original Broadway cast album of *Sincerely, Yours*.

Once the Marlie Rose album ended, the silence was noticeable, pulling Reid out of the game. The defining silence made it incredibly easy for Sadie's absence to haunt her mind. Everywhere she turned, she thought of her and how much she would have loved staying in this place.

Grief had to be one of the most tumultuous things humans had to go through in their lives. It was insidious, the way it slithered in and out of the depths of one's mind and wrapped itself around them at the most random times. One minute, she was finding pure entertainment in screwing over Audrey in *Uno*, and then the next, she was trying to hold it together.

"You okay, Reid?" Emma said as the three of them packed up the game. "You got quiet all of a sudden."

She swallowed the lump in her throat. "Yeah. I just…I just suddenly missed Sadie. I wish she was here."

The lingering glare in Audrey's eyes softened, and Emma squeezed her shoulder. "I wish she was here too."

"I guess I haven't gotten used to it just being the three of us yet," she said. "Is it always going to feel this incomplete?" She wanted Sadie to come back. As a ghost, a dream, a song on the radio, or a purple sunset. She had been obsessed with purple, and one of the more serious things she'd told Reid as she was dying was that she would come back as a purple sunset one day while Reid was out scuba diving.

She wanted and needed something to fill the giant hole in her heart. She'd take anything at this point. Even another letter.

"It's more like you get used to things feeling incomplete," Audrey said low and soft.

Reid noticed her somber eyes. She'd been so concerned about getting through the bucket list unscathed by Audrey's passive aggressive comments that she'd totally forgotten that this wasn't the first time Audrey had lost someone in her life. She had lost her mom a few months before Reid had met her. She couldn't imagine the pain she must have gone through at such a young age, losing such an important person.

"What do you mean?" Reid said. She needed any kind of insight, even if it came from Audrey. She just wanted to know when she'd start feeling more like herself again.

"It means this is our new normal," Audrey said. "Things never go back to what they were. You just get used to their absence and the heaviness in your chest. I guess if you're surrounded by ghosts all the time, you get used to them being there." The profound loss sparkled in her eyes as she turned away, almost as if she was ashamed to show emotion in front of Reid.

"I have seven years of psychology education under my belt," Emma said, "and even with all of that—even though I've had clients who come to me to help them with their grief—going through it myself, I feel so unprepared…and lost. It's one thing to study it. It's another thing to live through it."

"It doesn't get better," Audrey continued. "It just becomes… normal."

When the three of them went to bed, Reid ruminated on Audrey's words. *It just becomes normal.*

Ever since she'd known she was going to lose Sadie, she'd tried so hard to find a way to equalize herself to her new "normal," like a diver adjusting to the pressure of deep water. No matter how many attempts she made to adjust to all the changes that had happened in the last three months, the pressure continued to mount in her chest, stomach, and head, and if she didn't figure it out soon, it was just a matter of time before she suffered from the barotrauma.

Chapter Seven

Reid glanced up at a bright yellow sign that said, *The Roadkill Café*, welcoming them into the parking lot in Seligman, Arizona. "This place sounds very appetizing," she said, making sure the sarcasm was rich in her tone.

"Sadie's list of stop recommendations says this is, like, a quintessential Route 66 stop," Emma said as she unbuckled in the back seat. "She put it in the binder, and the binder is the Bible so…"

"I wouldn't say that loudly in these parts," Reid said. "It reeks of Trumpers."

"I'll take eating at this place over sleeping in a haunted cave again," Audrey said.

Even though they were only thirty minutes into their two and a half hour drive to Sedona, Emma had told Audrey to veer off to the small brick building with the dubious name and a giant elk statue off to the right.

The hot dry air greeted Reid once she got out of the car and stretched. She was skeptical about the name, but she also trusted Sadie's—and Emma's—research. They hadn't ever led them astray.

Inside, thousands of signed dollar bills covered the ceiling and walls, also dotted by taxidermy animals. They definitely were not in Southern California anymore. It was very clear they were in what had once been the Wild West.

"Well look at these beauts," a middle-aged man said from behind the bar. He had a white handlebar mustache and wore a crisp tan cowboy hat with a feather tucked into the leather-studded hatband. "Come on in, and take a seat anywhere you'd like." His accent was thick and sounded exactly how one would think a man with a low white ponytail and handlebar mustache in the middle of Wild West, Arizona would sound. He handed the three the menus and flashed a friendly smile.

You kill it, we grill it, was at the top of the menu. Every item was named after something someone could run over. Rigor Mortis Tortoise: a hungry man breakfast. Armadillo on the Half Shell: breakfast burrito. Flat Cats: buttermilk pancakes or Belgian waffles.

"Do you think he got that feather from a bird he ran over?" Reid whispered, leaning into the table so her words didn't travel.

"Yes, absolutely," Audrey said dryly.

"Do you also think he knows I'm a flaming homosexual? I feel like he knows. Thank God for the token straight friend." Reid patted Emma on the back.

"I'm so glad to be filling in a few of those boxes," Emma said. "Truly."

"I'm going to use the bathroom," Audrey said, standing. "Could you order me a water and a coffee, please?"

"Sure thing, boss," Emma said.

Once Audrey disappeared into the bathroom, Reid pointed her glare at Emma. It took Emma a few seconds to look up.

"What's that look for?"

"Why the hell did you tell Audrey I had a crush on her in high school?"

Emma's eyes widened. "Did I say that?"

"Oh yes. When you were all 'brusced out. You told us to kiss and make up already and that I've been wanting to do that since I was a teen, which is absolutely not even true, by the way. The crush didn't even last all of freshman year."

"Shit, Reid. I'm so sorry," Emma said, her tone genuine and partially embarrassed.

"It's already so awkward, and now I have to deal with that."

"I really didn't mean to. I barely remember saying something but—"

"*I* even forgot I had a crush on her. That's how long ago—and extremely short—the crush was. Thank God, she hasn't said anything about it since that night. The cave helped distract her from it, I guess."

"Do you want me to do damage control? I can—"

Reid raised a hand to stop her. "Please don't. I really hope she just forgets about it because it's the last thing I want to talk about."

"I'll swear off drinking for the rest of the trip."

"You don't have to do that, but you do owe me, at least, several drinks until the embarrassment leaves my body."

Emma held out her hand to shake on the promise. "I can do that."

As Audrey came back from the bathroom, Reid noticed a horrified expression crossing her features, her eyes plastered on her phone. She slid back into her seat next to Emma without saying anything.

"Did you see a ghost in the bathroom or something?" Reid said.

"Excuse me?" Emma said and leaned over to check Audrey's phone. "What are you doing?"

"She posted a picture with Maya," Audrey said, eyes glued to the image. She showed it to Emma.

"Who's Maya?"

"The girl she was flirting with in the comments. They went to the You Hall together."

"Oh no," Reid said.

She had no idea what image Audrey and Emma were staring at on Audrey's phone, but she knew all too well about the You Hall, a queer woman bar in Oceanside. It was bad news for Audrey for a couple of reasons. One, if Becca lived in Temecula, which Reid assumed, that meant she'd committed herself to an hour drive to Oceanside. A commitment like that just days after a breakup most likely meant she went there on a mission. Reid knew because she had also gone to the You Hall after Shelby had broken up with her to find a woman to help her forget. And two, if Becca was at the bar with another woman, the same woman she was flirting with in her Instagram comments, Reid was pretty sure they'd gone together. The bar drew young queer women and singles every weekend. It was where they went if they wanted a fun dance floor make out or to find a rebound.

Audrey looked over at Reid. "What do you think it means?"

Reid's mind sputtered. She wasn't sure if Audrey needed consoling or the hard truth. "Can I see the picture?"

Audrey flashed her the phone.

There Becca was, dolled up in sexy clothes, her brown hair coifed in curls and her makeup done to perfection. Right next to her with their cheeks pressed together was who Reid assumed to be Maya, almost a clone of Audrey with light brown hair and dark brown eyes that appeared almost black.

The fact that she resembled Audrey, plus how both Becca and Maya had dressed to impress, with tops that showed off the perfect amount of cleavage to grab any woman's attention, was a clear indication that Audrey's fears were most likely accurate.

"Wait, what? What's the You Hall?" Emma said.

"A lesbian bar," they both answered at the same time.

"In Oceanside," Reid added.

"Oceanside? That's a drive."

"That's partially the point," Audrey said.

Emma furrowed her eyebrows. "I don't understand the name."

"We can tell you all about U-Hauling later," Reid said. "But I think the point Audrey is getting at is that it's not a good sign. You go to the You Hall to meet women. I get why Audrey is concerned now."

"Thank you," Audrey said.

"Auds, you really need to stop checking. It's not good for your mental health or your healing. Watching her social media is just going to keep reopening those wounds."

"Mute her," Reid said and set her coffee mug down like an exclamation point. "Muting is your friend."

"I just want to know when she fell out of love with me," Audrey said softly. The deflation in her voice was loud and clear.

Reid wished there was a way to ease her pain, but they were not in the place where Audrey would even be open to hearing advice from her.

Emma rested her hand on Audrey's back. "You're not going to find that answer on her social media," she said sympathetically.

"She just broke up with me five days ago, and now she's trekking more than an hour away with her hot new 'friend,'" Audrey said. "I don't understand how she can just move on so quickly."

"You can't control what she does," Emma said soothingly, placing her hand on Audrey's wrist. "But you can control what you consume, and I strongly recommend you stop checking. At least throughout the rest of the vacation. Just focus on the present and what we're doing for Sadie."

"I just don't understand," Audrey said, shaking her head. "I don't understand how she can say all these nice things to me just a week before, tell me how much she loves me while I'm crying in her arms, and then decide to be done with me and move on to someone new in five days."

"I mean, we don't know if she really moved on, do we? She could just be going out with friends."

"No," Audrey and Reid said at the same time.

Audrey looked up at Reid. They both seemed to have an understanding, and Reid made sure to soften her stare so Audrey knew that all the feelings she was currently wrestling with were valid.

"What do you think?" Audrey said, looking at Reid.

"Who? Me?" Reid said, genuinely confused as to why Audrey was seeking advice from her instead of Emma, her more trusted friend.

"No, the other queer person behind you."

Reid gave her a side-eye. "Don't be an ass," she said jokingly.

"Emma's too straight for this conversation."

"Hey!" Emma shot back.

"I mean, of course there's a chance that she's there to distract herself, like Emma said," Reid said. If Audrey was fishing for her honest thoughts, she was going to give them. Sugarcoated opinions would just be detrimental to Audrey, and as someone who had been in that same spot before, she knew what Audrey needed. While it might hurt, she was better off in the long run. "It's something I would probably do right after a breakup. I definitely did that after Natalie and Shelby because I didn't want to sit with my feelings."

Emma coughed into her closed fist. "Avoidant."

Reid rolled her eyes. "Or maybe I'm self-aware." She turned back to Audrey. "I think the probability is pretty high that she's looking for a distraction. If not with Maya, then with a random chick."

"Really?" Audrey said, deflating with defeat.

Reid noticed Emma tightening her jaw as if telling her to knock it off.

"What?" Reid said. "False hope post breakup isn't healthy either."

Audrey downed another large gulp of her orange juice. "This is just great."

❖

Audrey knew she would regret not eating more than a few bites of her pancakes. An hour out from Seligman, her stomach growled for lunch despite the heartbreak coiling into knots in the pit of her gut.

She turned her comfort music up a couple of notches to distract herself from her hunger. She didn't care that Reid was just a few inches away in the passenger seat. A small, petty part was excited to subject Reid, the biggest critic of her music tastes, to whatever she felt like listening to. The car rules were firmly intact. Plus, Emma was awake to enforce them—

She checked the review mirror to find that Emma was already out. Eyes closed. Pillow against the window.

Okay, she was on her own again with nothing but her breakup playlist, Reid, and the emerging pine trees on the side of the road that had replaced the barren lands of the American southwest.

At least they were finally approaching civilization.

With an hour left to go, she tried breathing through the pain. The heartbreak mixed with anger. Anger about Becca, about the situation, about the fact that Audrey knew better and still chose self-sabotaging behaviors, and anger that her best friend wasn't there to give her the sympathetic yet tough love that she wanted and needed.

It was times like these she really wished her mom—and Sadie—was still alive. While her dad being there meant the world, she knew that the special bond she had with her mom would have really helped. She was always so nurturing and wise, and God, Audrey wished she could vent and cry to her mom about her heartbreak. They'd never had that chance. Her mom had died before Audrey had her first boyfriend.

Sadie and Emma were her go-to people for when she really needed a distraction or a sympathetic ear. Emma was great, but she was also a therapist, and sometimes Audrey just wanted a feral bitch session without any therapy talk.

It was a shame that she and Reid had their falling out before she'd realized she was bisexual because she also really needed a queer friend. Since she didn't have one or her mom, Sadie, or even Emma, who was passed out in the back with her mouth wide open, she had to rely on her music.

"Can I make a suggestion?" Reid said out of nowhere while Audrey navigated her way through Flagstaff, veering off Route 66 to head down to Sedona.

Ah, the peace and quiet since Seligman was nice…and short-lived. "If it's about my music, then no."

"It *is* about the music, but hear me out."

Audrey laughed. Of course it was about her music. She knew the peaceful two hours were too good to be true.

Audrey let out an annoyed sighed. "Okay, what?"

"You want to get over Becca, right?"

She didn't know how to answer that. "I don't know," she said, exhaling languidly. "I just want everything to go back to how it was."

"But that's not going to happen."

"Thank you for the reminder," she said plainly.

"Look, what I'm trying to get at is that I don't think these songs about longing and reminiscing are going to help you. It just feeds into what I'm sure you're hoping for: that she'll come back. But that's a dangerous way of thinking."

"Why? It could happen."

"Do you really want someone back who let you go? And if your suspicions are correct, broke up with you for someone else?"

She knew she shouldn't want Becca back. If she had moved on five days after their breakup, any secure person would say, "Fuck you, I'm too good for this." She just wished she was strong enough to truly believe that.

"I don't know," Reid continued. "If someone wanted to throw away a year relationship for someone else, I wouldn't want them back."

"I don't know if I'm at that point in my healing journey yet," she said softly. If Becca wanted Maya, she should let her go. But that was easier said than done when all their good moments keep replaying in her mind.

"Want to hear the biggest thing I learned in therapy?"

Audrey wanted to know when the hell Reid Haley had gone to therapy. Surely, it wasn't until *after* their friend breakup, but that was for another time. "Sure."

"Anger is your friend. It helps you detach. You should stop listening to your sad girl cover of 'Winner Takes It All' and start listening to the angry songs because once you hit your angry stage, God, it makes it easier to let go. Trust me."

"I don't."

Reid let out a hollow laugh. The silence filled the car as the sad girl version of "Winner Takes It All" finished.

The sad music might have made her feel less alone, but it didn't help tame her sadness. Maybe she needed to try a different approach. Trying out anything Reid suggested made her skeptical. Reid had a history of running from her feelings and not handling conflict well. But if, at any point, Reid led her astray, Audrey knew she could hush her up with a country song.

Audrey exhaled defeatedly. "Okay, what kind of angry song did you have in mind?"

"This song helped me get over my situationship," Reid said as she fiddled around on Audrey's phone.

She didn't know anything about Reid's situationship. She made a mental note to ask about it later.

Reid played the song, and on the dashboard touch screen read, "Silver Springs" by Fleetwood Mac. She wasn't someone who listened to seventies music too much, though she had nothing against it at all. As she focused on the road ahead, she took in the lyrics, and every line Stevie Nicks sang resonated, as if Stevie was knocking the nonsense out of her through that bop of a song. While she could still hear Stevie's heartbreak, it was the anger that really shone through her voice.

Each verse, more and more of Audrey's sadness boiled into betrayal and anger but the empowering kind. Stevie Nicks sang each word like she knew what she'd had to offer should have been cherished, and it was her ex's loss for not letting her love them.

And it finally unlocked a new feeling: anger. Anger about Becca breaking up with her when she was mourning the death of her best friend. Anger about Becca not appreciating all of Audrey's love for her. Anger about Becca fleeing to someone new and shiny in a matter of five days.

By the end of the song, Stevie Nicks and Reid had convinced her it was Becca's loss. She was the one who'd ended things and run off to find something shallow and temporary, and Audrey knew for a fact that what she had to offer was so much better and valuable than shallow and temporary.

She pressed the button on the steering wheel to repeat the song. From her peripheral, she noticed Reid smirking victoriously. She suppressed the urge to roll her eyes because at least the song was working. It ran through her and killed all the weepy sadness in her blood like a vaccine.

"It's a good one, right?" Reid said. "You know the story about this song?"

"No, not at all."

"Oh it's good. So you know that Stevie Nicks and Lindsey Buckingham dated, right?"

"I think so?"

"Well, they did. So Stevie writes this song about their breakup, and it gets nixed from *Rumours*, their biggest album, and Stevie is devastated. Twenty years later, they have this reunion performance where she finally gets to sing the song for the first time. And she just sings with her whole heart and stares daggers into Lindsey, as he has to stand there, playing guitar and singing backup vocals to his own diss track. Stevie Nicks said it was therapeutic to sing it to him and how it gave her closure."

"Maybe if we keep replaying it, it will give me closure."

"I don't care how any times we repeat this song. This is hands down the best breakup song ever written. A hill I will die on. This song helped me through it."

"Helped you through what? The situationship?"

"Yeah, Shelby."

"She was...after?"

"Yeah. We broke up a year ago. We were only together for six months, but she still crushed me."

"What happened?"

"She broke my heart."

Typical Reid answer. Short, sweet, and zero details. The more questions Audrey asked, the more she felt Reid's sturdy walls. "I gathered that," Audrey said and decided not to fight through them. "But how?"

"She dumped me out of the blue and ghosted me. We never spoke again. I tried multiple times, but she never responded."

"Wow. That's pretty…awful."

"Honestly, it was horrible. I have no idea how you go from finally calling me your girlfriend to then ghosting me two weeks later with very little explanation. It really crushed me. Took me a while to recover from that. Sometimes, those situationships get you hard." She motioned a stab in the heart.

"Do they? I wouldn't know."

"Consider yourself lucky."

"Lucky that I barely know how dating works?"

"Exactly that."

"I just had Trevor and Becca."

"And that guy you were talking to after Trevor. What was his name? Peter?"

"Paul."

"Trevor and Paul. Such boring straight dude names."

"And just like that, you turned into an ass and ruined a relatively nice moment."

Reid laughed. "What? How am I an ass?"

"Because you have an opinion about every aspect of my life."

"It's not an opinion about your life. Just the names of the dudes you've liked."

"Are you guys arguing?" Emma asked in her thick, groggy, sleeping voice.

Audrey checked the rearview mirror. Emma's eyes were still closed as she repositioned herself in her spot.

"No," Audrey and Reid said.

"Okay good," Emma mumbled.

As the highway took them up the mountains, the sinuous roads and sharp turns silenced Reid. Audrey didn't suspect anything abnormal until a sad country breakup song started playing, and Reid said nothing.

She snuck in a quick glimpse and found Reid with her head against the headrest, eyes sealed shut, and her sun-kissed face had paled to what could have been similar to Audrey's light complexion, leaving the tiny freckles on Reid's nose much more visible than before.

"Are you going to vom?" Audrey tried to say it with the same inflection and tone as when Reid had asked her yesterday.

"Mm-hm," Reid hummed against her tightly pressed lips.

Audrey gently slowed the car and cracked open Reid's window. She hated how the hot Arizona air filtered through their perfectly air-conditioned CR-V. Audrey loathed the heat. There was a direct correlation between heat levels and her bitchy levels. But as gross as the fresh air felt, as the strong southwestern sun followed them like a spotlight, she'd have rather felt the heat than smell Reid's vomit.

She pocketed this sacrifice for later.

"These are pretty awful turns," Audrey said.

"Mm-hm," Reid groaned.

The fresh smell of pine commingled with the heat and reminded Audrey that their journey through Coconino National Forest would end with the relaxation and decompression she desperately needed for the next day and a half. The four of them had been so incredibly wise at the young age of eighteen to add, *stay at a spa resort*, to their bucket list.

"Oh my God, these views are amazing," Emma the Sleepy Beauty said, waking up ten minutes away from the resort.

She'd woken up just in time. The pine forest and luscious vegetation grew on top of and all around the emerging red rocks. Audrey was pretty amazed of how drastic the scenery was compared to the first two days of driving. Flat, barren desert that barely had anything to look at except some patches of dry vegetation or a single cactus, to now being surrounded by luscious pine trees, juniper, and giant red rock buttes. For the first time since driving out of San Bernardino, rich colors saturated the ineffable scenery. Clear cyan skies, red rocks that bathed the entire city in a glow of crimson, and rich, forest green vegetation.

When they pulled into the Oasis Spa and Resort, southwestern casitas poked through the groves of pinyon and ponderosa pine. According to The Binder, Sadie had booked them a casita. Inside, wooden beams lined the ceiling, southwestern blankets lay on the ends of both queen beds, and the view of the red rock towers contrasted against the bright white walls.

They hadn't even seen the entirety of the resort, and Audrey was already blown away.

The resort was a secret, luxurious enclave on the edge of the woods, and it was home for the next two nights.

"This place is insane," Audrey said. "Sadie and Jeremey didn't have to do this."

"No, they didn't," Emma said, pulling another envelope out of The Binder. "But they did, and I don't think any of us could have said or done anything to change her mind." When Reid emerged from the patio, Emma waved the letter in the air, signaling to the two of them that it was letter time.

They were only a few letters in, but Audrey found herself enjoying them. She missed Sadie so much, and hearing her own words was almost like she was traveling along with them.

"Who wants to read?"

Audrey was shocked when Reid was quick to raise her hand. She was used to feeling Reid's walls, but she saw them go right up anytime they read one of Sadie's letters. Each time, Reid seemed to deflate, and her stare drifted away from the conversation. It was clear that the letters made her uncomfortable, maybe a reminder of what she lost, while Audrey viewed each letter as the last connection to Sadie.

"You sure?" Emma said, sounding just as surprised.

Reid nodded. She took out the letter, unfolded it, and let out a heavy sigh before reading it:

Hi friends!

How amazing is the five-star resort? Jeremy helped me do extensive research, and when he showed me this place, I knew this would be perfect for the three of you. I'll let you in on a little secret: this is one of my favorite things I have planned for you all.

For every time you say out loud, "OMG, Sadie, this is too much. Why?" I will find a way to haunt you. Hopefully by then, I'm hooked up to the Afterlife Wi-Fi. I genuinely want you three to have the best time. A silver lining to Jeremy and I not having enough time to have kids means I get to treat three of my best friends to an unforgettable trip when they need it the most. I'm so excited for you guys to experience this place...and the SPA.

I also treated you all to a pool cabana, not only to spoil you but because Audrey is as white as a ghost, and her skin needs to be protected. PLEASE lather up on the sunscreen.

Unwind from the long drive through the desert, get a fabulous massage and facial, and enjoy the red rocks—and maybe check out one of the famous Sedona vortexes.

Love you!

XOXO Sadie

"What the hell is a vortex?" Reid said, lowering the letter.

"Let me grab The Binder," Emma said. She pulled it out of her book bag and flipped through the pages until she found it. As usual, she skimmed before reading it out loud.

"The Binder says a vortex is a specific site where it's believed energy can produce a range of physical, emotional, and spiritual effects. Other known vortexes include Machu Picchu and Stonehenge."

"Oh, so some new age Sadie thing?" Reid said.

"I guess so," Emma said. "Who wants to check out the pool?"

After driving for three hours and being alone with Reid for most of it, unwinding by the pool and admiring the red rocks with a drink sounded exactly like what Audrey needed.

The pool was an oasis. It was quiet; the only sounds were soft chatters from other guests lounging around the deck and the soft trickling of the infinity pool situated in the shade of pines and greenery, and the other side of the woods offered a gorgeous panoramic backdrop of red rock buttes, spires, and mesas that bathed the view in a deeper shade of crimson. The cabana was equipped with a lounging sofa, cement circular coffee table, a mini fridge stocked with water, sodas, and a saran-wrapped charcuterie board.

Audrey plopped herself on the lounge sofa and took in the view. It wasn't anything like she'd seen before. It was absolutely breathtaking. She kept her eyes fixated on the beautiful rock formations off in the distance while she lathered up her fair skin with SPF 50 sunscreen since she notoriously burned after just thirty minutes while Emma and Reid naturally tanned.

She felt Sadie's loss once again. Those summer days spent at the Lins' pool, she and Sadie had passed the sunscreen back and forth like a bottle of wine. Sadie's porcelain skin was more of a victim of the UV rays than Audrey's. She always had to hide under the shade or her bathing suit coverup.

Audrey put on an extra slather of sunscreen just for her.

"Oh, I'm breaking this open for sure," Emma said, opening the mini fridge door to bring out the charcuterie board.

"And I'm testing out this pool," Reid said as she untied her white crochet swimsuit coverup. She slipped out of the fabric—revealing a black bikini—tossed the coverup on the chair on the opposite side of the cabana, and pulled her blond waves back into a messy bun. Her arms and legs were toned from what Audrey could only assume was from her scuba diving job, her tan had been perfected before June even started, and Audrey couldn't even deny that her breasts looked amazing. Captivating.

She couldn't believe that Reid had a crush on her in high school. She felt even more blindsided by that news than she had been of her breakup with Becca. She couldn't help but wonder if she would have realized she was queer much earlier than in her mid-twenties if she'd known that Reid had a crush on her.

And then she remembered the cleavage she was checking out belonged to Reid Haley, her ex-best friend, and she quickly flitted her attention back to the original task at hand.

Sunscreen.

She couldn't let Reid notice her checking her out. Her poor brain was already at capacity for anxiety, worry, and grief.

Reid slipped into the pool, and once the water reached her collarbone, she submerged. Audrey would have always sworn Reid was part mermaid. During the summers in high school and even college, Reid and her brother, Cameron, had made frequent trips to Oceanside for surfing and swimming. While Emma and Sadie hated getting their hair wet, Reid was always the first one to do so, and sometimes would just swim underwater like an actual mermaid, back and forth and back again.

Watching her float on her back with her black sunglasses in her natural habitat was the most at ease Audrey had seen her since reuniting at Sadie's funeral.

Audrey and Emma stayed behind in the wooden cabana, sipped their piña coladas, and snacked on the complimentary charcuterie board that, thankfully, didn't include goat cheese, making it a perfectly crafted charcuterie board. And yet, the absence of goat cheese on the perfectly crafted charcuterie board brought her mind back to Becca.

Her disdain for goat cheese rapidly increased as the residual anger unfurled in her.

"You doing okay, Auds?" Emma said after she popped a prosciutto and parmesan cracker into her mouth.

Audrey took a long drink until the brain freeze hit. She winced and put her tongue on the roof of her mouth, a trick her mom had taught her as a kid. Once the pain faded, she said, "I'm okay. Are you doing okay?"

"I guess so," Emma said with a shrug. "I'm more worried about you. You have a lot going on."

Audrey sighed. "I feel more angry than sad right now. Reid made me listen to some Fleetwood Mac. She said anger was my friend. She sounded very much like you."

Emma laughed. "I think anger is definitely an appropriate emotion for what you're going through." She paused. "How are you and Reid doing?"

Audrey glanced at Reid still floating on her back as if she had zero cares in the world. "Eh, fine for the most part."

"I think she could help you, you know. With the breakup, I mean. She's been through some real tough ones. Sadie and I were consoling her in her bed during the last one. She was looking really rough for a bit. Sometimes, those short situationships get you more than long relationships."

"What happened with the situationship?"

"Shelby? It was another blindside breakup. Avoidants, man. I pegged her from the first time I met her."

"Really?'

Emma nodded and slurped her piña colada. She had always been good at reading people long before her psychology degree. Now with her therapist training, Audrey wholeheartedly believed that Emma had adapted a sense of smell for red and green flags. It was the only explanation. The first time they'd all met Jeremy at the Lins' Fourth of July barbecue, Emma had leaned into her and Reid and whispered, "Those two are getting married. I'm calling it now."

"What was your read on Becca?"

Emma lowered her drink. "What? No, Auds, we're not doing this—"

"What? I want to know. It's over anyway. It doesn't matter."

Emma grunted. "Fine, if you actually want to know—"

"I do."

"She didn't give off anything alarming at first. But some of it was questionable toward the end."

"How so?"

Emma paused for a second as if debating whether to tell.

"I'm a big girl, Em. I can handle the truth."

She pressed her lips into a thin line. "Near the end, it seemed like the spark might have gone out on her end."

How come she had so easily picked up on that, and Audrey had still felt blindsided? Was love really blind? She needed to learn how to read people better. "What did Sadie think?"

Emma lowered her drink, and Audrey knew the answer from that gesture. "Audrey—"

"Just tell me, Em. Please? Maybe this will help me detach."

Emma exhaled. "She told me that she hopes you find someone who looks at you the way you look at them."

That one hit her right in the chest. Both Emma and Sadie had seen the expiration date to a relationship she'd thought would last longer than eleven months.

"And Becca didn't look at me the way I looked at her?"

Emma hesitated before barely shaking her head.

"Oh, wonderful." She was going to need their server to keep a steady stream of cocktails coming her way.

"I know this is about to sound very cliched, but they're out there, Auds. I promise. And when you find them, you'll realize how you're better off without Becca. Someone who doesn't break up with you three weeks after your best friend dies, someone who doesn't go to a club with someone new just five days after you broke up, someone who looks at you like you're their world. And it's probably for the best that it isn't Becca because you were always too good for her."

"That's probably true," Reid said, dripping into the cabana and reaching for a towel.

"You don't even know what we're talking about," Audrey said as she fought tears.

"I'm assuming it's Becca."

"You don't get to have an opinion about her. You never met her."

Reid looked at Emma. "Was Audrey too good for her?" Emma sipped and nodded. "See? There."

"Emma!" Audrey said.

Emma lowered her drink. "I'm sorry. The alcohol is making me honest."

Reid fixed herself a cracker of salami and gouda, popped it in her mouth, and said, "I mean, was it a secret? I knew you guys didn't really like Becca."

"Thanks, Reid," Emma said flatly.

"You can be mad at me, but everyone is right that Audrey is better than her."

"And how do you know? We haven't spoken in six years."

Reid laughed. "I see the booze is making you honest too. And I can tell based on how she broke up with you. Shouldn't it be a sign that your two best friends, plus a former best friend, didn't like your girlfriend? Isn't it a universal sign that if friends don't like someone you're dating, they're probably a red flag?"

Ouch. Those double insults sliced through her like a knife to the front and back. "You didn't meet her," Audrey said. "Your opinion doesn't count."

Reid fetched a Coke from the fridge, planted herself in the chair next to Audrey, and cracked open the can. "I'm not sure why you're still defending her. I think she's shown that she doesn't deserve you. One day soon, it's all going to click, and you'll see what we see."

She hated that Reid made a good point. She hated how the one person on this trip who could help her through the breakup was the one person she didn't trust.

Chapter Eight

"What the hell is a eucalyptus steam room?" Reid said, reading a door labeled, *Eucalyptus Steam Room*. She frowned. She figured that, after the morning of a fantastic massage, no muscle on her body had the ability to contort, but she was starting to find out that Sedona was filled with new aged things like sunrise meditation with crystals, hiking guides through the vortexes—whatever the hell that was—and an entire steam room devoted to one single essential oil.

"You know…if I were to take a wild guess, it's probably a steam room that smells like eucalyptus," Audrey said.

"Thank you for that profound assessment. I don't know how I would have figured that out without you."

"Then it's a really good thing I'm here on this trip. I say we go in. Why not?"

"Okay, I'm sold," Emma said.

Reid opened the door. "Let's go smell like eucalyptus." She didn't know what to expect. A sauna that smelled like eucalyptus? But inside, iridescent aquamarine tiles made up the walls and floors. In the middle was an oval-shaped pit for them to sit in. The smell of eucalyptus saturated the humid air.

"So what are you supposed to do in one of these?" Emma said as she took a seat.

"You smell like a Yankee Candle and, I don't know, talk?" Reid said.

Emma put a hand on her chest. "Oh my God. Does Reid Haley want to talk? We're already feeling the power of the vortexes."

"What do you want to talk about, Reid?" Audrey said, playing along.

She thought for a moment. "You think there are any queer bars between here and Nashville? You need to go to one."

"Yeah, I heard Oklahoma City is the San Francisco of the Great Plains," Emma said.

"Are you encouraging a rebound?" Audrey said skeptically.

"Not necessarily a rebound but a fun distraction."

"I'm not interested."

"Why?" Reid said. "You know America only gets straighter from here, right?"

"Well, getting dumped doesn't make me feel all that great."

Reid knew that all too well. It was the reason why she also had no interest in any relationship because most likely, it would end. The breakup would either be like her first: Natalie, who was extremely toxic and had made Reid's life a living hell when she finally had the guts to walk away. Or the second heartbreak: Shelby.

Both had broken her in different ways, and she finally felt like she had just recovered.

She couldn't fathom having her heart crushed from losing Sadie and then having a relationship unexpectedly end. She looked back at Audrey and felt her stare softening when she thought about all the pain she must be feeling. Sure, Audrey really needed to stop checking social media, but for having gone through a blindside breakup just weeks after her best friend had died, she seemed perfectly fine. A little quiet at times, sure, but she held herself together much better than Reid would have.

At least on the surface.

"Want to know what doesn't make you feel like shit?" Reid said. "A lesbian bar. You're hot. You'd get plenty of external validation."

Audrey raised an eyebrow. "Apparently, you used to think so."

Reid rolled her eyes and grunted. "Look, I might have had the smallest crush on you for, like, a semester during freshman year, but you were my 'straight' friend. So I killed it. End of story."

Skepticism contorted Audrey's facial features. "Mm-hm. Sure."

"All you need is a little bit of confidence, and you'd do pretty well at a queer bar. See, this is why we need the You Hall."

"But that's the thing, I have no confidence," Audrey said. "Becca went from saying how much she liked me to breaking up with me and posting a bunch of new pics of her hot gym friend in a matter of two weeks."

"But doesn't that say more about her than it does about you?" Reid said.

"Well, damn," Emma said. "Things I didn't have on my bingo card: Reid getting all therapist in a eucalyptus steam room."

"You know I'm right," Reid said.

"You are right. It does say way more about Becca than it does about Audrey."

"That's easy for you to say," Audrey said. "You and Matt have been together for seven years. You and Sadie were the ones who went one and done. You never had a devastating breakup."

"You mean, you don't feel like the vortexes and the eucalyptus are melting your heartbreak away?" Reid said. She was happy to see that Audrey gave her a little smile.

"Unfortunately, no."

"Sounds like we need to take a trip to a queer bar," Reid said. "I'm looking into it when we get back to our room."

"And is that what you did after your breakups?"

"Absolutely, and I went to the You Hall."

"Can one of you queer women please explain the name to me," Emma said as she wiped the dripping sweat off her face.

"I can't tell you," Reid said. "It's part of the gay agenda. You straights have everything else. It will be okay."

Emma rolled her eyes. "Auds?"

Audrey smiled. "It means U-hauling."

"As in the moving company?"

Audrey nodded. "The entire joke is that when two queer women start dating, they move in together incredibly fast."

"One minute, they're your one-night stand, and the next, both your names are on the title of your Subaru, and you share custody of a cat," Reid added.

Audrey rewarded her with a knowing laugh. Emma sat there, eyebrows furrowed, clearly irritated by how much she was sweating. Reid made a bet with herself for how much longer Emma would last in the sauna. Both Emma and Audrey loathed the heat, and Emma found no enjoyment in sweating. She only lasted about twenty minutes in a hot tub until she announced that she was "overheating" and either headed inside or just dangled her feet in the water.

"This makes sense now," Emma said with another wipe to the face. "I had a client who moved in with her girlfriend after two months, and inside, I was like, 'girl, you gotta slow down.' But obviously, I had to voice support."

"Sometimes, a queer girl can't slow down," Reid said. "Hot women sometimes do that to you. They drive you a little crazy. And don't get me started on the hot straight women."

"I'm so glad I have zero experience with that," Audrey said.

"Consider yourself lucky."

"Okay, I'm overheating," Emma said as she slapped her thighs and stood. "You guys want to come with or stay here longer?"

"I'll probably jump in the pool for a bit," Reid said and looked over at Audrey.

"I'll probably do the same," she said.

"All right, well…behave," Emma said, eyeing them.

They all left the steam room at the same time and parted ways in the lobby. Emma waited for the elevator while Reid and Audrey meandered through the hallways until they reached the outdoor pool, which was just as tranquil as the day before.

Reid submerged herself in the cool water, washing the sweat off her body. For a moment, she enjoyed how being in her happy place stilled her thoughts. Even a five-foot deep pool immersed her in a different world than whatever chaotic one she lived in.

As she resurfaced, she wiped the water from her face and found Audrey waist deep, watching her. She wondered why Audrey had decided to join her rather than go back to the hotel with Emma. She eyed her skeptically.

"What?" Audrey said, as if her following Reid to the pool wasn't something out of the ordinary, as if they had been transported back in time and were best friends.

"You're not with Emma?"

"I actually am. This is just a figment of your imagination," she said, gesturing to herself.

Reid rolled her eyes. "You're a pain."

Audrey must have heard the teasing in her tone based on her laugh. "And you're a walk in the park?"

"I must not be so bad if you followed me to the pool. I figured you'd want to be with Emma."

"I, um, I kinda wanted to talk to you about something," she said, her voice dropping, all shy.

Reid held in her next breath. She really hoped Audrey wasn't about suggest they talk about their falling out. They had been successfully dancing around it for the last four days. She knew that was temporary. Either Emma would pressure one of them to have the conversation, or it would be Audrey, someone unafraid to have vulnerable conversations, unlike Reid. Part of her was glad Audrey was distracted by her breakup instead of their riff. She wondered if they really even needed to have the conversation. They'd finish the road trip and bucket list and go their separate ways: Reid's life continuing in Oceanside, Audrey's life continuing in Temecula. And maybe, at most, they'd be cordial enough to attend the same events.

"Okay…what about?" Reid said.

"Emma suggested I talk to you. She said you've had rough breakups in the past and could maybe give some advice."

Reid blew out a heavy sigh of relief. She'd absolutely talk about her heartbreaks over having The Talk in her happy place. The heartbreaks were much easier to talk about now that she had buried her feelings years ago. The Talk was still too raw for her comfort. "I thought you didn't trust me?" she said. Audrey's mouth pressed into a tight line. "Your words, not mine."

"I don't trust you fully, no."

The insult didn't hurt as much as it probably should have. Honestly, Reid didn't trust herself. In fact, she wasn't sure if anyone in her twenty-nine years had ever come to her for relationship advice. She hadn't ever really been in love. She'd thought she was in love with Natalie until she'd realized she had been caught up in a toxic relationship with someone who Emma claimed was a textbook narcissist. Then, there had been Shelby, everything Natalie wasn't, until six months into their…whatever it was…Shelby had decided to break up with her, claiming she was "too busy" for a relationship. She'd started dating someone three weeks later, and a mutual friend of theirs had told Reid that Shelby claimed to be "in love" with her, twisting the knife harder into her back.

And then, if someone like Emma wanted to psychoanalyze Reid's mess of a love life, they could just look at her parents, Terry and Caroline Haley, who'd rushed into marriage at twenty-three and had Reid ten months later. Terry never listened. Caroline always nagged. She'd never seen her parents go out on dates, hold hands, or have adorable moments together in their house. Their relationship was like a partnership, their only goals were to raise the kids, pay the mortgage, and get through the day without one of them grunting at the other.

It had been ten years since her parents had finalized their divorce. It was honestly a blessing in disguise, better for the entire family. But it left Reid having no example of what kind of love she wanted.

Or the kind of love she deserved.

"And you really trust me with relationship advice?" she said, feeling her eyebrow rise.

Audrey thought for a moment. "I'm not sure."

How could Reid give someone "good" relationship advice when she had no idea what healthy love felt or looked like?

She'd try, though.

Audrey sighed. "I just feel…really fucking sad."

Empathy swelled in Reid's chest. Audrey wasn't a simple woman by any means, and she might have caused Reid quite a bit of hurt six years ago, but she still didn't wish heartbreaks on anyone. "Because they're really fucking sad," Reid said.

Audrey finally lowered her torso into the pool as if settling into the conversation. Reid still wasn't sure how she felt just talking about her heartbreaks on the fly with someone she also didn't fully trust yet.

"I don't know how you and Natalie ended," Audrey said.

Reid buzzed her lips as the dormant feelings tangled up in all her Natalie memories snaking around her sternum. So she told Audrey.

She'd broken up with Natalie just two months after she and Audrey had stopped talking. Their friend breakup was actually the catalyst for Reid to snip herself free of Natalie.

"She's a mean girl, Reid," Sadie had said one night when she, Emma, and Reid had killed two bottles of Magnolia Springs wine at the Lins'.

"You and Audrey just cut ties, and that was a clash of personalities," Emma had said. "So how come you have a higher tolerance for Natalie, who doesn't even treat you right?"

"But sometimes she does," Reid had said.

Emma had given Reid a stern side-eye. "She's a textbook narcissist, Reid. She's only 'nice' to you after horrible arguments, and that's a manipulation tactic to get you to stay."

"I honestly don't know what else you see in her," Sadie had said.

Sadie hadn't disliked many people. She'd liked to see the good in everyone, which had been to her own detriment during middle and high school, when she had been too nice to girls who'd also treated her like shit. So when Sadie had said, very frankly, that she didn't like Natalie, the light bulb had clicked in Reid's head.

"Yeah, I knew the two of them didn't really like Natalie," Audrey said when Reid finished telling her story.

"I'm surprised it took me long to figure it out, Why didn't you say that during our fight?" She attempted to tease, but she didn't see it land on Audrey's face.

"Because our fight wasn't about her. I'm glad she's gone, though."

"Me too. She just left behind some mild trauma, but hey, at least I went to therapy for a few years."

"That's a big step," Audrey said, sounding genuine.

"I think it really helped me. Made me a better person."

"What about Shelby?"

"Ugh. That one hurts more. Looking back, I was too scared to leave Natalie. But I actually wanted to be with Shelby. I was very smitten with her, but right when things got a little real, she ran so fast, I swear she should have been an Olympian."

Audrey belted out an empty laugh. "That sounds familiar."

Reid offered a half-smile. "I know. I really do. Except Shelby and I were just a thing for six months. I had asked her to be my girlfriend two weeks before she broke up with me. When I asked her, she seemed really excited. I would never have guessed that two weeks later, she'd ghost me and completely write me out of her life for reasons I'm still not sure about."

Audrey's mouth dropped. Sure, the breakup was a year ago, and Reid had mostly healed from it, but she couldn't lie, the mouth drop from Audrey was extremely validating. "Wow," Audrey said in disbelief. "Doesn't that bother you? Not knowing what the hell happened in those two weeks? The fact that you never got closure?"

Reid shrugged one shoulder. "It did for a bit. I can see what you're doing because I did it too. You're keeping your heart open for the possibility of a next chapter with her, not realizing the book finished when she gave up on you and your relationship. At the drop of a hat. So when I say trust me, I really mean it. Keep that book closed, Audrey. Trying to keep tabs on her is only going to hurt you more. I did that with Shelby for about a month, and it was a stab in the back every time I looked. Even when she wasn't doing anything bad. She could just post an Instagram story, and it would still crush me. It was just another reminder that she'd tossed me without looking back. So let my mistakes be a lesson."

Audrey looked at the ripples between them. "Yeah, I guess you're right."

"I *am* right, and I know you know that. Look, we clearly aren't perfect people. I think our failed friendship is a testament to that." Audrey met her gaze again with a little hint of a smile. "But even with our imperfections, we don't deserve Shelbys and Beccas, and I could have a whole Ted Talk about the Natalies."

"Then, what do we deserve?"

Reid thought for a moment. "We deserve someone who looks at us like Sadie and Jeremy looked at each other until the end."

Audrey's smirk faded a degree. She extended her hand. "Let's make a pact that we do that."

That was easier said than done. Reid thought everything she knew about love was so hazy and chaotic, she questioned if she even had the ability to have a love like Sadie and Jeremy. But she boxed up her doubts and pushed them to the back of her mind. She cared about Audrey walking away from the breakup in less broken pieces than she had. So she tacked on a smile and told herself that if she might not find the love Sadie and Jeremy had, she would at least lower her guard a bit to start thinking about it as a possibility.

She clasped Audrey's hand, and at contact, something curled in her stomach. She had no idea what that was about. Maybe it was her body telling her she'd reached her vulnerability quota for the day.

"Deal," she said and swallowed the mysterious tugging in her throat.

CHAPTER NINE

Just one more look, and I'm done for the rest of the trip, Audrey thought.

They were two hours into their five and a half hour journey from Sedona to Albuquerque when their conversation reached a lull. Emma was on driving duty, and Reid stared out the passenger window at the desert surrounding Route 66 that dissolved into the shimmering mirage along the horizon.

With nothing to stare at and no conversation topics popping up in her mind, Audrey mindlessly scrolled through apps on her phone until she opened Instagram. Going against her better judgment, she clicked on Becca's profile. She breathed a sigh of relief when she saw that Becca hadn't posted any new stories.

Put your phone down, her brain warned.

Instead, she went back to Becca's profile to look at the picture that contained her flirty exchange with Maya.

She let out a gasp.

Embarrassment erupted in a wave of hot heat that traveled down her arms and legs when she noticed the solid red heart she'd just put next to Becca's: *I have plenty of water at my place if you wanted to stop by*, comment.

She quickly unliked the comment.

Error.

She pressed the red heart again.

Error.

Her pulse quickened as she tried again.

Error.

"What the fuck?"

"What?" Emma said in a panic, pushing slightly on the brake enough to jolt Audrey forward until her seat belt locked.

She couldn't pull her gaze from the red heart that wouldn't go away no matter how many times she pressed it. She looked at the top of her phone, all the icons letting her know she had zero service. The Wi-Fi was as plentiful as cacti in whatever desert they were driving through, apparently.

"You good?" Reid said, peering around her seat.

"You can't just gasp like that," Emma said, collecting her breath. "I thought I was about to hit something."

Audrey blinked back a couple of tears. "I did something absolutely mortifying."

"What?" Reid and Emma asked.

"You know that flirty exchange Becca and Maya had? Well, I accidentally liked one of Becca's comments."

Reid grunted. "Audrey! Stop looking. I thought we made a pact yesterday."

"You guys made a pact yesterday?" Emma said.

"That's karma right there for doing something you shouldn't be doing," Reid said.

"I know, all right? I just need service ASAP to unlike it."

"I hate to break it to you, but we're *really* in the middle of Bumfuck, America. Did you not see the ghost town sign a mile back?"

"No, I was trying to unlike this comment a mile back. I need to get service. There has to be a little town with Wi-Fi."

"I wouldn't count on that," Emma said. "It looks pretty empty between here and Albuquerque."

"I wonder if the ghost town has Wi-Fi?" Reid said with a chuckle.

"I'm glad this is amusing you," Audrey said with a bite. She should have known better. She had been so desperate to feel some kind of relief yesterday that she'd attempted to lean on Reid, the last person she'd thought would actually help. Right as she thought she and Reid had reached an intersection of common ground, of course Reid had to ruin it by laughing at something that caused Audrey's anxiety to spiral.

"It's going to be okay, Audrey," Reid said with a little less smile to her tone.

Audrey grabbed a fistful of hair. "Oh my God. It's just going to sit there until we reach civilization. She probably thinks I'm so pathetic."

"Honestly? She's probably not even thinking about it," Emma said. "She's most likely trying everything she can to run away from her feelings about the breakup and you that she's not going to dwell on it."

"Can we please stop at the next town we drive through that looks like it has civilization?"

"Yes, we can do that," Reid said with what sounded like a hint of sympathy in her voice.

Audrey was pretty shocked by how she didn't put up a fight. She'd take that as a baby step of progress between the two of them.

Her phone didn't work until they got to Albuquerque. Three hours of staring at desolate desert until signs and buildings started to pop up. She didn't take a full breath until her phone finally allowed her to unlike the comment, but undoing it didn't ease her anxiety like she'd hoped it would.

The feeling of embarrassment and being discarded still hung in her chest.

When they got to their Airbnb, Audrey walked into the closest bedroom with a queen bed and plopped face-first into the pillow. The three of them had agreed to some rest time before they went out to dinner and explored parts of the city.

Just a few minutes into her decompression, there was a knock on her door. She turned over on her back and told the knocker to come in. When the door opened, Reid stepped in. "Emma is running to the store to get more car snacks. If you want anything, you should text her now."

Audrey felt so out of sorts that the thought of car snacks didn't even excite her. "I'm fine with whatever she gets."

"You don't have any special requests?"

"Not really."

Reid's eyebrows rose. "Audrey McCann not caring about car snacks? The most important thing on a road trip besides music?"

Audrey shrugged. "I'm not hungry and too tired to think about snacks. I'm fine with whatever she buys. I trust her."

"Wow," Reid said, resting her back against the door frame and crossing her arms. "You okay?"

Audrey faltered once the stinging reached her eyes. There was a lot on her mind, and she hated that since their talk in the pool the day before, she'd wondered when the hell they would address what had happened years ago. Once they talked about what happened, they could finally close that chapter and maybe start a new one.

Sadie and Emma were right; the three of them all needed each other, and Audrey couldn't help but wonder if that sliver of familiarity was slowly mending their friendship again. After losing both Sadie and Becca, God, she could have used another friend.

She breathed out a trembling sigh, worried The Talk would excavate all kinds of buried feelings. But if she wanted answers, now was the best time. Emma was at the store, Reid was offering a helping hand, and Audrey was feeling vulnerable enough to say everything she wanted to say.

"Are we ever going to talk about what happened?" she said.

"About what? You breaking the pact we made yesterday?"

"I didn't break any pact."

"Yes, you did. We agreed that we were both going to at least be open to finding the Jeremy to our Sadie, and then you went back to stalking Becca."

"That's not what I'm talking about. I'm talking about what happened with us. We've been avoiding it rather successfully."

"Oh," Reid said, her voice softening. "You want to talk about that? Now? Are you in the right headspace?"

"I'm definitely in the right headspace."

Reid pushed off the doorway and ran a hand through her waves. The late afternoon sun beamed through the bedroom window and fell on her face, highlighting the light freckles on the flat of her nose in a way Audrey hadn't noticed before. For a moment, Audrey found herself surprisingly captivated by her beauty.

"I guess we should probably talk about it," Reid said, as she sat on the cushioned chest at the foot of the bed.

Her words snapped Audrey out of her trance.

Thankfully.

"I'm just…well…you know I'm not good at these things."

"I'm not here to argue," Audrey said calmly. "I don't have the energy to argue, either. It's just one last thing I want looming over me, you know?"

Reid nodded. "I get it."

"I can start?"

"Sure, go for it."

"What the hell happened?"

Reid let out an uncomfortable chuckle. "I don't know, you tell me. It seemed like you had a lot of resentment toward me."

When Audrey thought back on the last few months of their friendship, Reid wasn't wrong. If she had to put a word for how she felt about Reid near the end of their friendship, that term would have been "resentment." She had continuously pushed aside all the annoying things about Reid until all those things accumulated into a mountain she could no longer ignore.

"I guess, in a way, that's true," Audrey said. "There wasn't a specific big thing that you did. It was just a bunch of things all added together."

"Like what? Because I didn't hear about any of it until we were yelling at each other in the hotel. Like 'pulling a Reid' and 'Reid time'?"

Audrey looked away. The fight replayed in her mind, and being six years older, there were so many things she would have done differently, things she would have reworded or not said at all. She heard the hurt still present in Reid's voice, and the guilt began to wash ashore inside her.

"I shouldn't have worded it like that, and I'm sorry," she said. "What I meant to say was that you were notoriously late. There were times when we were all waiting on you for, like, twenty minutes. It started getting old very quickly and came off as disrespectful."

"I get that," Reid said, lowering her head. "I didn't do it to disrespect anyone. I just had very bad time management."

"You had bad time management at Sadie's funeral?"

Reid's body deflated, and for a second, Audrey felt bad for bringing it up and seeing her so wounded. Reid pulled her stare off Audrey and ran another hand through her hair. Audrey wondered if it was a nervous tic she had picked up during their time apart, or if it had always been a habit, and Audrey just noticed from her sudden, radiating beauty.

"I actually wasn't late for her funeral," Reid said softly while staring at her fidgeting hands in her lap. "I just…I…had a panic attack."

Immediate guilt washed over Audrey. She shouldn't have said anything. She should have given Reid the benefit of the doubt that maybe something had happened if she was late to her best friend's funeral. She just wished all those times Reid had been late for no reason didn't cloud her judgment. "I'm…I'm sorry, Reid. I didn't know."

Reid shook her head and met her gaze again with a forced smile. "It's okay. I got there twenty minutes before because…well…I wanted to check in with Jeremy and say hi to her parents. I just…I never had a panic attack. I didn't know what was happening—"

"You don't have to explain, really. I shouldn't have said anything."

Reid shrugged. "I get why you did. I don't have a good track record."

There was a pause as the bedroom thickened with tension.

"Look," Audrey said through her heavy exhale. "I just wanted to say that I'm sorry for how everything panned out the last trip. I was angry, and I let some things build up. I was twenty-three and had no idea how to handle all my feelings. We saw each other only a few times a year, and during those summers we were all home, it felt like you were more interested in getting laid than us. And I don't mean that in a judgmental way. That was just the impression I used to get."

Reid thinned her mouth and nodded. "That's fair."

"And you were always unresponsive to texts, which made planning anything way more complicated because we were always waiting on you, and when we finally managed to get everyone in the same room, it felt like you didn't really want to be with us."

Reid looked up with hurt sparking in her eyes. "What? That's not true at all."

"I'm just telling you how it felt at the time. Anytime we tried talking to you about it, you shut down, and we wouldn't get anywhere. It was an endless cycle."

"I'm sorry that I shut down, Audrey. I really am. It's just that, sometimes, I'm terrified about talking about my feelings. I needed to feel safe and—"

"You didn't feel safe?" Audrey said. That was news to her.

Reid shook her head. "No, I didn't. I knew something with us had been off for a while, and I was afraid anything I said or did would be met with criticism or judgment, so I thought it was better to distance myself. It was a defensive mechanism, not a healthy one, but I'm still trying to work through it. On the trip, I think both of us were at the end of our ropes for different reasons. You were tired of my flaws, which is all fair. I understand now, and for me, I was tired of feeling constantly under scrutiny, and that's why I reacted the way I did."

She had no idea Reid had felt that way. Hearing her open up and finally being vulnerable made discomfort grow inside Audrey like a field of weeds. She hated that she'd made Reid feel uncomfortable, and most importantly, she hated that she hadn't made Reid feel safe. It was no wonder why the two of them had blown up on each other in the middle of a random hotel in Springfield, Missouri.

Reid sighed and pushed her hair back again. "I know I wasn't perfect, and I had some annoying tendencies. I was young, dumb, and, well, toward the end, I was lost. I was with Natalie, and she tried to control every aspect of my life, and I let her because I just wanted to be wanted. I know that Sadie and Emma were disappointed with me too, and by the time I opened up to them about what was really going on with Natalie and how controlling and toxic she was, I'd already lost you. But I'm not that person anymore, and as I can see from spending the first few days of this trip together, neither are you. Losing Sadie has really put this situation into perspective, at least for me."

"It has for me too," Audrey said. "Before everything got complicated, I really enjoyed our friendship, and I, well, I miss it. I don't think I realized how much I missed it until this trip."

Reid smiled, her eyes sparkling. Seeing her genuine smile, Audrey felt, for the first time since high school, that she and Reid had clicked themselves back in place. It was so familiar, yet slightly foreign, but God, did it feel good to lift that boulder off her.

Finally.

"I missed it too," Reid said.

The moment was so sweetly tender, Audrey had to force her gaze away to keep from tearing up. She'd wondered all this time if Reid had missed her, and hearing that she had unlocked the last bit of hurt still lodged in her chest. After all this time, Audrey had finally found the closure she'd been hoping to get.

They might have grown up and apart, but their roots were still tangled around each other no matter how hard they tried breaking free.

"I missed you too," Audrey said softly. "Can we…hug? Would that be weird?"

Reid laughed. "Not at all." She stood and walked over to Audrey, her arms wide. Audrey hugged her back and was surprised how easily she let herself sink into Reid's embrace. She did feel safe in her arms, protected and cared for, all feelings she'd never thought she'd ever feel from Reid just five days before.

But it was the hug that glued them back into place.

And Reid smelled really good, like a soft, sweet perfume mixed with a splash of something musky and woodsy. Audrey inhaled a deep breath of the scent sticking to the shoulder of Reid's shirt.

Why was her heart racing?

"I have a surprise for you," Reid said in her ear. The words sent a shiver down her spine right as Reid broke the hug.

Audrey furrowed her brow. "A surprise? For me?"

Reid nodded proudly. "I hope you packed a top that shows off your tits."

CHAPTER TEN

Reid was very spoiled living in Southern California, a special land where people had to came out as straight, Pride flags hung from homes and business, and every gay bar had memorable punny names.

When the Uber dropped them off at what was supposed to be Albuquerque's famed gay bar, the building in front of them was completely unassuming from the outside. A plain white, territorial-style building stood on the corner with a black sign above the entrance that just said, "Nob Hill Community Bar."

"Are you sure this is it?" Emma said.

"The building feels closeted," Audrey said.

It was the straightest looking building Reid had ever seen. "I'm positive," she said, disappointed in the lack of rainbows. "Let's just check it out."

As they stepped through the front door, a cold blast of air-conditioning welcomed them. She let out a sigh of relief when she spotted an array of Pride flags hanging from the ceiling right above a small stage where a Cher drag queen performed "Believe." People of all ages mingled around the place.

"Oh my God, it's like a queer oasis," Reid said, feeling her entire body replenish with gay energy after the long haul through the southwest. She scanned the patrons to see what they would be working with for Audrey. She also scanned Audrey from head to toe, ignoring her quizzical frown. She didn't expect that an assessment would cause a spark of attraction to run through her body. That was a…surprise. Since Audrey hadn't brought a sexy top, Reid had let her borrow a black halter top with a low neck that really flaunted her assets. And damn, they caught Reid by surprise. She'd always thought Audrey was beautiful, but she'd always tucked her attraction away in the name of friendship. Her friendship was much more important to Reid than her attraction.

But now, they weren't friends; they also weren't enemies. She actually wasn't quite sure how to describe her relationship with Audrey now that they had just patched things up. But if she had to put it in words, she would have described it as standing on neutral territory that looked optimistic. They hadn't been friends in six years, and with that label no longer in the way, Reid finally discovered Audrey's new beauty that had been enhanced with age and time.

Emma leaned into the bar to try to grab the bartender's attention, but Reid remained focused on Audrey's fabulous cleavage. Her top did a fantastic job.

"My eyes are up here, Reid," Audrey said, holding in a smile.

"I'm just admiring my top on you," Reid said, trying her best to recover. "You look great. I feel confident about tonight. Now let's get a drink."

They approached the bar, and the hot bartender caught Reid's eye. She had to be in her late thirties, and her tanned arms were covered in tattoos. Her dark and moody vibe was enhanced by her head-to-toe black outfit and long dark brown hair. She was definitely Reid's type. Maybe after she successfully wingwomaned Audrey, she would spend some time back at the bar.

Damn, it had been a long time since Reid had been with another woman. Even a nice, steamy make out. She realized as she scanned the drink menu that she had put her dating life on hold since Sadie's diagnosis in early February. She needed to resurrect the dating apps when they got back. She needed some kind of release, and she needed it soon.

"What can I get you, ladies?" Hot Bartender said, finally noticing Emma. She walked over with a confident smirk, her dark brown eyes locked on Reid.

Reid knew she could work with Hot Bartender's smile and flirtatious tone. Sure, she was doing that to get tips. Reid knew that, but it didn't mean she was going to ignore the bait and not flirt with an incredibly attractive woman. "What's your specialty?" Reid said and leaned in with a smile.

Hot Bartender's smirk grew into an impish grin. "The Lesbian Kickboxer."

"I'm intrigued. Tell me more."

Hot Bartender leaned her arms on the bar, offering a perfect view of her cleavage. "It's a whole lot of alcohol that tastes like peach raspberry."

"So if my friend here is trying to mend a broken heart, you would probably recommend the Kickboxer, right?"

"Reid," Audrey said with a bony elbow nudge. Deep red embarrassment slammed onto her cheeks and lingered down her neck. It was kind of cute how easily she got embarrassed.

"Oh, definitely," Hot Bartender said without a beat. "Why do you think its named the Kickboxer? It punches the heartache right out of you."

"Great. We'll take three of those," Emma said, pulling her credit card out of her purse.

"Who said I need one?" Reid said.

"I do. If Audrey drinks it, we all drink it. We're in this together."

"Yeah, what she said," Audrey said, hooking a thumb at Emma as her victorious smile grew.

"You don't think you can handle the Kickboxer?" Hot Bartender said.

Apparently, she knew exactly what she needed to say to get Reid to acquiesce. "I'm not afraid of the Kickboxer," she said. That was definitely a lie. She was afraid of it when she had the first driving shift the next day, and not just any driving shift, the most boring leg of the road trip, from Albuquerque to Oklahoma City. "Maybe I just want to remember tonight…and the very attractive bartender who made me the drink."

Audrey let out a cackle. Reid shot her a quick side-eye.

"Three Kickboxers coming right up," Hot Bartender said with a wink and turned to the bottles of liquor. Orange and strawberry vodka, plus raspberry, melon, and peach liqueurs, a splash of sour mix, cranberry juice, and Sprite.

"What's so funny?" Reid said and faced a snickering Audrey and Emma.

"How many times have you used that horrible line?" Audrey said.

"I've never used it, and please. I don't need any sort of line."

Audrey rolled her eyes. "Oh, okay, Cassanova."

Emma shook her head. "Nah, she didn't do her voice thing."

"What voice thing?" Reid said.

"I know when you're into a woman when your voice goes up an octave." Emma rested an arm on the bar, got into character, and twirled her hair. "Maybe I just want to remember tonight."

Audrey bellowed, any last trace of embarrassment on her face fleeing to Reid's.

"That doesn't even sound like me," she said.

"I always knew when she was talking to Shelby on the phone because of that voice," Emma said to Audrey, continuing the impression. "And she did *not* have that voice with Natalie."

"Because Natalie was horrible. I was absolutely infatuated with Shelby."

"I know," Emma said. "Because of your voice. Sadie and I laughed about it all the time."

Reid rolled her eyes as the heat continued to warm her face. "I don't have a voice."

"You can say it as adamantly as you want, but that's not going to change the fact that you do, indeed, have a voice."

"You know, now that I'm thinking about it, you really do," Audrey said. "I remember it coming out when you were dating that girl in college sophomore year."

"Whatever," Reid grumbled. "Hot Bartender winked at me. Don't worry, your time is about to come to impress us with your skills." She shook Audrey's shoulder.

Audrey pulled away. "What does that mean?"

"It means that we're not leaving this bar until you talk to a woman. I've already scoped them out. There are a few contenders."

"I didn't agree to this."

"You didn't have to. It's what you need to do, especially after you accidentally liked your ex's flirting exchange with Marathon Girl."

"Don't worry, babe. You came to the right place for a pick-me-up," Hot Bartender said as she slid all three Kickboxers over in pint mugs.

Reid flashed the bartender a smirk before turning to Emma and Audrey and raising her glass. "To forgetting women not worthy of our thoughts."

"Yes," Emma said, as if she, the straight friend in a long-term relationship, had gone through a brutal sapphic breakup.

They clinked mugs and took a cautious first sip. Reid winced. Damn, she could taste all five liqueurs in it. For what seemed like ninety percent alcohol, the Kickboxer was tart and dangerously tasty. She needed to just sip on this one for the rest of the night if she didn't want to be hungover during her driving shift.

"Okay, so since the last time we saw each other, like, six years ago, you came out as bi, and now I have no idea what your type is besides women named Becca who run marathons and suck in general," Reid said, facing the stage where most of the patrons stood watching the drag show. "What's your type?"

"I don't know," Audrey said. "I've only been with one woman."

Reid glanced at Emma. "What's Audrey's type?"

"Reid, I just learned what U-hauling means," Emma said. "I don't think my role as the token straight friend is to educate you on Audrey's type."

Audrey scanned the place as if trying to find her answer. She stayed close to the bar, sipped her Kickboxer a little too long, as if using the drink as a way to kill time, and how her shoulders curled forwarded indicated to Reid that she wasn't feeling confident.

God, this Becca chick had really bruised Audrey's ego, and it sucked to see. She really needed more experience. With women and feeling wanted in general.

Reid glanced at Hot Bartender. She might not have known Audrey's type, but it was an indisputable fact that Hot Bartender was universally hot for all genders and sexualities. "Can you please reassure my friend here that she's hot and doesn't need to keep thinking about her ex-girlfriend?"

Audrey finally lowered her straw. The blush claimed her face once again. "Reid!"

"Oh, hon, you're too good for her," Hot Bartender said. "I think you'll do just fine without her. You're gorgeous."

"See? Now, you need to wipe yourself clean of Becca. Get her off you."

"The therapist in me says it's time for you to start setting healthy boundaries with yourself on how much you focus on Becca," Emma said. "But the friend in me says, 'What the fuck is Becca doing? Why is she being so shitty to you? Also, fuck her. Stop dwelling on her. She's not worth it.'"

"What Therapist Emma said," Reid replied.

"And how do I do that?" Audrey said.

"You find someone to fuck."

Audrey choked on her drink. "What? I've never even done that—"

"At a minimum, we need to find you a DFMO."

"A what?"

"A dance floor make out, obviously."

"You know, you're not the only one here doing that tonight," Hot Bartender said.

"What do you mean?" Emma said.

Hot Bartender nodded to the stage. Reid turned and spotted a group of five women singing and dancing along to now Drag Celine Dion performing "That's the Way It Is." "The brunette over there. She's having a divorce party. Hence the Kickboxer in her hand and the sash."

The woman in question had short, curly brown hair; black, denim shorts; an open, floral button-up; and a black sash that read, "Just Divorced" in silver. She slowly swayed back and forth and sipped on her Kickboxer. Reid could only see the side of her face, but her profile was very attractive. A femme face and masc of center attire.

"What are your thoughts on the divorcée?" Reid said.

Audrey checked her out. She pursed her lips and went back to sucking on the Kickboxer for a second. "She's pretty hot."

"Right?" Reid said. "Is she your type?"

"Has a similar vibe as Becca," Emma added.

"Go talk to her," Reid said.

"What? Absolutely not!"

"What? Why not? Would you not make out with her?"

"I mean, yeah, I would. But I'm not going to go up to her and strike up a conversation just to make out with her."

Audrey was the shyest one out of the four, always had been. Reid should have remembered that. Of course she wasn't going to willingly go up to a stranger and start a conversation. She couldn't do that with men back in the day. Women were much more intimidating than men, according to her bi friends. It was no surprise to her that Audrey was rooted in place at the bar despite the fact that a very attractive woman stood just a few feet away from them.

Luckily, she wasn't shy or afraid to initiate. "Okay, fine," she said and snatched up her Kickboxer. "This is the ultimate truce. I'm going to be your wingwoman."

"Reid—"

She headed straight to the group of women and stood right next to them. For a few seconds, she watched Celine Dion perform before turning to the brunette. When they locked eyes, Reid smiled.

"I love your sash," she said over the music.

The brunette smiled and looked at it. It said "Just divorced!" in a black, sparkling font. "Oh, thank you. I wasn't sure about it, but my friends insisted."

"I think it's great. My friend back there at the bar thinks it's really great too." She hooked her thumb behind her, and the woman turned to look. "The brunette one in the black top. She's a little shy, but she thinks you're very cute. She's mentioned it several times."

Reid followed the brunette's gaze to where Emma and Audrey still sat at the bar. Emma smiled and waved, while Audrey continued being her shy, awkward self and focused on her Kickboxer instead.

"*Aw*, really?" The brunette said. "She's cute."

"She's a catch once you get through the first awkward two minutes."

Emma nudged Audrey to look over. Audrey shot her a quick glare before facing Reid and the brunette. Reid wiggled her fingers in a wave and watched as Audrey's face turned beet red once again.

Okay, so she was learning that Audrey had very little game with women. On the surface, it was very entertaining to watch, but Reid knew the root of it came from insecurity and a lack of confidence.

"I'm not afraid of awkward," the woman said.

"Great. Oh, I'm Reid, by the way. My friend is Audrey."

"I'm Casey."

"Nice to meet you, Casey. Let's get you talking to a hot woman on your divorce party night."

Reid waved Audrey over. When she didn't move fast enough, Reid's wave turned assertive. Once she directed a stern look, Audrey got off the barstool and walked over with her emotional support Kickboxer.

"Audrey, this is Casey. Casey, this is Audrey."

Casey stuck out her hand and smiled. "It's nice to meet you, Audrey. Your friend Reid is doing a great job of talking you up."

It was foreign to be referred to as Audrey's friend, but she brushed it off in the name of trying to find Audrey someone to make out with.

"Oh, has she?" She eyed Reid skeptically.

"Audrey is also a big Celine Dion fan," Reid said, nodding to Celine Dion, who'd just walked off stage.

"I'm surprised you weren't over here with us while Celine was singing," Casey said.

Reid leaned into Casey's ear. "You'll see her freak out if she hears 'It's All Coming Back to Me Now,'" she said loud enough for Audrey to hear. "Once that piano plays, she goes feral."

"Reid!" Audrey said.

Casey let out a laugh. "I can't wait to see that happen. What are your thoughts on Beyoncé? Because she's about to come back out."

"Anything from *Lemonade* or *Cowboy Carter* will also make me go feral," Audrey said.

It was like sending a child off on their first day of school. Reid was proud that Audrey just leaned into the setup. See, there was hope underneath the sadness, Reid thought. Audrey just needed a little bit of encouragement and a strong cocktail.

"I'll let you two talk," Reid said. "I think you have a lot in common." She patted Audrey on the shoulder and headed back to the bar where Emma was talking to Hot Bartender.

"Look at you playing matchmaker," Emma said and nodded to Audrey and Casey chatting away.

Reid playfully flipped her hair back. "I know. It's a talent of mine."

Emma took a step forward and said, "So Audrey and I were just talking. Apparently, you two had The Talk?"

She was always amazed by how fast word traveled with two very emotionally available people. She pulled one last liberal sip from her drink, knowing she would need it. "Yeah, we did."

Emma laughed. "That's it? That's all you have to say about it? That's a pretty big deal."

Reid shrugged. "I'm sure Audrey filled you in on everything."

"How do you feel about all of it?"

"It was a good talk. I'm glad we finally had it. It's been nice the last two days."

"I think she really appreciates your help with her breakup."

"Yeah, well, I've been through it before. I've got the toxic relationship down and the earth-shattering, unexpected breakup down. I'm glad at least one of those can help someone, especially Audrey. I'm not sure how she's dealing with Sadie and Becca at the same time. I can barely deal with Sadie."

Emma thinned her lips and rubbed Reid's back for a moment. "You doing okay?"

Being best friends with a therapist meant that sometimes, Reid couldn't hide from the emotions she was actively trying to bury. Yes, she knew that she needed to give herself plenty of time to properly grieve, but wasn't there a time and place? She wanted to revel in the fact that she and Audrey seemed to have found themselves in a good place for the first time in years. She wanted to enjoy the fact that Audrey had let her pick out a hot outfit, take her to a queer bar, and play wingwoman. She could think about the painful things on her long drive tomorrow.

Reid tacked on a smile. "I'm doing okay. I promise. Are you?"

Emma gave a one shoulder shrug. "I'm doing the best one can be given the situation. I'm just very glad you two talked. I really didn't expect it to happen this early."

"I really do feel for her," Reid said and turned back to find Audrey and Casey smiling and singing along to Drag Beyoncé performing

"Single Ladies," the perfect song for both their nights. "And she was in an actual relationship with Becca. Shelby and I were…well…it's been a year, and I still really don't know what we were. All I know is that whatever it was, she crushed me."

Emma squeezed her shoulder. "I know you really liked her."

"Eh, what can you do besides help your friend with her breakup?"

Emma smirked. "You just called Audrey your friend. I never thought I'd hear that again."

"Yeah, well, sometimes weird, magical things happen during really shitty times."

By the time Celine Dion came back onstage about a half hour later, Audrey and Casey had yet to part ways. Reid sat at the bar with Emma, so proud of herself for setting the two up and also so proud of Audrey for carrying her own.

Then, dramatic piano music filled the bar. Audrey stopped in midsentence and started drunkenly singing "It's All Coming Back to Me" to Casey with a microphone fist. When Celine pointed to her during her performance, Audrey pointed back and sang with just as much passion.

"Our little Audrey is growing up," Reid said.

Emma's mouth dropped. "Oh my God. Our little Audrey is making out with a woman."

"What? Seriously?" She turned back and found Audrey and Casey in the middle of the dance floor, full on making out. Casey held Audrey's hips close. Audrey clasped Casey's face. Casey's friends nudged each other and pointed with smiles on their faces, as if they too were hoping she would kiss her heartbreak away.

"Oh my God," Reid said, amazed of her matchmaking skills. "She's really doing it. They're, like, fully making out to Celine Dion." She hoped that by letting loose and receiving attention from an incredibly hot divorcée, a few small pieces of Audrey's broken heart had started to mend.

CHAPTER ELEVEN

The past few days had flown by, much to Audrey's surprise since it was through a very uneventful Middle America. At least the drive was peppered with roadside attractions. Sadie had included an entire page of "cute stops" on the route.

They made a pit stop at Cadillac Ranch in Amarillo where ten, colorful, graffiti-painted vintage Cadillacs were buried nose first in the ground. They snapped a picture of the Leaning Tower of Texas, which was just a rusty old leaning water town with "Britten USA" on it. They checked out the iconic soda store, Pops, in Arcadia, Oklahoma and took a picture by the sixty-six foot LED soda bottle sculpture in front. They walked through the mouth of the famous Blue Whale of Catoosa in Catoosa, Oklahoma and pulled off in Baxter Springs, Kansas to take a picture of the "Field of Dreams" baseball field for all their dads.

Now, they only had one more stop to make before they could officially cross Route 66 off the bucket list: Springfield, Missouri.

Audrey had never heard of anyone who'd intentionally gone to Springfield, Missouri to visit for fun, and yet, here they were again for the second time. This go around, she hoped they made it out of the city with their tentative friendship intact.

Emma drove from Oklahoma City to Springfield. Reid sat in the passenger seat, glancing out the window, and Audrey couldn't help but wonder what was going through her mind. Was a little part of her worried about being back in the city where their entire friend group had unraveled? Luckily, they were only crashing here for the night, and

Audrey's guilt would hopefully alleviate once they hit the road the next morning.

"I might be really biased, but if this city's big claim to fame is having the original and largest Bass Pro Shop that is also attached to the NRA Museum, we really need to get out of here as soon as possible," Reid said.

"I think this is good for you, Reid," Audrey said. "You gotta expand your world beyond California."

"I have," Reid said, turning in her seat. "I have a diving bucket list written down and everything. I've been to the Bahamas, Mexico, Iceland, Belize—"

"Okay, we get it," Emma said, teasing. "You have a really cool, non-corporate-America job."

"Key word: cool. Bass Pro Shop and the NRA? Definitely not. Remind me, why did we stop here instead of, like, I don't know, St. Louis?"

"Because now we can officially brag that we drove Route 66 in its entirety. Last time, the trip blew up at the Best Western."

"Don't look at me," Reid said and faced Audrey. "It was her fault."

She heard the smile in Reid's tone as she kept her eyes focused out of her window, searching for the "Birthplace of Historic Route 66" sign. A few minutes later, she spotted the red banner attached to a light post right in front of a thrift store. She remembered looking for the same exact sign six years before as the four of them had followed Route 66 into Springfield and pulled aside to take a picture.

Emma parked the car, and they hopped out. Sadie's absence was palpable as they snapped a selfie. Except this time, instead of Sadie and Emma squeezing in the middle to separate Audrey and Reid, who had already been bickering, Reid slung her arm around Audrey's shoulders, and Emma took the photo.

Just a few miles away, they pulled into the infamous Best Western parking lot, neon lights illuminating the mid-century-styled buildings. Several pastel colored vintage cars welcomed them in the parking lot. As they walked into the building to check in, a memory crossed Audrey's mind of six years prior, when she, Emma, and Sadie had walked silently along the black-and-white checkered floors of the office with disappointment and anger trailing behind them like a shadow. It was the morning after Reid had booked her one-way ticket home in protest. The guilt had consumed Audrey so much, she'd thought she might have a breakdown or throw up right in front of the reception desk.

As Emma checked in, Audrey glanced at Reid, searching for a sign that she was also struggling, but she seemed too preoccupied with admiring the retro gas pumps right outside the propped open front door.

Once Emma got the keys, they walked to the building next door that was lined with rooms. Inside, they were greeted by a king-size bed where the actual tail end of a retro pink Cadillac had been converted into a combination footboard and sofa. Just a few feet away from the bed was a Jacuzzi tub. Just like the outside of the property, the inside felt like they were stepping back into the 1950s.

"This room is ridiculous in the best way," Audrey said.

"Everyone settle in," Emma said. "And we'll read the letter. This is going to be a big moment."

Once they changed into their pj's, the three of them sat on the king bed. Emma held the letter, crossed her legs, and opened it. "Anyone want to read it?"

"You do the honors," Audrey said.

Emma took a deep breath and unfolded the letter.

Hi friends!

Welcome back to everyone's favorite city: Springfield, Missouri. Some call it the birthplace of the Mother Road. We call it the start of the Fall of Rome. Whatever you three decide to call it this time around, it's your last Route 66 stop, which means if you three made it this far without another Caesar-Brutus situation, then...CONGRATS! You have not only conquered Springfield but all 2,448 miles of Route 66.

I'm so very proud of the three of you for making it all this way through the mountains, the prairies, treacherous roads of Bumfuck, America, the scariest thing Reid will ever have to endure in life, and the oceans white with foam.

I hope you three can redo the picture of the "Birthplace of Route 66" sign, and yes, you're staying at the same hotel as the first time around. But at least this time, I instructed Emma to book the Elvis suite. Get comfortable sharing a king-size bed where Elvis slept in 1956 after one of his shows. Maybe a group spooning session is just what the three of you need to bring the friend group back together. I'll be watching with some afterlife popcorn. Rumor has it that it's better than movie theater popcorn, but I'll be the judge of that.

Or if that's not the vibe, don't worry. I asked Emma to request a rollaway bed.

See y'all in Gatlinburg. The fireflies are waiting for you.

XOXO Sadie

"Wait, who the hell called our friend break up 'the Fall of Rome,'" Reid said, frowning.

Emma looked up from the letter. "Sadie and I did behind your backs. The Fall of Rome, the Ides of Springfield, depended on our mood."

Audrey let out a laugh only half filled with humor as Reid's mouth dropped.

Reid wasn't sure if she considered that funny or offensive, but she refused to let whatever weird vibes Springfield had floating around affect the rest of their night. "But wait," she said. "Who stabbed who?"

Emma lowered the letter and gave her a side-eye. "Are we really going to reminisce about the Fall of Rome in Elvis's bed?"

"Yes," Reid and Audrey said.

"It's an important detail," Reid added.

"Is it?" Emma said.

"Yes," they both said again.

"Ugh, fine," Emma said, exhaling. She set the letter on the nightstand and faced them. "Sadie and I said Reid was Caesar—"

Reid held up a hand. "Whoa, wait. You actually assigned roles?"

"Of course we did," Emma said casually. "Audrey started the fight, so she was the one who stabbed you."

"I did *not* start the fight," Audrey said, sounding only mildly offended.

Reid bit her lip to hide her laughter as embarrassment crawled up Audrey's neck and face. They might have patched things up and decided to move forward as friends, but Reid would have been lying if there wasn't the smallest part of her that was happy Emma and Sadie had agreed that Audrey was the one who'd initiated it.

"You did, Brutus," Emma said, and the red deepened on Audrey's face. "The entire fight started because we were all waiting on Reid to get ready, and you said, 'The entire world doesn't run on Reid time.'"

"This is true," Reid said, nodding. "That was, indeed, the first stab. I still have a scar." She grabbed the hem of her T-shirt and lifted it a few inches to show off a faint pink scar on the side of her stomach.

"I didn't stab you," Audrey said, evidently deciding to play along. "You got in the way of my knife."

"The scar begs to differ." Reid snatched the bucket list and the purple pen from the nightstand. "One of you want to do the honors?"

Audrey raised her hand. "I will since, apparently, I started the fight. It's the least I can do."

Reid laughed, hearing the slight teasing in Audrey's tone. Audrey pressed the letter up against Reid's back, clicked the purple pen, and gently scratched Route 66 off.

"There," Audrey said and handed Reid the bucket list over her shoulder. "I hope that makes up for the backstab."

"The twenty-three backstabs," Emma corrected. "Brutus stabbed Caesar twenty-three times."

"I know," Reid said. "I was there."

Audrey rolled her eyes. "You know, I learned more about the Fall of Rome just now than I ever did in school."

"Great! The more you know." Emma said and took back the list. She scanned it, and as she did so, a soft smile landed on her face. She glanced up. "We did it. We actually finished Route 66."

Reid couldn't believe it either. A week ago, she couldn't have fathomed feeling like she had gained a friend in Audrey in the very city where they had fallen apart.

"I'm really proud of us," Audrey said. "I was really nervous about this, but I'm so glad we did it." She met Reid's gaze.

"Me too," Reid said. "Maybe Sadie was on to something. Apparently, this was exactly what we all needed."

"And I'm sure Sadie is smirking in the afterlife, saying, 'I told you so,'" Emma said through a giggle.

"Oh, she's for sure saying that," Reid added. "In the most obnoxious way."

Audrey shrugged. "I feel like it's warranted."

After the long day of driving, it didn't take long before the three of them got situated in bed and turned off the lights. Emma insisted on taking the middle to maintain their hard-earned peace. But after not even an hour of tossing and turning, she announced in a dramatic sigh, "I'm burning up. I'm taking the rollout bed."

"Are you sure?" Reid said. "Just take my spot. It's fine."

"It's okay. I kind of want my own space. Just…behave."

"Tell that to Audrey. She's the one with the knife."

Emma moved to the rollout bed, leaving an Emma-sized space in between Reid and Audrey.

"Do you think we should spoon like Sadie suggested?" Reid whispered.

It seemed like a wild idea even to Reid, but something about being in Springfield, completing Sadie's Route 66 dream, and just all around missing her terribly, she wanted—and needed—some kind of nurturing, some kind of physical touch to ease the heaviness inside her.

"I'm not sure if I trust you," Audrey said lightly.

"I have to earn back your trust somehow. It can be a trust spoon session."

"Fine," Audrey said, flipping over on her opposite side, her back facing Reid.

Reid scooted closer and wrapped her arm around her.

"Are you two actually spooning?" Emma said from the foot of the bed.

"Just listening to Sadie's suggestion," Reid said. "We'll see if we can build Rome back in a night."

"I feel like this is a big moment."

"Don't make it weird, Ems," Audrey said. "I haven't been held in a long time."

Reid tightened her grip. She hadn't been held in a long time either. It was nice to feel a warm body settling into hers. She found her hand naturally tracing invisible lines up and down Audrey's arm. For not have cuddling someone in ages, the habit happened as a reflex.

Audrey sighed. "Oh, this feels nice."

"I think we should have just done this six years ago."

"I don't know. I'm at a disadvantage with my back facing you."

"Maybe it's all part of my master plan."

Soon, Emma's heavy breathing filled in the silence that settled into the room. "I never noticed the scar before," Audrey whispered.

"You didn't? You saw me in my bathing suit in Sedona."

"I know but…I didn't notice it. Where did you get it?"

"From you, Brutus."

Audrey kicked back and clobbered Reid's leg. She laughed. "Answer the question before I stab you again, Caesar."

"Fire coral. I took a diving trip to Belize last summer and was free diving with some friends. I was being a bit careless and brushed against it. I don't know if you know anything about fire coral, but its venomous, so not only did it cut me, but I got this insane rash for the rest of the trip, and it burned like crazy. Now, I have a battle scar."

"You have to be careful."

"I usually am."

There was another pause. "Is it weird how nice this feels?"

The vulnerability in her voice was as loud and clear as Emma's heavy breathing.

"Maybe," Reid said, tightening her arm. Audrey snuggled closer. "Or maybe we both just really need it."

"Yeah, maybe we do."

Chapter Twelve

Finally, they made it to Gatlinburg.

They pulled into the driveway where a cozy log cabin in the midst of a forest of oaks and white pines awaited them. It was their beacon of the road trip, signaling that they were no longer lost at sea in the flat, barren parts of Middle America.

Audrey had especially enjoyed their time in Nashville, walking down Lower Broadway, experiencing the heart of country music. She had expected Reid, the vocal hater of country, to complain as they listened to live country music at Tootsie's Orchid Lounge, the oldest honky-tonk in Nashville, but she hadn't complained once, with the exception of uttering, "Wow, we're definitely not in California anymore." Instead, Reid had stood close to Audrey's side, occasionally nodding along to the music as live bands performed. Audrey had even successfully convinced Reid to line dance with her with only a little bit of resistance. She'd snatched Reid's hand and pulled her onto the dance floor, and Emma had tried holding in her laughter at Reid, the born and bred, surfer-scuba diver Californian, fumbling her dance moves to the twangiest country music.

Something about the Albuquerque bar and line dancing in Nashville had caused an undertow of emotions in Audrey because every night since Albuquerque, Reid had been creeping into her dreams. Right as they pulled into the driveway of their Gatlinburg cabin, she was jolted awake and snapped out of the dream of her and Reid slow dancing to live music at Tootsie's, the flutter in her chest still active when she blinked herself awake.

Audrey rubbed her eyes and stepped out of the car. She breathed in the deep scent of fresh, woodsy air, which smelled so much better than the stale, dusty air of Oklahoma. The smell pushed away the last remaining dream fog from her brain, and the fluttering slowed.

What the hell was happening?

Their cabin had an open floor plan with high wooden ceilings, a balcony overlooking the back of the property, and to Audrey's delight, a hot tub. She rested her elbows on the balcony, taking in the peaceful silence and the breathtaking views of the mountains.

"Oh wow, it's really beautiful back here," Reid said behind her. She came up beside Audrey, leaned into the balcony railing, and savored the view.

Out of all the space on the deck, Reid had positioned herself right next to Audrey, leaving barely an inch between them. "Isn't it?" Audrey said. "I'm definitely going to enjoy the hot tub and all of this later. Care to join?"

Reid put a hand over her chest. "Are you inviting me to decompress with you?"

"You have five seconds to accept or reject, or I'm taking the offer back," she said playfully.

Reid smirked. "Count me in."

"You guys," Emma announced from inside on the other side of the sliding screen door. "It's Sisterhood of the Traveling Syrah Time."

She and Reid exchanged a glance.

"The moment has come," Reid said and gestured Audrey to go first.

"I'm absolutely ready to crush this bottle of Syrah," Emma said, peeling off the gold foil. "But part of me feels a little guilty for breaking it in. Is that just me?"

Audrey hadn't thought about it until she studied the bottle and the black label spelling out "Sadie and Jeremy Barnes" in gold cursive. Emma tossed the foil into the trash beside her feet and handed Audrey and Reid empty wineglasses. They paused and stared at the bottle.

Audrey had never expected this moment to be heavy. They had a delicious bottle of wine in front of them, personally made by Sadie, Jeremey, Mr. Lin, and Magnolia Springs' head winemaker just a few weeks after their engagement. A year and a half later, they had drunk the Syrah at Sadie and Jeremy's low-key reception on the back patio of Magnolia Springs. Audrey hadn't had the chance to fully enjoy the taste because she had been too focused on staying well away from Reid and the extreme awkwardness and discomfort that came with it.

This bottle of Syrah, the letters, and the time capsule they'd made on graduation night were the only things they had left of Sadie. As much as Audrey wanted to actually taste and enjoy something created by her best friend, she didn't want to lose even more of her.

"I feel a little weird," she said softly.

Emma looked at her sympathetically. "What do you think we should do?"

"I feel like Sadie would tell us to drink it," Reid said. "I can hear her saying that she worked hard to create something so magical, and she'd pretend to act all offended if we didn't try it. Plus, Jeremy wouldn't have given us the bottle if he didn't want us to drink it."

"I think we should drink it," Emma said. "You don't go through all the effort of making wine for your wedding and then encourage people to just admire the bottle."

"I agree," Audrey said. She slid her wineglass over.

Emma gave her a thin smile. "Okay, let's drink." She opened a few kitchen drawers until she found a corkscrew. She popped the cork and poured them each a liberal glass. As she held on to hers, Emma glanced at the envelope labeled *Gatlinburg* in purple pen handwriting.

"Anyone want to read it?" she said.

Even though her heart clenched, Audrey knew that this moment, with Sadie's wine and one of the last letters of their trip, was important. She noticed a faraway look in Reid's eyes and had a feeling it would be too much for her.

"I'll do it," Audrey said and opened her hand for the envelope.

When Emma slid it across the kitchen island, Audrey pulled the letter out.

Hello friends!

You've finally reached your final destination, which means Reid survived Bumfuck, America—too soon? I'm so proud.

I hope you guys made it because Gatlinburg is gorgeous…and so is this cabin. Auds, I hope this log cabin matches the vision you had when you added it to the bucket list. You can finally live out your Little House on the Prairie *dream…except without bonnets or a covered wagon. Hope that doesn't ruin the experience for you.*

I wish I had the chance to go back one last time, even if I couldn't see the fireflies. It means the world to me that the three of you have taken this trip to experience something that has meant so much to me my entire life. It's peaceful and serene, and after driving across the country, it's a perfect way to end a road trip. I hope you enjoy your log cabin in the woods and take some time to decompress and enjoy the trees, mountains, and moonshine. If I've hooked up to the Afterlife Wi-Fi by now, I'll try my best to live vicariously through you. Maybe I will know how to send you guys a little sign that I'm with you…a cute haunting. Unless you guys are arguing or not wearing bug spray, then the haunting won't be cute.

You want to know who also loves this place just as much as I do? Ticks. Wear the damn bug spray.

I'll see you when it's firefly time.

Love you guys!

XOXO Sadie

"Well, " Reid said and cleared her throat as Emma scratched it off the bucket list. "Make sure we don't forget about the ticks."

"I think I saw bug spray in the upstairs bathroom," Audrey said.

Emma held up her wineglass. "We should toast to Sadie." She and Reid raised their glasses. "We made it. Over two thousand miles later, we're here in one of Sadie's favorite spots, and tomorrow, we get to see something she talked about every summer throughout our entire friendship. I think we were all a little nervous about this trip, given everything that has happened." Audrey stole a glance at Reid, and an unexpected warmth washed over her. "And I'm just really incredibly proud of all of us for doing this…for Sadie and for us. I'm kind of sad that tomorrow is our last day. It's been, I don't know, nice having us back together. Well, not fully back together but…you know what I mean."

Audrey walked over to Emma and put an arm around her. "I'm really glad too. I was obviously hesitant, but being with the two of you has been exactly what I needed, and I'm grateful that during this really hard and shitty time, I had both of you by my side."

"I'm glad you weren't alone for that," Emma said.

Audrey snuck another glance at Reid and smiled at her, silently thanking her for showing up as a friend for the past ten days instead of the foe she had mentally prepared for.

"Cheers to us and to Sadie," Reid said, holding her glass over the kitchen island. "And to *finally* making it here. I was worried we wouldn't survive Middle America."

"Is that why you were nearing a hundred miles an hour on our way to Oklahoma City?" Emma said. "Don't think I didn't notice."

"It was an open road in the middle of Bumfuck, America. Of course I was going to spice things up and try to go a hundred."

"You could have run over an armadillo," Audrey said.

Reid smiled. "When you were asleep, I saw one. I almost woke you up, but I didn't want to disturb your sweet dreams. Another cheers to not running over an armadillo."

They clinked their glasses and took their first sip. One taste of the Syrah and Audrey was transported back to the Magnolia Springs back patio. She pictured Sadie in her A-line wedding dress with the classiest plunging neckline. She looked absolutely gorgeous in a dress so simple and laidback. Audrey remembered the looks that Sadie and Jeremy had exchanged all night like they were the center of each other's universe. Even though by the time they had their reception, they had been married for three months and together for five years, up until Sadie died, they had acted like they were in the honeymoon phase. Audrey and Emma had joked that their love was disgusting in the most adorable, envious way.

Drinking the Syrah brought a flood of Sadie memories, and they were equally happy and heartbreaking all at once.

The three of them brought their glasses and the bottle out to the deck. The tree canopy opened up to a perfect view of the western sky where pale pinks and oranges blended in with the remaining daylight. The string patio lights flickered on and illuminated the deck with mood lighting. The night bugs slowly came out, one by one, and chirped and sang in the shadows.

Audrey stretched out her tired legs and basked in the scene in front of her. Reid played some indie folk music from her portable Bluetooth speaker that stitched together the soundtrack into the warm, piney air accented by the faint smoke from nearby fires.

The three of them enjoyed the scene, sipping Syrah and chatting about random things as the sunset morphed into a natural painting. Bold streaks of oranges emerged from the horizon where the sun had fallen behind a thin blanket of clouds. The clouds soaked up various shades of pink, but right above them in the older night sky, violet hues imbued the clouds, sky, and even the rolling mountains in front of them.

A heavy pang clenched around Audrey's chest as she noticed the purple in the sunset.

Her heart sank, and the stinging in her eyes was almost instantaneous. Purple was Sadie's color. It was the color of her childhood bedroom, her bicycle, her JanSport backpack in high school, the color she'd dyed a streak of her hair once when they were twenty. She had multiple pairs of purple scrubs, and the purple in her veterinary practice's logo was absolutely intentional, whether she admitted it or not.

"Does this mean she finally hooked up to the Afterlife Wi-Fi?" Reid said, looking up.

Maybe I will know how to send you guys a little sign that I'm with you...a cute haunting.

"It must be," Audrey said, her eyes glued to the gorgeous sunset.

"Out of all the sunsets we've seen on this trip, we get a purple one our first night in Gatlinburg," Emma said.

"You think it's just a coincidence?" Reid said.

"It could be," Audrey answered. "But I'd like to think that it's Sadie showing this place off for us."

They sat in silence and watched the purples in the sky deepen until the sun finally set.

This had to be Sadie's doing. She would show off like this, Audrey thought.

Her absence had hung over them for the majority of the trip. But watching that sunset, Audrey felt her presence as if she'd pulled up a chair behind them to admire the view. The air was full of her. It was the closest thing Audrey knew she would ever feel to Sadie being back with them.

As she finished her second glass of Syrah, she studied the tattoo on her inner right wrist and the last triangle out of the four. She hated thinking that their tattoos were no longer complete without Sadie. Her absence was more permanent than their ink.

"I just had an idea," Audrey said. "What if we filled in the last triangle with purple ink?"

"Oh, I like that," Reid said and glanced down at her tattoo as if she needed to visualize it. "Maybe, like, an orchid color. That was her favorite shade."

"Wait, I love this idea," Emma said. She pulled out her phone and searched for something on it. "How wild would it be if we got it after we fly back home? I feel like that amazing sunset is the sign to do it."

"That's where I got the idea from," Audrey said.

"I'm down," Reid said.

"Me too."

Emma reached for the bottle of Syrah that sat between her lounge chair and Reid's. When she poured the rest of it, only a modest sip came out. That was unfortunate, as the wine was starting to make Audrey the perfect level of tipsy.

"Is it time for the margaritas?" Reid said. "Isn't that the right thing to do when you're sad, Ms. Therapist?"

"Not at all," Emma said, but an impish grin still formed. "But let's do it."

Reid smiled. "Three strong margaritas coming right up."

Those were the famous last words. After one margarita, Emma tapped out, claiming drunkenness and exhaustion.

"Reid, your margs killed Emma," Audrey said after Emma went inside.

Once she'd left, something in the air had shifted. Before, Emma's presence had shielded them from their passive aggressive comments and unresolved issues, but now, it had served as a buffer for a spark Audrey felt growing between them.

Reid laughed and sipped on the remains of her first margarita as if it wasn't as strong as a Kickboxer. "The girl has never been able to handle anything other than wine. She even struggled with Mike's in high school. I have no idea how she's going to handle moonshine tasting if she can't handle my margarita."

Audrey took another sip and winced when the strong taste of tequila overpowered her taste buds. "I mean, in her defense, these are wildly strong."

"Gotta drink it by tomorrow night, or it'll be a waste of money." Reid's stare drifted over Audrey's shoulder. "We also need to try out the hot tub before tomorrow."

Audrey checked her phone for the time. "It's almost 10:30."

"Your point?"

She would have usually considered 10:30 as "winding down" time. But when Reid directed that coaxing smirk at her, she didn't have to think before she stood and said, "My point is, it's hot tub time."

Emma was in bed, Audrey and Reid were tipsy, and the night was filled with possibilities.

Chapter Thirteen

Wrapped in a towel, Audrey headed downstairs to find Reid standing in the doorway of the open fridge in her black bikini. Audrey's eyes fixated on Reid's small nipples protruding against the fabric. Without even stepping one toe into the hot tub, her body temperature skyrocketed.

What the hell was happening? She'd seen Reid in a bikini countless times and had never had a reaction. She didn't need a hot tub. She needed an ice bath.

Reid, seemingly oblivious to Audrey's locked stare, turned and poured another round of margaritas in their empty glasses. "Hot tub margs."

She headed toward the sliding porch door, and once her back was turned, Audrey held the cold glass up to her face. She needed to get it together. She followed Reid onto the deck where the hot tub waited for them, bubbling in the glow of purple neon lights.

Reid was quick to slide into the bubbles. She let out a sigh as she sank into her spot, and damn it, Audrey's mind started to replay that soft sigh over and over again, each replay sounding more sexual in her head.

She settled into a seat as far from Reid as she could manage in the tiny tub. She looked up to find Reid's eyes locked on her while she nursed her drink, eliciting an electric current to travel from Audrey's chest to her clit.

"And then, there were two," Reid said with a smirk. Drops of water dotted her face, down her neck, along her collarbone.

God, this had to be because it was so long since Audrey'd had sex. That must have also sparked the sex dream she had right before waking up when they had pulled into the driveway. Adding wine and tequila into the mix would, of course, cause Audrey's body to hum with arousal at sharing a hot tub with an attractive, scantily clad Reid.

She pulled her gaze away. She had to. Staring at the moisture shimmering along Reid's collarbone in the violet glow of the LED lights was getting her riled up, and she refused to tap out too early because of her body temperature...or because she really needed to relieve the pressure and frustration mounting within her.

As she looked around to find something to stare at, she spotted speckles of yellow light flickering in unison against the thick curtain of night.

Fireflies.

She hadn't seen them since she was a kid in Ohio; lightning bugs, as Ohioans called them, weren't the synchronous ones. Her heart swelled when she saw the light show invade the draped darkness. "Hey, look, the fireflies," she said with an eager point.

Reid turned around and gasped. "Are those *the* fireflies?"

Audrey slid over to the side of the hot tub closest to the trees and rested her arms on the side. For a moment, the two of them got lost in the light show. While Reid watched the fireflies with the smallest trace of a smile touching her lips, Audrey admired just how great her smile was. Had it always been so fantastic? She'd always thought Reid was attractive, but she'd never found herself thinking just how contagious her smile was.

Or how sexy she looked with her hair in a messy bun.

Or how sexy her neck was collecting water droplets.

"I think I get it now," Reid said, still staring at the fireflies. "Why Sadie was so fascinated with this place. I've been hearing about this since middle school and never understood what the fuss was about. Until now. It's oddly cathartic."

Audrey quickly turned back to the woods. "They really are."

They sat on the edge in silence, sipping their drinks and admiring the natural strobe lights pulsating against the night. She knew that the next morning, when they told Emma about the fireflies, she would regret going to bed early.

"Can I be honest with you?"

The softness in Reid's voice pulled Audrey's gaze to her. She was surprised to see the vulnerability sparkling in her eyes. It was...nice, observing Reid in a raw state and not hidden behind walls or jokes.

"Of course you can," Audrey said.

Reid didn't open up easily, so whatever she had to say, Audrey would welcome the depth with open arms. She was surprised that, given their history, Reid felt comfortable enough to even consider her a safe space. "I was really worried about this trip."

"Why's that?"

Reid shrugged and sat back into the corner of the tub, facing Audrey with a haunting look of regret. "Our last trip together didn't really go over well, and I was worried this was going to be a repeat, and none of us could handle that. Not when we're grieving Sadie. Plus, I thought you hated me."

A pang erupted in Audrey's stomach, the guilt starting to stack back on top of her. "Reid, I never hated you."

"I didn't know—"

"Well, I'm telling you now. I never hated you," she said sternly for added measure. "I was sad, angry, heartbroken, all because I didn't hate you. I just wanted my friend back."

Reid glanced at her margarita. "I never hated you, either."

"I know."

"You just used your teacher voice on me."

"I want to be sure you know that I never hated you."

"The teacher voice is kind of hot, I'm not going to lie."

Audrey rolled her eyes. There was the typical Reid joke that squashed the sweet moment. "You always have to ruin a moment."

"Gotta stay true to who I am." After another glance at the fireflies and a moment of silence filled with the cacophony of night bugs, Reid looked back at Audrey and said, "Did you really mean what you said?"

Audrey furrowed her brow in confusion. "What do you mean?"

"When we had the Sadie toast. You said you were glad that you had the two of us by your side during this shitty week."

"Of course I meant it. I wouldn't say something I didn't mean. I really appreciate everything you've done for me. You could have easily been, 'eh, well, fuck you.'"

"I wouldn't ever have done that."

"I mean, I don't know. We hadn't been on good terms for six years. It would have made sense if you did."

"It wouldn't have. All those feelings you've been feeling—between Sadie and getting your heart broken—I've felt all those before. It would make less sense if I said 'fuck you' knowing what it's like to really go through it."

Audrey shrugged. "Well, I really appreciate you being there for me. I know you didn't have to, but you were, and well, it really means a lot. I know there were times I was being really stubborn, but even in those moments, I knew you were right. I knew you were genuinely trying to help me."

Reid gave her a soft smile. "I'm glad I could be there for you. Truly." She turned around and situated her body against one of the bubbling jets in the corner. "You know, we've never really talked about your hot steamy make out in Albuquerque."

Heat crawled up her face. She washed it down with a drink. "That was a hard transition."

"It's what I'm best at. You know this," she said. "I'm feeling tipsy and gossipy."

Audrey slid off the side of the tub and sat in the opposite corner from Reid. "What do you want to know?" The water bubbled around Reid, and Audrey hated how her eyes went straight for the bubbles around Reid's perfect cleavage. For a minute there, she had forgotten all about just how sexy Reid looked in that bikini.

"Was it good? Did it make you feel any certain way?"

"Well, if you really want to know—"

"Oh, I want to know."

She smiled, knowing that Reid was fully enthralled with what she had to say about her dance floor make out. "It was good. Hot. Turned me on a bit."

Reid's eyebrows rose. "Oh really?"

"That's not saying much. It's been, like, a million years since I've had sex. So that didn't really help tame anything."

"You think when we get back to California, you'll join dating apps?"

Audrey laughed. "God, no."

"What? Why not?"

"Because I've heard horror stories."

Reid waved off her comment. "It's just an initiation. If you get past that, you'll eventually find the love of your life…so they say."

"And how well have they worked for you?"

Reid pursed her lips and nodded. "Fair point. But in my defense, after finding Shelby on one of those, I haven't really tried. I'm not in the mood to get my heart broken again."

"I get that. I'm not sure if I want to get back to dating. It seems… exhausting, and I'm at a spot in my life I want something fun. Actually, I need something fun. Getting dumped right after my best friend died isn't necessarily a fun time."

"You need to tell yourself that you're the tequila. You don't chase," Reid said and wiggled the margarita in her hands.

"Wait, I actually like that. A lot."

"Good. Once you fully embrace being the tequila and let go of the lime mentality, it works wonders. Trust me." She pulled a sip of margarita. "You know, people *do* use dating apps for fun. Pretty sure most of the people on Tinder aren't looking for anything profound."

Audrey smirked. "Are you one of them?"

"I have on occasion."

"Recently?"

Reid raised a curious brow as a mischievous smirk grew. "Why are you asking?"

Suddenly, the hot tub was a little too hot for comfort. Audrey drank her margarita, hoping the ice would tame the heat of embarrassment crawling across her face.

Damn it, that smirk told Audrey that she was being a little too transparent. "I'm just continuing the conversation you started," she said with the hope that it was enough to prevent Reid from reading her cards.

"I haven't recently, if you want to know," Reid said and took a casual drink, eyes locked on to Audrey's.

"You're not interested in dating?"

"It's not that I'm not up for dating. I'm just, I don't know, I guess I'm a little—"

"Scared?"

Reid exhaled. "I guess I am. It's one thing to have a random, meaningless hookup. It's another to let someone into your life. The more you let someone in, the more they might hurt you."

"I get it. I'm afraid too."

Reid held up her margarita. "Cheers to hopefully not getting fucked over by women in the near-distant future."

Audrey clinked her glass. "Cheers."

"We should go to the You Hall when we get back," Reid said. "Sometime this summer. Find you a proper rebound."

"Rebound has a negative connotation," Audrey said. "I'd call it more like a reminder that there's better women than Becca out there."

"Oh, there are for sure. No question about it. Becca is the one who lost out."

Audrey rolled her eyes. "You have to say that."

"I don't," Reid said confidently. She floated into the middle of the tub about a foot away. "You're a pretty awesome human," she said, her voice dropping.

Audrey let out a laugh. "I don't think your twenty-three year old self would have thought that."

"My twenty-three year old self had her own issues to deal with." Reid gave her a soft smile.

"I still can't believe you used to have a crush on me in high school," Audrey said. She tried tucking her foot underneath her, and instead, she slipped along the seat, only catching herself as her chin hit the bubbles. She quickly stood and wiped the water off her face. God, did she have any smooth bones in her body?

Reid laughed hysterically. "You okay there?"

Audrey realized the only way to stop her face from consistently getting attacked by a blush was if she just went to bed, even though that was the last thing she wanted to do. "I slipped," she said and sat back in her spot. The damn traitorous spot.

"Yeah, I know. I saw the whole thing."

"So back to your crush. Stop avoiding it."

Reid laughed. "I'm not avoiding it. I had a small crush on you during our freshman year of high school. Keyword, small." She held her pointer finger and thumb an inch apart.

"Don't joke," Audrey said and flicked water at her.

Reid winced and wiped her face. "I'm not joking." She pushed a wave at Audrey, nailing her right in the face.

She blew out the disgusting warm water from her mouth and nose. "I still don't really believe you."

Reid laughed. "What? Why not? I've been crushing on girls since I was, like, five. You were the new, cute, gym class girl. You have a nice smile. I always thought so. I couldn't help it."

"Why didn't you ever tell me?"

"Because we became friends shortly after, and I didn't know you were bi until literally a year ago when Sadie and Emma were gossiping about you and your new girlfriend."

"How long was this crush?"

Reid shrugged. "I don't know, like, fall semester? And we became good friends, so that fizzled. Also hearing you, Emma, and Sadie constantly talking about boys did the trick too."

Audrey's heart pounded. If Reid had once found her attractive—and during her most awkward years—surely there had to be some attraction still there, right? Audrey didn't see herself as any Margot Robbie, but she did have a glow up in college. She would give herself that.

But if she didn't ask a follow-up question, the moment of knowing if she was the only one feeling this sparking tension would be lost, and she didn't know if she would get another chance. Maybe in this new chapter of her life, she needed to take more risks, follow the things that made her feel something other than the loss she'd experienced over the last few months.

So she decided to take the leap. "And what do you think now?"

Reid's smirk bloomed again. "What do I think now? I think you're very attractive, but probably the hottest thing about you is that you are just seemingly unaware of it." Those deep blue eyes never once wavered, as if Reid wanted to send a stern message, one that would be strong enough to get past all of Audrey's insecurities that had sprouted from Becca.

She hadn't heard a compliment like that in months. "Don't fuck with me."

"I'm not fucking with you."

The moment was so sweet and tender that looking Reid in the eyes became almost impossible. She looked at the bubbles to try to calm her racing heart. "I mean…am I even your type?" she said but continued to look at the water bathed in purple lights. "What the hell is your type?"

"Well, I have my type on paper that I usually go for but shouldn't and the one I need to start dating. Which do you want?"

Audrey took an encouraging drink of her strong margarita. "Both."

"What I usually go for that I need to stop chasing? Fit, femme, tatted brunettes who look like they could physically—and emotionally—hurt me."

Audrey almost choked on her drink. "Wow. That's oddly specific."

Reid shrugged. "It's true, though. Shelby. Natalie. The women in between."

She wasn't sure if it was a good or bad thing that she didn't fit that description. "What's the type you should be going for?"

"Kind and secure women who want to take care of me, not hurt me. Women who give off good vibes. And if they're brunettes, well, that's even more alluring." Reid's confident gaze locked on to Audrey, causing her to come undone. "What's your type?" she said, seemingly unaware of Audrey's internal sexual frustrations.

"I don't know. I only have Becca to compare to."

"Yeah, we really need to go to the You Hall. Figure out what your type is, what attracts you to a woman—"

"Oh, I know what I like about women."

Reid raised a curious brow. "Oh, do you?"

"Isn't that what makes you realize you're queer in the first place?"

"I guess. So what do you like about women? What's your favorite part?"

The effects of Reid's flirtatious voice collided with the alcohol in Audrey's veins. She wanted to embrace this feeling of excitement and anticipation bubbling alongside them in the tub. So she decided to lean into the moment. She had nothing to lose. "How about I show you?"

Reid's eyebrows rose as Audrey met her in the middle of the tub. She hooked her hands around Reid's hip bones, right where the hem of her bikini met her skin. A jolt went straight to her clit at the contact. She looked up and found Reid's eyes hooded with want. Audrey gently rubbed circles around Reid's hips and moved her thumbs to wander along the hem of her bikini. Reid closed her eyes as if savoring her touch.

When Reid opened her eyes, they fell to Audrey's lips, and a wave of arousal curled underneath her bathing suit. The way Reid stared at her, determination mixed with vulnerability, turned her inside out. She didn't have time to think about the consequences or what all of this meant. She slid her hands to the small of Reid's back and leaned in, waiting for her to take the next step.

Reid closed the rest of the space between them and kissed her. At the first swipe of her tongue, Audrey melted, a moan escaping her. The kiss deepened, starting from a seed of uncertainty and blooming into a scorching kiss. She pushed Reid against the ledge, pulled her closer until their bodies meshed together, and let her hands wander back down her body to her perfect hip bones. In response, Reid sucked her bottom lip and nibbled. That soft bite unlocked another level of desire, and all the fluttering and flickering in Audrey's chest made it feel like those fireflies lighting up the darkness were inside her.

She pulled away to collect a breath, and when she opened her eyes, she found Reid's still closed, lips pursed, clearly still reveling in what had transpired.

God, had Reid Haley always been this damn sexy?

"What's happening?" Audrey said softly through a ragged breath. She wanted to make sure they were on the same page. Was this just the two of them caught up in the emotions of the evening and alcohol, or was there an unspoken truth stitched into that kiss?

Reid opened her eyes. "What's happening? You made a move on me."

That snapped Audrey out of her daze. Damn, she really had made a move. But when she examined the look on Reid's face, her lips were curved upward as if basking in the remnants of the kiss. "I guess I did. Is that okay?"

"It's more than okay," Reid said, gliding her hand back onto Audrey's burning cheek and pulling her in for another searing kiss.

Reid guided her so she was in one of the seats. When Reid straddled her lap and deepened the kiss with her tongue, Audrey's clit throbbed and begged for more. She let her hands wander the expanse of her bare skin not covered by her bikini. Reid kissed her with skilled precision, another nibble to her bottom lip, gently pulling on it, and God, Audrey was putty in her hands. She pulled Reid's waist into hers, their bare stomachs meshing together.

Reid wrenched her mouth away and moved to Audrey's neck, sucking a spot that unlocked another moan. She glided her tongue up to Audrey's ear and softly kissed it. "You're sexy," Reid whispered and gently pulled Audrey's earlobe with her teeth.

Audrey unraveled. At this rate, she wasn't sure she would make it out of the hot tub without melting. "No, I'm not," she said, eyes closed and loving how Reid's soft words and breath tickled her earlobe.

Reid pulled away. "What? You are." Audrey laughed. "Why are you laughing?"

"Because. It's just…I don't know. I never thought we would be here. We're making out in a hot tub."

"We *were* making out in a hot tub. Past tense because you decided to laugh," Reid said, not too seriously.

Audrey positioned both her hands on Reid's hips, and Reid melted in her grip. A soft moan escaped her, and she quickly recovered by pressing her lips together. But the moan had already landed and lit up Audrey.

"You, um, you really do like a hip bone," Reid said breathlessly.

Audrey loved how Reid instantly deflated at her touch. She felt powerful. She felt sexy. She felt wanted. Before she had the chance to lean in, Reid must have found a last bit of strength because she pulled

Audrey back in, their tongues picking up the dance from moments before.

Reid had blindsided her in so many ways. How forgiving she was of Audrey once they finally spoke. How she'd owned up to all of her mistakes so quickly. How she'd kept her crush a secret for nineteen years. How she kissed Audrey as if they hadn't once been best friends. How she seemed so confident and adamant about Audrey being sexy.

All of the versions of Reid she'd known over the years were not the same person straddling her and making her throb and ache for more of her mouth. This version of Reid she wanted all over her, inside her.

At the realization of how desperate she was for more, she rested her hand against Reid's chest, stopping her from adjusting the kiss. "Reid," she said. The desperate moans of desire and pleasure that she muted in her throat made her voice hoarse.

Reid's eyes remained closed. "Hm?"

"I'm enjoying this way too much."

"Hm."

"Maybe we should stop before we get too carried away."

Reid opened her eyes. She tucked a loose strand behind Audrey's ear and cupped her face. "You're probably right."

She let out a sigh of relief that they were on the same page. "I don't want to stop but—"

"You don't need to explain. I get it. Really."

"I just don't want this to be a caught-up-in-the-moment thing because we had some strong margaritas. Our friendship is too fragile for that."

"I know. I agree. Maybe we should head up to bed? I'm sure Emma has a full schedule packed for us tomorrow."

"She absolutely does. I bet you she has the itinerary on her Notes app."

They got out of the hot tub, patted themselves dry, and wandered upstairs to their separate bedrooms. At the top of the steps, Reid stopped and faced her. "If you think there's a chance I'm going to regret what happened just because we had a few margaritas, I'm not going to," she said. She gave Audrey a soft smile before heading into her room for the night.

When Audrey's head hit the pillow, she closed her eyes and immersed herself in the fresh memories of all the kissing. Her lips tingled as the kissing played out in her head like a movie. She couldn't believe what had transpired. If she hadn't stopped it, what the hell would have happened? Would they have fucked in the hot tub? Because she really believed they were well on their way to doing just that, given how desperately she wanted more of Reid all over.

However, the most unexpected thing was Reid saying she wouldn't regret what happened, making Audrey wonder if Reid thought about her just as much as she thought about Reid.

Even as Audrey lay in bed, willing her heightened senses to simmer for sleep, she couldn't tame the tingling dancing on her lips or the arousal pulsating on her clit. She tossed and turned, trying to find a comfortable spot so the alcohol could rock her to sleep.

After twenty minutes of trying, she knew she had to be more proactive.

So she closed her eyes and slid her hand under the hem of her sweatpants, fully savoring the lingering kiss still attached to her mouth and the tip of her tongue. When her fingers met her folds, she felt just how turned on she was. She applied pressure on her clit, and an involuntary gasp escaped her lips, fighting against the desperation that consumed her. She could feel her entire body tighten from so much desire and sexual frustration that each stroke and circle unwound all the knots that had collected inside her. She stifled a moan and got lost in the replay of the kiss. Reid's soft lips against hers, the little nibbles on her bottom lip, Reid's tongue moving in and out of her mouth. Audrey imagined being underneath her in bed and how those tongue movements would feel against her clit. She wished Reid's sexy, warm mouth was on her, tasting her like the top-shelf tequila she'd told Audrey to be, moaning along with her.

Her free hand fisted the comforter as the pleasure spread to her toes.

As she moved her fingers up and down in measured strokes, she imagined Reid running her tongue down Audrey's wet length before pushing inside her.

She twisted the comforter again and muted another moan with her closed lips.

"I want you to come for me," she imagined Reid saying, that same darkened look in her eyes boring into Audrey, as if her only mission was to make her come. "Please come for me, Audrey. I want to hear you and feel you."

Her hips bucked, feeling the pressure rising to the surface and ready to claim her entirely. She let go of the comforter and threw an extra pillow over her face. Muting herself was only causing her to hold back, and she needed to come. She needed to rid herself of all the frustrations and have the dopamine rush reverberate in her limbs.

She opened her mouth against the pillow, bit the cotton case, and let out a groan. She moved her fingers faster and harder as the current of arousal spread up her arms and down her legs until it reached the top of her head and the tip of her toes. "God, you taste amazing," she could hear Reid saying as she moved her tongue inside her. The orgasm slammed into her hard and fast. She bit even more of the pillow, wishing it was Reid's shoulder, and filled her ears with the sound of her own orgasm.

Feeling the much needed release from her sexual frustration, Audrey was finally able to calm her mind and fall asleep.

Chapter Fourteen

The smell of delicious bacon wafted from the kitchen up to Reid's room, making her stomach growl and her mouth water. She remembered the way Audrey kissed her last night, her lips still sizzling from that searing make out session in the hot tub.

Her eyes shot open and fixated on the rotating ceiling fan.

Holy hell, what had happened last night?

As the memories materialized in her mind, her body went from a sleepy fog to alert with desire. Oh, she and Audrey had made out… for a while. She recalled pinning Audrey to the seat and straddling her while Audrey salaciously rubbed her hips. That was a newly discovered erogenous zone, thanks to Audrey.

Fuck, was it bad she wanted to feel all of that again? While sober? Was she allowed to want that? It was Audrey, for crying out loud. The woman who she'd thought had hated her for the last six years.

Now, she ached to have her mouth latched on to hers again.

She guzzled her water bottle on her nightstand, hoping that would nurse her arid throat before she went downstairs and acted like nothing unusual had happened the night before. She took her time going to the bathroom and brushing her teeth, attempting to buy some time before she donned a casual mask.

As she walked down the stairs, she heard Emma and Audrey's chatter. Once she walked into the kitchen, her eyes immediately landed on Audrey making herself a plate of scrambled eggs, bacon, and hash browns. She still was in her pajamas: a black Midnight Konfusion concert T-shirt and black sweatpants, her hair in a messy bun with a few wavy strands poking out of the hair tie.

Reid smiled at Audrey's shirt. She remembered when the four of them had gone to a music festival headlined by Midnight Konfusion the summer after they'd graduated college, one of the bucket list items they scratched off. It was also one of her last solidly good memories before their fight.

"Nice shirt," Reid said, gesturing to it.

Audrey looked down and smiled. "Oh, thanks." She had such a nice smile. Seeing her lips curve like that caused Reid's heart to race, as if her crush from when they were fourteen had bloomed again overnight. There was something so sexy about her in her pj's and bed hair. Reid took pride in herself that their kissing in the hot tub was likely the reason why Audrey's hair was up in a bun instead of her usual straight look.

Because damn, that was a good kiss. That kind of passion usually ended with her and the other woman in her bed instead of parting ways.

"Good morning, sunshine," Emma said, breaking the silence.

Right. Emma was here.

Reid had almost gotten completely lost in Audrey and the memories of last night. She needed to act like nothing was out of the ordinary so Emma didn't pick up on what had happened, but that was a challenge because it felt impossible to tamp the electric current flowing between them. She felt completely exposed, as if that electricity now highlighted all the spots where Audrey had kissed her.

She was brave enough to fix herself up a plate just a few feet from Audrey.

Right as she spooned the scrambled eggs, Emma asked, "How late did you two stay up?"

She and Audrey exchanged a glance. "Uh, like, midnight?" Audrey said, and Reid was a bit shocked she'd told the truth because she was about to lie and say, "Just shortly after you went to bed." It was less conspicuous.

"Midnight?" Emma said as if she couldn't believe it. "You two stayed up talking…to each other…until midnight?"

See, this was exactly why they should have just said ten-thirty.

"We had a lot to talk about," Audrey said. Thank God because Reid felt too exposed to answer. "Obviously."

"And?"

"I think we got to a good place," Reid responded through the dryness still in her throat. Audrey looked at her, and as their eyes connected, Audrey sent her a small smirk.

"Really?" Emma said, totally buying it. "Wow. So you two finally kissed and made up?"

Fuck, Reid thought, they'd been caught, and embarrassment started crawling up her spine.

"We did," Audrey said calmly. Reid let out a small sigh of relief, realizing Emma was just using the expression, not making an accusation. It was a good thing they were going moonshine tasting today. Clearly, she was on edge. "Yeah, it was hot. You should have been there."

Emma laughed and rolled her eyes. "Yeah, right. Well, I'm really glad you two got a chance to talk and work things out. Does that mean we're all good?"

Audrey nodded, and Reid breathed another sigh of relief, one that seemed to scoop up and discard the remaining feelings of doubt inside her. "Yeah, I think we're good," Reid said. Based on the blush spreading across Audrey's cheeks, Reid also gathered that she was relishing the memory of their late-night escapade.

Emma clapped. "I love this so much. We can celebrate over moonshine. I've never tried it before."

"I can tell you that if you struggle with Mike's Hard Lemonade and my margaritas, then moonshine might not be for your grape-loving palate."

Emma shot her a side-eye. "I haven't had Mike's since we were teenagers, and your margaritas were all tequila and a splash of mix. I'll be just fine."

"Famous last words," Audrey said as Reid joined them at the table.

As they ate breakfast, Emma went over the itinerary for the day. Moonshine tasting, sobering up at the cabin before dinner, and then getting to the park in the evening. Reid only half listened. She was too focused on Audrey sitting right next to her and how their kiss still skated across her lips. God, if that was how it felt when Audrey kissed her lips, she couldn't imagine how the rest of her body would feel if Audrey kissed her in other places.

She desperately hoped she would find out.

The distillery sat on top of a mountain, offering gorgeous, panoramic views. Even if the Smoky Mountains were foothills compared to the mountains in California, it was a rarity for Reid to sit on top of one while drinking. Between the view and Audrey in that emerald floral dress, her eyes were going to be busy.

She loved sundress season.

The distillery was a huge barn with an outdoor patio and a live band. People surrounded the stage, talking, laughing, dancing, and taking pictures of the rolling mountains around them.

They found three empty spots at the main bar. As they took their seats, Audrey's bare leg brushed up against Reid's, and just a simple brush of a leg made her as warm as the hot tub had.

And probably that sundress. Definitely the sundress.

A bald man who looked to be in his forties with a salt-and-pepper goatee approached them with three menus. He had a name tag that said, "Dale" pinned to his black distillery shirt.

"Hello, ladies," he said, his Tennessee accent just as strong as Reid would have guessed it would be for someone working at a moonshine distillery. "Are we interested in doing a tasting today?"

"Absolutely," Emma said. Her enthusiasm was already high. Reid couldn't imagine the levels of enthusiasm after drinking a few shots. Moonshine was on a different level than what she was used to.

This will be very interesting, she thought.

"Have you ever been here before?"

"We're from wine country, Dale," Reid said. "Temecula. Her family owns a winery. We're about to embark on an adventure with you today."

He laughed. "It sounds like it. This ain't California wine. A bit stronger, so I hear."

"I have a diverse palate," Emma said. "I can handle it."

Reid covered the side of her mouth where Emma sat next to her and loudly whispered to Dale, "She can't."

"Listen, Dale. We've been on quite the cross-country journey," Emma said. "I'm ready for some moonshine. *We're* ready for some moonshine."

He slid them each a glass of water and a napkin. "A cross-country journey?"

"Started in San Diego and went up Route 66."

"Why are you here? You know that road ends in Chicago," Dale said with a teasing grin.

"That's another story," Emma said, waving him off.

The three of them ordered a tasting, each of them selecting a different flavor moonshine so they could try as many flavors as possible. As the other bartender fixed up their tasting flights, Dale handed them each a shot glass filled with some amber-colored moonshine.

"This is our apple pie, one of our most popular flavors," he said. "I figured after your long trek across the country, the least I could do is have you sample our best flavor. On the house."

"Really? That's so kind," Emma said. "Thank you."

Reid sniffed the glass. Instead of apple pie, her nose was overcome by the strong smell of alcohol. She was positive that Emma wouldn't survive this tasting.

"To Sadie," Reid said, holding her shot glass up to Emma and Audrey.

They clinked their glasses. Reid downed hers, and the powerful moonshine contorted her face. Even though Emma was making hilarious faces as she sipped her moonshine, Audrey pulled Reid's attention. She smacked her lips as if trying to decipher whether she liked the taste. Reid wanted to know what apple pie moonshine tasted like off her tongue, savoring it until she got drunk from her kiss.

Audrey noticed Reid's stare and nudged her arm. "What?" she mouthed so Emma wouldn't hear. She was too busy sipping her shot like a child with a sippy cup.

Reid shook her head. She didn't have the right words to articulate her confusing feelings, and this was certainly not the place. Tomorrow, they would fly back home to LAX in their first-class seats, where they would scratch off one of the last remaining items on their list. Then, it was back to regular life, and that prospect terrified her. With real life came the random urges to text or call Sadie, the loneliness of grief, and reckoning with what had happened between her and Audrey.

She resolved to enjoy every moment of their last day. The hard stuff could come later.

"You don't need to be afraid of the moonshine," Dale said to Emma.

Reid snapped back to reality to find Emma still nursing her shot.

"Her tastebuds are used to sweet, gentle, red, California wine," Reid said.

"Speak for yourself," Emma said defiantly, taking another taste and cringing.

Reid laughed. "Do you remember all the liquor we drank when we celebrated my birthday in Vegas?"

"I do not."

"Exactly."

"Just because I'm sipping it doesn't mean I can't handle it."

"She's really doubling down on this," Audrey said, leaning into Reid.

She smelled another wave of her bodywash. She wanted to be wrapped up in it, in her.

Instead, she pushed her desire into a little box inside her and closed it tightly.

Once they got their flights, they tasted, passed, and traded the different flavors to each other while Dale educated them all about the history and making of moonshine. By the time they were done with their flights, Reid's limbs felt lighter, and a pleasant buzz softened the edges of her worries. They ordered their own specialty cocktails. Reid got the blackberry lemonade with blackberry moonshine. When she sipped it, she let out a sigh of relief. It tasted like summer, a perfect complement to the live folk music filtering from the outside patio through the open barn doors where they sat.

"I'm off to break the seal," Emma said. "Don't drink too much without me."

And then, it was just the two of them.

Again.

"Which one was your favorite?" Audrey said.

"The blackberry," Reid said and held up her full glass of lemonade. "Yours?"

"Blueberry muffin," Audrey said and pointed to her Bomb Pop cocktail. "You know I like those weird flavors. It tastes like childhood."

Reid didn't really want to talk about moonshine. She wanted to talk about the kiss. She wanted to continue to relish how her mouth craved more of her and how kissing Audrey in the middle of all the synchronous fireflies had made her lips feel like they'd glowed along with them.

But for now, she would talk about her favorite moonshine. At least it would help her very distracted mind.

"Can I try?" Reid said.

Audrey nodded and slid over her drink. Reid sucked on the straw, the closest thing she could get to tasting Audrey at that moment. She kept her stare set on Audrey's gorgeous eyes. She had almost forgotten how dark her eyes were. A rich dark brown that appeared black at first glance, but when she really studied them, she saw the richness in the irises. If someone wasn't careful, they could easily get lost in them. Like she was at that current moment, diving straight into their depths like a deep water cave she hadn't explored yet.

"Wow, this does taste like childhood," Reid said, blinking out of her trance. She slid the cocktail back to Audrey. "That's good. Very weird. Very you."

"I bet you Sadie's favorite would have been the sour blue raspberry."

"There's always a correlation between blue drinks and the chicken tender friend," Reid said.

"I'm still surprised she allowed Emma to add a Michelin restaurant to the bucket list. She wouldn't have eaten anything."

"Emma was getting sassy with us teasing her, but we all know full well Sadie would have been the biggest shit talker. She absolutely would have made Emma stop at In-And-Out or Raising Cane's."

They shared a laugh, and as the light moment came and went like a breeze, the familiar heaviness pushed its way between them, a reminder of how much space Sadie's absence left.

"So," Audrey said, her voice dropping low. She leaned into Reid, causing her pulse to sprint. "How are you doing with, you know, last night?"

Damn, they were going to talk about this after an entire moonshine tasting with Emma returning any moment? But as much as she felt exposed, Reid wanted to know where Audrey stood. She knew that if she wanted Audrey's lips on hers and her hands on her hip bones again, having a quick check-in was probably necessary.

"How am I doing?" Reid said. Audrey pressed her lips together and nodded. Reid tilted toward her ear, allowing the moonshine to deliver her next words on a silver platter. "I've been wanting to kiss you since I woke up this morning." When she pulled away, she smiled at the blush blossoming on Audrey's cheeks, hinting to Reid that she probably wanted the same thing.

"Yeah, um, it was a pretty good kiss," Audrey said. "I'm glad it wasn't just me."

"I promise, it's definitely not just you." She paused for a moment as salacious thoughts ran wild.

"What are you thinking about? You have this look on your face that you're up to no good."

"You're correct." Reid placed her elbow on the table and rested her cheek against her hand. "When Emma comes back, we should sneak away."

Audrey laughed. "What? Reid, we can't—"

"But we can."

"I do want to kiss you again," Audrey said, barely above a whisper.

"Well, I *need* to kiss you again."

Audrey's eyes widened. "Well, fuck," she muttered under her breath.

Reid rested a hand on her knee, feeling her warm skin underneath her palm. She wanted to explore the expanse of Audrey's smooth legs until she was under her sundress.

"Reid," Audrey said in a sexy, breathless voice that just enticed her to keep her hand wandering.

"What?"

"Emma's going to catch us," Audrey said.

"I'm simply consoling you during this incredibly hard time."

"And what's the really hard time I'm going through?"

Reid leaned closer, resisting the urge to nibble on Audrey's earlobe. "Trying not to kiss me. I can see it in your eyes that you want to kiss me as badly as I want to kiss you." Reid pulled away, and tension sizzled between them. God, what the hell was happening? Was this feeling real or coming from the moonshine? Reid swallowed and felt the warmth crawl up the center of her back and around her neck.

Audrey glanced over her shoulder and pulled away. She reached for her cocktail and took a long drink, and without checking, Reid knew that Emma was heading back from the bathroom. She swiveled in her chair and retrieved her hand from Audrey's knee to nourish her arid throat with some spiked lemonade.

"Okay, better," Emma said through a sigh and sat across from them. "What did I miss?" She looked at the two of them, completely clueless with the tension still hanging in the air like humidity.

Reid tacked on a smile. "The band covered 'Jolene.' There was a wild banjo solo," she lied. "It forever changed me."

"In a good or a bad way?" Emma said. "Because you said the same thing after we went on It's a Small World at Christmas at Disneyland."

"Don't you dare compare the two," Reid said, directing a point. "I lost part of my soul on the ride."

"I think that banjo solo finally healed you," Audrey said.

"Damn it," Emma said. "I love that song."

As Emma focused on the band, her back to them, Reid whispered to Audrey. "I think the moonshine and the hot tub finally healed me." She loved how red Audrey's face turned.

After Ubering back to their cabin, they gave themselves a few hours to sleep off the moonshine before they headed to Elkmont Campground for the firefly show. They climbed the stairs to their separate rooms. Emma stopped in front of her bedroom door and said, "We leave at seven," she said and directed a flimsy point at the two of them.

Yeah, Emma couldn't handle anything that wasn't wine. Maybe she needed to sleep off her moonshine, but Reid had other plans. "Yes, Mom," Reid said.

"And don't forget to drink water."

"Okay, Mom. Good night."

Emma blew them each a kiss and closed her bedroom door behind her. Reid and Audrey hovered in their bedroom entrances.

Reid winked and propped open her door. She turned and headed to her bed, hoping that was enough to lasso Audrey to follow her. She waited only for a moment before Audrey appeared in the doorway. Without saying anything, Audrey shut the door, locked it, and slipped into the empty space next to her. Reid wasted no time crawling onto her to kiss her. At first, their tongues met gently. But then, Audrey's tongue slowly skimmed her bottom lip, and their bodies molded together. Reid felt the kiss cascading downward, filling her up with the intoxicating feeling she had been desperate to be reacquainted with all day.

They picked up right where they left off as if they'd been starved for years. Warms lips, eager tongues, and soft moans. Reid moved her legs on either side of Audrey's, pressing one into Audrey's center. A moan escaped her lips and lit Reid's entire body up in goose bumps. She rocked her hips along Audrey's leg, desperate to feel some relief of the sexual frustration building around her clit.

She held Audrey's face, deepening the kiss as Audrey ran her fingers through Reid's hair. Her desire obscured all the questions that came with kissing Audrey. Those didn't matter at the moment. What mattered was Audrey curing the desperate need taking her over.

Reid pushed herself up and slipped her hands underneath Audrey's dress, finally feeling her warm, soft skin. She noticed the goose bumps that sprouted underneath her palm and followed the path of her hand as she wandered up to her bra. She cupped Audrey's breasts, trying so hard not to come undone right then and there. She couldn't do that. Not when Audrey's damn bra was in the way of feeling her nipples. She couldn't be *that* easy.

Audrey pushed Reid's shoulder until she fell backward. Without any time wasted, Audrey straddled Reid's hips, and her hands soon followed, holding on to her hip bone like a railing. She leaned back in, removing one hand so she could hold Reid's face as she deepened the kiss. Her hips undulated against Reid's right in the perfect spot that needed more touching. Fingers. Mouths. Moans. Something needed to be done.

She grabbed Audrey's dress and pulled it up just a few inches, waiting for Audrey to respond. She did so by sucking in Reid's bottom lip and nodding. Reid lifted the dress, and Audrey pulled back, lifting her arms while her ravenous stare stayed locked on Reid's. Once Reid tossed the dress aside, she took a moment to absorb the sight of Audrey, and God, if she thought Audrey's breasts felt amazing in her hands, they looked just as perfect filling her black bra.

Audrey went back in for more, securing her leg between Reid's and applying pressure. If they continued like this, Reid knew she wouldn't be able to remain in control. Not when the moonshine and Audrey's mouth made her aware of every erogenous zone in her body. Every kiss Audrey planted on her lips, ears, and neck sparked life into her numb nerve endings. The arousal mounted, especially when Audrey started softly rocking her hips.

Reid wrenched her mouth from Audrey's and bit her neck. The unexpected mix of pain and pressure must have snapped Audrey out of her moonshine trance because she placed a hand on Reid's chest and gently pushed away.

"What are we doing?" Audrey said in a soft yet authoritative way.

Reid opened her eyes and grinned when she noticed Audrey's sexy, swollen lips. "Do we really need to figure it out right now?" she said, gliding her fingertips up Audrey's sides, feeling her shiver. She loved that Audrey's body reacted to her just from a simple touch.

"I'm straddling you in my bra and underwear."

Her hands wandered up Audrey's back. "I know. It's a marvelous sight."

"Don't you think we should talk before you take off my bra?" she said lightly.

Audrey's question pulled Reid's mind from her fog of arousal. "You're probably on to something."

"Aren't you concerned at all by how good this feels?"

Reid's stare bounced from the swell or her breasts to her eyes. "I'm not at all concerned."

"I am."

"Why?"

"Because…we're supposed to be friends. Childhood best friends. Childhood best friends don't make out and hump each other."

"Well, technically, we haven't been best friends since we were twenty-three, so it's more like we are…friendly acquaintances making out and humping right now."

Audrey laughed. "Is that what you're calling us? Maybe we should pause and sober up a bit."

"Yeah, you have a point." Reid scooted up, exhaling frustration. Though her mind agreed with Audrey's plan, her libido had strong opinions about it.

"It's just that we've been doing pretty well. I just…maybe we need to think about this more when we're sober and with a bit of time. I don't want it to get weird and make things more complicated."

Reid let out a sigh. Usually, when she was incredibly turned on, she shut off her brain and let her body lead the way. But Audrey was different. She wasn't just some random person Reid used to satisfy her needs. This was Audrey McCann, a woman she'd known for the better part of her life and not someone also using Reid for sex.

Thank God she'd packed her vibrator.

"I hear you," she said and tucked a loose strand of hair behind Audrey's ear. "You're probably right, and I don't want things to get weird again either. We absolutely should talk about this after we sleep off the moonshine. But you've also turned me on, so I might need you to leave so I can deal with it before I can nap."

Audrey got off the bed and slipped back into her dress while a wide smirk claimed her face. As she headed to the door, she stopped and faced Reid. "I know how you feel. I did that last night." She winked before shutting the door, delivering Reid her privacy.

Reid's mouth dropped. *Audrey had…she thought about…fuck.*

If she didn't relieve the throbbing stuck in her clit, she was going to drive herself mad.

She thanked her past self for throwing her vibrator in her bag as a "just in case." One never knew when a release of tension might be required. Once she pressed the toy into her clit, she closed her eyes and moaned into her pillow the sounds she wished Audrey could hear.

Chapter Fifteen

After their naps, plenty of water, and Reid's much needed time with her vibrator, Emma drove to their most important destination of the entire trip: Elkmont Campground in the Great Smoky Mountain National Park.

They followed the crowds of people trekking through the path through the woods and found a spot to set up their blankets. Reid felt calm in the midst of all the people, the trees, and upcoming firefly show because she could focus on the activity rather than Audrey sitting next to her and their recent clandestine make out session.

Once Reid fanned out her blanket and took a seat, Audrey and Emma set their blankets up on either side of her. Her body hummed with anticipation and want when Audrey sat crossed-legged next to her. They were at least a foot apart, and that foot that she'd considered too close for comfort at the start of their trip was now too far away.

Audrey pulled a long sip from her water bottle. When their eyes locked, Audrey smiled around the rim, and just that little smile caused a flutter in Reid's stomach. "How was your nap?" Audrey said with a playful smirk.

"Rejuvenating, thank you for asking."

"Well, we still have about twenty minutes until it gets dark," Emma said, snapping them out of their moment. "Should we read the letter?"

Damn it, the letter.

"Who wants to do the honors?" Emma said, holding the envelope. She looked at Reid.

Reid wasn't surprised. She had been hearing about the fireflies since she and Sadie were in middle school, long before Audrey and Emma had come into the picture. Throughout their middle school sleepovers, Sadie had told Reid stories about visiting her grandparents, how magical the fireflies were, and how she wished Southern California had them. She could hear Sadie's voice clearly in her mind: "We have almost everything here: mountains, the ocean, endless sunshine, and all the wine, but we don't have the fireflies. We're really missing out on those."

Once the night took over, those little fireflies would come out and remind Reid of the thousands of reasons why she missed Sadie so much. As if Emma had X-ray vision, she offered her a sympathetic grin. "It's okay. I'll read it."

Her heart started thudding as Emma opened the envelope and pulled the letter out. Reid's breath caught when she took in Sadie's handwriting.

Emma cleared her throat and read the letter out loud.

Hello friends,

Welcome to the most magical place on the east coast!

Is Tennessee considered the east coast? I don't know, and quite honestly, I don't have enough time for a Google search. Literally.

Now that I got my dark joke out of the way, indulge a dying woman in retelling why I sent you three on a road trip to Tennessee.

When I was a kid, my family took trips to visit my grandparents every summer. They retired to this beautiful log cabin in the heart of the Smoky Mountains with an enormous backyard. Bryan and I always had so much fun running around and going down to the end of the property where the creek met the woods. We always called it the Enchanted Forest because the woods—which are really the national park—had synchronous fireflies, and these fireflies are only in three spots in the US.

My grandma once told us that a forest full of fireflies is like a thousand tiny promises of hope in the darkness. I couldn't fathom the impact of her words until now, as I'm writing you this letter, knowing that when you actually read these words, I'll be long gone.

I've been reflecting on her words ever since my diagnosis, and honestly, I think it's memories of her that have kept me from falling apart. It's hard to completely fall apart—emotionally and physically—when I have so many specks of light. I have you three, Jeremy, the love of my life, my soul dog, Charlie, my vet clinic and ALL the animals I cared for, my parents, and my brother. All of you have been my fireflies throughout this cancer journey, and God, I'm so fucking lucky, which I know is a weird thing to say since I'm literally dying of cancer. But I am. I think it has taken death approaching to fully see the brightness you all bring to my life. I hope this journey has helped the three of you become each other's fireflies.

I wish so much that I could be there with you. I haven't seen the fireflies since I was ten, the last summer with my grandma, and I've always wanted to go back. It was the first thing I wanted to add to our bucket list because I knew witnessing them with you three would have been just as rare, magical, and special as when I was a kid. But that damn lottery kept getting in the way, and then things fractured in our group. Of course, life likes to play jokes on us, and I finally got tickets on my deathbed.

How fucked up is that?

But hey, at least I can finally say, "I won the lottery."

I'm so excited for you three to experience the Enchanted Forest. I'll be there with you in spirit. I'm haunting you in my cute, loving way. I promise. Please take it all in. Remind yourself of all the things you have in your life and the good things that surround you.

Thank you so much for continuing to check off items on our bucket list and finishing this trip. I hope you all know how much I love and adore you.

XOXO Sadie

P.S. I'm really fucking serious about this. PLEASE wear bug spray and do a tick check. My haunting won't be cute and loving if you disregard this warning.

Reid's heart plummeted to the ground. No matter how hard she tried holding back her swelling emotions, she couldn't do it. Tears streamed down her face as Emma lowered the letter.

Silence and stillness blanketed them despite the children running around and people laughing and talking to pass the time as the sun continued to set behind the trees. Sadie's presence was the loudest and strongest it had been since the last time they'd seen her.

Reid wiped the moisture from her eyes and tried finding her voice to no avail.

After what felt like an eternity, Emma blew out a heavy sigh. "Well…fuck."

Reid looked at her hands, picking blades of grass and twirling them between her fingers. Missing Sadie as much as she did cut so deeply that she might break apart. All the conversations she'd had with her about this place flooded her mind, especially the times when Sadie had talked about going back as adults, one of many tiny promises they had made to each other since they were eleven.

"She should be here," Reid said softly, still rolling a piece of grass in her fingers. "It doesn't feel right that she's not."

Emma squeezed her shoulder. "I know. I really miss her too," she said, her voice shaking.

Her eyes brimmed with tears, and Audrey swatted at both of her eyes too. There they were, the three of them, together in Sadie's favorite place in the world, forever missing their last puzzle piece.

About forty minutes later, dusk had fallen. They waited in a heavy but calm silence, not wanting to break down around hundreds of people. Once the trees morphed into silhouettes, the first few fireflies glowed through the darkness. A few people pointed straight ahead to the woods.

"Did you guys see that?" Emma said, also pointing.

The woods glowed in neon yellow, and with every breath, the spectators oohed and aahed like it was a firework show.

It had been easy to lose sight of why they'd taken the trip out here in the first place. Reid's excitement to see new sights, finally completing the trip they'd tried taking six years ago, and being absorbed by her changing relationship with Audrey had overshadowed the real purpose of the trip. As beautiful as the entire scene was, for Reid, it reminded her of what she'd lost and what they'd all missed out on: a chance to see this sight with Sadie, the very thing she had talked about since she was a kid.

Something on her face must have given her thoughts away because she felt Audrey's warm hand stroking the back of hers. She turned, and Audrey stared at her with worry.

"Hey, you all right?" Audrey whispered.

Emma was taking pictures on her phone, an amazed grin tacked on, seemingly unaware of the world Audrey and Reid had just created for themselves.

Reid looked at Audrey's fingers swirling invisible circles on her skin. She wanted to clasp her hand, something concrete to hold on to while fighting back tears and the tugging pain in her chest. She wanted all of Audrey wrapped around her, a life raft to save her from the drowning grief.

But that seemed too intimate—significantly more intimate than their steamy make outs.

Instead, she watched Audrey caress her hand while she tried to piece together her next words. The harder she tried, the more her eyes stung. The crowd fixated on the fireflies, kids smiling and laughing, reminding her that the world continued on while hers fell apart. "I'm hanging in there. Are you?"

Audrey gave a soft smile and nodded. "I'm all right. This is very heavy but also cathartic. It feels like she's here. Well, almost. I felt that way watching the sunset last night."

"That's because she's haunting us," Reid said and nudged Audrey's arm with her elbow. She figured the moment could use a little levity. "But, like, in a cute way."

Audrey smiled. "That must be it."

The sight was truly breathtaking. Reid had no idea a little bug could be so beautiful, pulsating in the woods like Earth's handmade strobe light. Reid was honored to finally witness something that Sadie loved so much. She viewed the scene through the lens of all the kids around her, finally understanding just how magical it must have been for a young Sadie.

Experiencing it with Emma and Audrey in Sadie's memory was so meaningful, especially now that she and Audrey had, at a minimum, mended their friendship. What gave Reid the most strength was that Audrey pressed herself into her side and didn't once shift away.

❖

When they got back to their cabin, Reid went straight to the fridge to treat herself to what was left of the margarita mix and tequila. She needed it. So did her body. Just enough to quell her sadness but not where she'd be hungover for their flight home in the morning. They still had to cross off flying first class on the bucket list, and there was no way anything was going to ruin her first time flying fancy.

When she turned, both Emma and Audrey stood behind her, arms outstretched, waiting for their own margarita. She quickly fixed them a glass, and when she handed Audrey hers, she noticed a small black spot right above Audrey's collarbone. She leaned forward to examine it and noticed her skin was swollen around the spot.

"Fuck," she said.

"What?" Audrey said.

"I think you have a tick on your neck."

"Are you serious?" Audrey yelled, set her glass on the kitchen island, and scampered into the half bathroom around the corner. Reid peered around the corner and watched Audrey flip on the flights, inspect herself in the mirror, and let out a shriek. "Get it off me!"

"I'll go grab tweezers," Emma said and ran upstairs.

Audrey came out of the bathroom with a look of absolute terror. "Get this thing fucking off me right now."

Reid tried holding in her laughter. "Hey, it's going to be okay. Just breathe."

"No, there's a bug literally crawling into my body right now." A shudder ran through her. "Please get it out before it lays eggs."

Reid placed both of her hands on her arms and rubbed them. "I'm going to. How about you sit on the couch."

"I'm coming, I'm coming, I'm coming," Emma said from upstairs. Her uneven footsteps pounded on the floor above them before she sprinted down the stairs.

Audrey sat on the couch, and Emma handed Reid the tweezers. She turned to Audrey, trying to figure out the best approach to get the little demon out of her skin. "Okay, I'm going to have to straddle you."

"What?" Audrey said in a panic.

She straddled Audrey and found herself as turned on as she was disgusted. It was a very confusing concoction of emotions. "This thing is on your collarbone, and sitting like this is the best and most stable angle for extraction." She dug her knees into the couch to get into the best position to pluck the tick from her skin. She studied it up close, and a disgusted shiver snaked down her spine. God, she hated bugs, and it was utterly nauseating to see a gross, multi-legged creature buried into Audrey's skin.

"Okay, do I just rip it out?" Reid said.

"I think so?" Emma said. "But slowly. You don't want to yank the body off the head."

"Ah!" Audrey bellowed in repugnance and squirmed underneath Reid. "Get it out of me!"

Reid pushed a hand into her other shoulder to stabilize her. Audrey shut up and looked at her with wide eyes. "Stop moving, or you're going to have a tick head forever inside you."

"Please get it out," Audrey said, holding still, her eyes pleading.

Reid leaned in again. The tick had picked a very good spot to bury itself in. If she recalled their moonshine make out correctly, she was almost positive that sucking on that exact spot had elicited moans from Audrey.

She steadied her fingers and clasped the tweezers around the butt of the tick. She suppressed another shiver as she slowly yet firmly pulled the little fucker out. Audrey let out another whine of disgust. Reid hopped off her lap, walked to the bathroom, and flushed the tick down the toilet. It was only a lingering sensation in her hips that made her realize Audrey had been holding on to her the entire time.

"The internet says you need to put some alcohol or soap and water over where it bit you," Emma said, reading off her phone.

Audrey let out a dramatic shudder. "I need to take a shower. I feel infested."

She scampered up the stairs, leaving Reid and Emma to unwind in the living room. As Reid settled into the couch, Emma took a seat across from her, tucking her legs into her chest and wrapping her arms around them. The vibrant smile usually on her face had dissipated.

"Hey, you okay?" Reid said.

Emma's shoulders deflated. "I'm just really sad."

"About what? Sadie?"

Emma nodded and looked at her lap. She quickly wiped her eye, and Reid's empathy swelled. Emma was the most stoic out of the group, always in control of her feelings, and always able to be everyone else's rock. Reid could count on one hand the number of times she'd seen Emma break down in the course of their fifteen-year friendship.

Emma needed her own rock in that moment. Reid left her spot on the couch and sat on the armrest of her chair. She put a hand on her back, and Emma let out a cry, immediately covering her mouth.

"Hey, it's okay. You can cry with me," Reid said softly.

The more she rubbed Emma's back, the harder Emma cried. Reid scooted off the armrest and wedged herself in the chair. She put an arm around Emma and pulled her close. She had no idea what to do. Nothing she said or did would make anything better, but she figured making Emma feel safe enough to feel her feelings was the only thing she could do.

"Do you want to talk about it?" Reid asked after a few silent moments of holding Emma in her arms.

"I wanted Sadie to be with us tonight, and I think it just hit me so hard that she wasn't. This whole trip, reading her letters, it felt like she was with us. But when we get back home, we go back to real life, and we won't have letters to look forward to or tiny things that Sadie planned. I know I'm really going to feel her absence, and I'm terrified. All of this fucking sucks. Missing her sucks, and the scariest thing about it is that there's no set timeline for when we'll stop feeling all this. It's dramatic and chaotic, and I'm tired, and it hasn't even been two months."

Reid pulled her closer and rested her cheek on the top of Emma's head. As a pang rippled through her, she tried piecing together some comforting words.

"I'm scared too," she said, continuing to rub her shoulder. "I think, for a while, it's going to be really scary. And debilitating. But at least we went on this trip, and we all have each other. Her letters aren't all over. We still have the time capsule to open with Jeremy when we get back. I know I'm an hour away, but I'll drive back home whenever you or Audrey need me. I promise you that."

Emma glanced up with watery eyes. "You will?"

"Of course I will. Doesn't matter the time. I'll be there."

"I hope that the end of this trip doesn't mean the end of us hanging out. I've really loved how much you and Audrey have been getting along."

"Me too," Reid said, taming the heat that threatened to consume her face. Luckily, Emma seemed too focused on hiding her tearstained cheeks to notice. "This trip isn't the end of us."

"You promise?"

She kissed Emma's head. "Of course I promise. I'm committed to making this friend group work, and I know Audrey is too. I know it's very hard and scary right now, but we'll be okay. We have our friend group back, and none of us will have to go through this alone."

By the time Emma calmed herself down and cleared her face from tears, Audrey came down from rinsing invisible tick families from her skin. She plopped on the couch opposite of Reid and Emma still cuddled together on the chair, and let out a deep sigh.

"I feel so much better now," she said.

"Did you use warm water and soup?" Emma said.

"I did. I scrubbed every inch of my body, like, three times. I'm tick free now."

"If that's the case, do you guys want to play the vacation game before bed?"

"What's the vacation game?" Audrey asked.

"It's when we go around and say our favorite thing about the trip."

"Sure, let's play," Reid said.

"I'll go first," Emma said. "My favorite part was staying in the cave. Oh, and watching you two become best friends again." She motioned to both of them.

For a moment, Reid's heart raced at the callout. She met Audrey's gaze. "Yeah, me too."

Audrey smiled back at her.

"Oh, and finally getting my Michelin restaurant experience, even though the two of you couldn't have cared less."

"It turned out to be fine," Reid said. "But I still prefer In-And-Out."

"Fair," Emma said and looked at Audrey. "Auds, you go next."

"Hmm, let's see. I could have done without the cave, but I loved the spa in Sedona…and making out with a really hot woman."

Reid was surprised Audrey would bring up their kiss until she remembered her dance floor make out in Albuquerque. She deflated slightly, assuming that was who Audrey meant. She couldn't help but wonder how their make out had compared.

Emma waggled her eyebrows. "That was a glorious moment," she said. "Therapist approved."

Audrey put a hand over her heart. "Thank you. It's called healing."

Emma smiled and looked at Reid. "What about you, Reid?"

Reid pursed her lips and thought about it. "I loved the cave. I miss the mummified bobcat." She exhaled languidly. "And then, I don't know, being here. Gatlinburg. Seeing the fireflies, drinking moonshine, the hot tub—"

Audrey furrowed her eyebrows. Reid bit back the smirk that wanted to claim her face. She could play this game too, especially if Audrey was trying to make her question which make out was a trip highlight.

"What?" Emma said, clearly confused. "The hot tub?"

"Audrey and I drank margaritas in the hot tub last night. It was… memorable."

Audrey quickly jumped in, "Because of the fireflies. We saw the fireflies. Last night. In the hot tub. We saw some flickering in the woods."

Reid bit back a laugh as Audrey fumbled over her words, clearly flustered about the callout.

Emma, clearly distracted by FOMO, didn't seem to pick up on the slight panic in Audrey's voice. "Oh, you did? What the hell? Why didn't you wake me up?"

"Babe, when you're tired, there's no stopping you," Reid said.

Emma grunted. "That's true. Well, damn. I bet that was awesome."

"It was a night I'll never forget," Reid said with a victorious smile directed at Audrey.

In return, Audrey clenched her jaw at her. She was cute when she was all flustered.

"So are we glad that we went on this trip?" Emma said. "Because I am."

"I really am," Reid said sincerely. She didn't break eye contact with Audrey. She wanted her to know that she really did mean it, and it had largely to do with how much the two of them had grown in just ten days.

Audrey's features softened. "I really am. It definitely helped with, well, everything. I really missed this. Us."

"What happens when we get home?" Emma said. Audrey locked her stare on Reid, almost as if searching for an answer in her eyes.

"We move forward together," Reid said, holding Audrey's gaze before she gave Emma the same reassuring look. "We still have a few things to scratch off the list, right? And the tattoo addition?"

"We can't forget about updating the tattoos," Audrey said.

"What if we open the time capsule with Jeremy right after we get Sadie's triangle filled in with purple?" Emma said.

"I love that," Reid said and tightened an arm around Emma's shoulder. "I'm down."

"Me too," Audrey said.

With an early flight the next morning, they soon headed upstairs for bed. Just like the night before, Reid lay wide awake, replaying her previous twenty-four hours. Her lips hadn't stopped tingling since her post-moonshine make out with Audrey, her chest hadn't loosened since she'd seen the fireflies, and her stomach hadn't stopped churning at the thought of going back to normal life again.

Just as she pulled out her phone to mindlessly scroll through apps, a text from Audrey popped up on her screen. It wasn't attached to their road trip group chat. It was a message only for her. It was a brand-new thread, like opening up a blank page of a book, the slate wiped clean from their past issues. They were officially starting over. No road trip or forced proximity had tied them together against their will. She smiled.

Come to my room? I'm in my feels and don't want to be alone.

She didn't hesitate for a second. She tiptoed down the hall and slowly opened the door to find Audrey tucked into bed, the glow of her phone highlighting her face. Without saying anything, she scooted over to make room and flipped over on her side, her back facing Reid. Reid slung an arm over her and held her.

She was grateful she didn't have to end this trip alone.

Chapter Sixteen

Is it weird that to say I sort of miss you?

Audrey's stomach fluttered when Reid's text appeared on her phone. A week had passed since they'd flown first class back home, scratching off more of the bucket list while drinking free champagne and reading another Sadie letter. Audrey had used that time the decompress, spend time with her dad, and catch up with teacher friends.

Even though it had only been a week, it felt like ages since she had seen Reid. *Not at all because I feel the same*, she texted back.

Would you be interested in hanging out sometime? Not with Emma? Love her but I kind of just want to hang out with you.

Anticipation flickered all over Audrey's body. She had no idea what the hell was happening between them, but she didn't want it to stop. Between grieving Sadie and her breakup, whatever was transpiring between her and Reid was the elixir she needed in that moment.

Audrey: *I'd love that.*

Reid: *I can either come back to Temecula, or you can come here... and I'm just a few blocks from the ocean. Just saying.*

Audrey: *I can come to you since I have all the free time in the world right now. Plus, the ocean sounds nice. I've missed it.*

Reid: *How about you come over on Saturday? I'm not working.*

Audrey: *It's a date.*

She nervously waited for a response, unsure how Reid would respond to her word choice. When Reid responded with a heart reaction, her chest inflated.

Maybe it *was* a date?

❖

Audrey hadn't seen the ocean in a long time. When she'd first moved to California, she'd assumed living in SoCal meant she would spend every waking moment on the beach. Even though the closest beach was only a forty-five minute drive away, it had been at least a year since she'd made it to the coast.

Her heart lurched when she pulled into the driveway of Reid's apartment building and saw her waiting outside, back resting against the building while looking at her phone. Her tousled hair was in a wild part, and she wore an emerald green, floral print button-down that matched her high-waisted boy shorts. Her shirt was open, revealing her green and white striped sports bra and her stomach.

Even with the AC blasting from her car vents, Audrey felt like chocolate left behind in the car on a summer day. Goddamn, was Reid attractive. Had she really always looked like that? Maybe Audrey had just been blind the entire time.

Reid noticed her and pushed off the building with a smile. She grabbed a beach tote that sat next to her on the ground and walked over. "Hey."

Audrey's heart twitched just from that simple word. "Hey," she said, forcing the greeting through her arid throat. She involuntarily scanned Reid yet again, stopping on her stomach for a lingering moment before meeting her gaze. "You look…really good."

"Do I?" But how she asked it indicated that she knew full well how hot she looked, and the subtle confidence drew Audrey even more into her. She nodded, and Reid playfully flipped her hair back. "Oh, thanks. You look great too."

"Do I?" Audrey said, wishing that her tone was as confident. She wasn't wearing anything eye-grabbing like Reid. Just jean shorts and a tank top that didn't show off any sexy parts of her body like her cleavage or stomach.

"You do," Reid said. "You usually do. Want to head to the beach?"

Audrey savored the compliment for the entire three-block walk to Pier View North Beach, where crowds of people scattered along the sand. To their left, the Oceanside Pier stretched into the water with

Mexican fan palms towering above them. People played volleyball at the courts in the shallow tides and relaxed on towels and blankets.

The beach was quieter than Audrey expected, so it was easy to find a spot in the sand just a few yards away from Lifeguard Hut 4. She set her tote down and pulled out a blanket, fanned it, and claimed the empty spot.

"Oh, I brought an extra sweatshirt in case you got cold," Reid said, pulling out a navy hoodie that said *Oceanside Scuba Adventures* in white with the company's logo: a sea turtle wearing a diving mask.

Audrey grinned at the surprisingly cute logo. "Oh, thank you," she said and slipped into it, knowing she was going to get cold. "I like the logo."

Reid smiled when her head poked out. "It looks good on you."

It smelled like Reid. Her natural smell mixed with the familiar woodsy perfume Audrey had caught whiffs of on their road trip. She felt her body relax in the fabric.

When the two of them sat, Audrey took in the sight. She fully understood why Reid had moved out here. For someone who loved the water and the beach, Oceanside had so much more to offer than Temecula.

"This is an amazing view," Audrey said. "I can't believe you live just three blocks from the ocean."

Reid faced her as the ocean breeze whipped her hair back. "I know, right? I kind of can't believe it, either. I got lucky. My boss owns my apartment, and I guess he likes me enough to rent it to me for a little discounted price. He calls me his second daughter."

"This is all just very…Reid."

She laughed. "What does that mean? Like 'Reid time'?"

Audrey heard the teasing and shot her a side-eye. "No, like, this is your element. Being near the water, having things to do and see, being free."

"I just feel like myself out here."

"I can absolutely see that."

Reid raised an eyebrow. "You do?"

"Mm-hm. You seem way more at ease. I know we just sat down, but it's pretty noticeable."

"I'm that easy to read? Damn, I'm failing at the mysterious vibe I was going for."

"Being easy to read isn't a bad thing. I personally like it. It puts me at ease. I don't have to question anything."

"Well, I'm glad I finally found a way to put you at ease," she said lightly and squeezed Audrey's knee.

The momentary contact left Audrey hyperaware of every nerve on her knee flickering with warmth. She wanted Reid's hand to stay there, touching her bare skin, maybe sliding up her thigh. It was probably for the best that Reid took her hand back on a public beach. The last thing Audrey needed was to be turned on surrounded by families just wanting to enjoy the view of the beach, not her losing control.

They spent the next few moments sitting in a comfortable silence. The sun had started dipping, washing the evening sky in bold reds, oranges, and yellows. The briny wind swept through their hair, and Audrey could feel the salty air sticking to her skin.

"Can I ask you a personal question?"

Audrey snapped out of her trance. "Of course."

"What do you think happens after we die?"

The question took her by surprise. Reid had metaphorically grabbed her hand and plunged them right into the murky depths of conversation topics. "Wow, that is an incredibly deep question."

The corner of Reid's mouth rose. "Don't you love these kinds of questions?"

"I do. I just…I wasn't expecting it." There was always something about the darkness taking over the sky that unlocked those deeper topics, as if finally granting them permission to explore the depths. But there was absolutely zero chance that Audrey would pull Reid back to the surface.

"Then, what do you think?" Reid continued. "You think there is some way we're connected to Sadie? Like that purple sunset we watched in Tennessee? Or is she completely wiped from the Earth?"

Even with pieces stolen by whatever universal force, Audrey still found memories scattered everywhere, pieces of her mom and Sadie in every song, every dream, and every place. Her mom and Sadie were stuck between a place she couldn't go and a place that didn't allow visitors.

"I want to believe there's something more," Audrey said. "Energy can't be erased, right? So based on that, shouldn't someone leave some of their energy behind? I don't know what that looks like, though."

Reid paused for a moment and ran her fingers through her hair. "Do you ever feel like your mom is with you?"

Audrey thought about the loss she'd felt after her mom died. Her heart had to learn to beat without her and never fully felt whole again. Even when Audrey tried to fill the emptiness with distractions, those memories found a way to bleed through like ink.

She wanted to believe so badly that Mom and Sadie were somehow still connected to her, but she was far too disconnected between what she wished and what was scientifically possible. She didn't want science to get in the way. She wanted to be able to tell Reid—and fully believe herself—that Mom and Sadie weren't "wiped from Earth."

"My mom and I used to stargaze in our backyard during the summer, and we would count how many shooting stars we saw. I think the most I saw in one night was eight. When she died, I tried stargazing, but the sky felt so empty. It was like I could see them but couldn't feel them. My first night in California, when I was trying to sleep, I looked out my window and saw a bright star right in my view. I didn't have to move or go outside. It was right there. It made me wonder if it was some sign from her. It probably wasn't. Just a coincidence, right?"

"Does that mean the purple sunset was a coincidence?"

"I really hope not. Anytime the stars are extra bright, I think of my mom. Sometimes, I like to think that's her in the sky. It's silly, I know—"

Reid grabbed her wrist and squeezed it reassuringly. "It's not silly at all."

"It is a little bit."

She shook her head. "I don't think so because I want to believe Sadie gave us that purple sunset. Does that make me silly?"

Audrey held her stare firmly on Reid as she shook her head. "No, not at all."

Audrey faced the ocean and observed the sky falling into darkness. A few more stars poked through the occasional streak of clouds. Even though their conversation faded, Reid still held her wrist. Her thumb rubbed invisible lines back and forth. The delicate touch made Audrey's heart sore out of her chest. She felt safe, seen, and heard with Reid, a feeling she would have never guessed Reid would ever make her feel again.

"You would have loved my mom," she said, feeling a trace of a smile.

Reid looked over. "What was she like?"

"She was amazing, very nurturing. Anytime I was sick, she would go buy my favorite juice boxes, candy, and a coloring book, and always rubbed my hair when I watched a movie. When I had friends over, she would come back from the store with all the best party food."

"That's one of the most important qualities in a mom."

"It really is. All my friends loved her, and she loved them. She was just so warm and friendly. And hilarious too. I loved her sense of humor and her sarcasm. It's wild to me she's been gone for fifteen years," she said softly, feeling her smile loosen. "It's wild that you guys never met her, that she was never part of my Temecula life. When I first moved here, every sleepover we had just made me think of her. The Lins always reminded me of her, how they were the kindest hosts and made the best food. How warm and inviting they are. I can't believe they never met her, either."

"Sounds like she was a very amazing woman." Reid grazed her fingertips down to Audrey's hand and clasped it. The assuring touch tugged on Audrey's chest as a few tears formed.

"She was," Audrey said through the growing lump in her throat.

"I really wish I could have met her."

She swiped a loose tear dangling in her eyelid. "Sometimes, I think about it, and I can't believe I lost her, and not only that, but I had to go through the pain of losing my mom when I was fourteen. That's an incredibly young age to lose someone so close."

She'd lost the very person who'd breathed her into existence only to watch her mother's existence leave her dark brown eyes, the same ones she'd inherited. It was hard for her to shake that moment from her mind. She wanted to remember her mom as she'd lived, not as she'd died. She tried to do the same when she thought about Sadie, healthy and full of life.

Reid shook her head. "I can't even imagine. This is my first major loss, and I'm an adult who sometimes feels like it's impossible to function."

"Because sometimes, it is impossible to function." A silence fell. Reid's stare was focused on the sand. "I'm sorry. I didn't mean—"

Reid looked up. "No, don't apologize. I want to know what I'm in for. Plus, it makes me feel, I don't know, less alone. It's hard to remember that what I'm feeling is considered 'normal' because it hurts so much, but knowing you and Emma are also going through it helps. I guess Sadie and Emma were on to something with this road trip. I didn't really feel alone until we came back, and I was literally alone in my apartment, going about my normal routine and wanting to text Sadie all about my day. At least on the trip, our minds were distracted."

"I'm glad you told me to come over then," Audrey said softly.

Reid put her arm around her. "Me too."

Reid didn't move her arm until the last warm hue faded into midnight blue. They packed up the blanket, and as they started trekking back, she already felt the absence of Reid's arm around her shoulders. She spent the ten minute walk coaxing herself to get the courage to make some kind of move.

But tonight was the first time that not a single drop of alcohol had encouraged them. Her clear brain had much more room to weigh the pros and cons of whatever the hell was happening. Her body craved being pressed up against Red; her lips and clit begged for Reid's mouth to take her in, but her damn brain kept questioning if all of this was a good idea.

"This is home," Reid said as they walked through her front door.

She gave Audrey the tour, showing off the floor to ceiling windows that no doubt filled the space with sunlight during the day. She had a large kitchen and an open staircase leading to a second floor. Above her couch was a gallery wall of sapphic art. Her apartment was gorgeous. She had been absolutely right. She'd really lucked out with this place.

"This place is amazing," Audrey said.

"Isn't it? Want to see the upstairs?"

Audrey's heart quickened as she nodded.

The upstairs was a loft with a queen-size platform bed, nicely made. For some reason, Reid having her bed made without a single crease in the comforter came as a little surprise. Audrey had figured that someone like Reid would have a more "lived-in" place, but that wasn't the case at all. Everything was clean and orderly but not in a way that made Audrey feel like she was in a museum.

She looked over the railing, admiring the view of the open apartment and the last bit of blue coloring the sky. "This is a great view to wake up to," she said.

Reid stood next to her, resting her arms on the railing. "Oh, it is. You have the palm trees and just the smallest sliver of ocean right there. I'm in love with this place."

"I can see why."

Reid retrieved her arms from the railing and tucked a tendril of hair behind Audrey's ear. The soft graze against her cheek caused her entire body to vibrate. She slowly leaned in to plant a soft, tender kiss on Audrey's lips. Even a sweet kiss like that had Audrey surrendering, her knees wobbling.

When Reid pulled away, she said, "I've been wanting to do that all night."

"Why haven't you?"

"I don't know. I got caught up in our conversation. I like talking to you."

"Even about deep things?"

Reid shrugged one shoulder. "Talking to you is easy." Her features softened, and vulnerability darkened her eyes. She was so incredibly sexy when she stood there, completely raw. The old Reid would have only shown a glimpse of this vulnerability before running back behind her walls. But now, Reid standing in front of her, flitting her stare between Audrey's eyes and lips, didn't seem at all bothered by showing that side of her, the real Reid underneath her hard exterior.

It was the sexiest Audrey had ever seen her.

"It hasn't always been like that," Audrey said, the nerves and anticipation collecting in her throat. "Talking to you in the past was quite the feat. Our own personal Everest."

Reid laughed. "I'm not a robot. I feel quite a lot, actually. I just don't let many people see that side of me. Except Cameron. He's, like, the only person who hasn't hurt me. I've never regretted opening up to him."

"I'm really sorry I hurt you, Reid. I wish we didn't have six years taken from both of us. And from Emma and Sadie too."

"I know," she said, caressing Audrey's cheek. "I regret it too."

"I hope you know that I'm here if you ever need someone to talk to. I know I haven't always been a safe person for you, but I'm also not that version of me anymore."

"I appreciate that. I really do. But I don't want to talk right now."

"What would you like to do?" Audrey said, her heart fluttering with anticipation.

"I want to kiss you. Soberly. For real this time." She moved her thumb to Audrey's mouth and glided her fingertips along her bottom lip as if trying to map out every curve.

Audrey parted her lips, granting Reid permission to take her.

Reid slid her hand around the back of her head and pulled her in for a kiss. It was hungry, demanding, and scorching, so much so that it melted any last strength left in Audrey's knees. To save herself from potential injury, she placed her hands on Reid's hips and guided her to the foot of the bed. But before they fell, Reid grabbed Audrey by the waist, twisted them around, and pushed Audrey onto her bed, crawling on top of her.

The look in Reid's eyes sent enough heat searing into her to set her on fire. Reid fastened her thigh between Audrey's legs and pressed into her as she leaned down to part her mouth with her tongue. The kiss ignited a fire deep inside her. She clasped Reid's face, their tongues meeting in heated passion.

They kissed like they had been in withdrawal during their time apart. It was confusing how amazing, how good, and how right it all felt. There was something about Reid that felt wild and untamed. Audrey had craved this feeling of anticipation, knowing that a secret moment with Reid could spark at any time. With every tongue swipe and nibble to her bottom lip, Reid revitalized her. Her touch lit up every nerve ending like a lighter to a cigarette.

Reid pulled away. "I want you to feel what you do to me," she insisted hoarsely.

Audrey's stomach curled in desperate arousal. "Yes, please," she said as she pressed her forehead against Reid's.

Reid's gaze remained firm on Audrey's as she undid the button of her own shorts. The moisture in Audrey's mouth evaporated. Gently, Reid slid Audrey's hand into her underwear. Her breath hitched when her fingers finally slid between Reid's wet folds. She closed her eyes and savored the feeling of just how much she turned Reid on. It was another struck match that ignited more ravenous need in her.

"Fuck, Reid," she said, goose bumps breaking across her skin. She curled her fingers just enough to collect more wetness. Reid let out a gasp. As Audrey slowly retrieved her fingers, Reid opened her eyes right as Audrey put her fingers in her mouth. She sucked on them and relished the sweet and intoxicating taste of Reid. She fastened her stare on Reid's sexy, desperate dilated eyes that offered a window inside that walled-up mind of hers. Nothing about her was walled. Reid's gaze dripped with vulnerability and rawness, completely at Audrey's mercy.

God, she needed more of her. Right now. "Reid," she said, and even she could hear her own desperation.

"Hm?"

She loved the fact that that was all Reid could manage to say.

"I want to feel full of you."

Reid's eyebrows rose. "Fuck, Audrey." There was a ruggedness woven around her name, and God, was it sexy. Audrey's legs parted at the sound of it, welcoming Reid to take all of her.

Reid grabbed the hem of Audrey's shirt and looked at her as if asking permission. Audrey pushed herself forward to help Reid slide her tank top off. She unclasped her bra and tossed it to the side, and Audrey did the same.

There Reid was, standing there topless in front of her, and now it was Audrey's turn to lose all ability to form words, only a whimper of desperate need. She was completely spellbound, absorbing the sight of the expanse of Reid's sun kissed skin. The air rushed out of her lungs at the sight of Reid's perfect breasts and how her nipples were already firm, begging for Audrey to pull them in between her teeth.

When she looked back at Reid, she noticed her gaze still locked on her body as if trying to memorize every inch of her naked torso.

"Fuck," Reid muttered, her voice soft yet thick, as if it was an accidental spoken thought. Her fingers trailed invisible lines from

Audrey's collarbone, down the swell of her breasts, and circled around her nipples. Audrey closed her eyes, attempting to seal the tingles that broke out over her skin, her nipples tightening with want.

Reid grazed her fingers down Audrey's stomach to her shorts and slowly unbuttoned them. She lifted her hips so Reid could pull her shorts and underwear off, and once she was finally freed, Reid took in every inch of her naked body. Her mouth slightly parted as if in awe of the sight beneath her.

Reid lowered herself in between Audrey's legs and wrapped her hands around her thighs. She paused and looked up at her, and the gleam in her eye and her faint smirk told Audrey that Reid was waiting for her to beg for it. Reid clearly knew what she was doing. No one affected Audrey like this, having her twitching and dripping when they'd barely explored each other's depths.

"Reid, please," Audrey said, the desperation grating against her throat.

That was the magical word because Reid wasted no time wrapping her mouth around Audrey's throbbing clit. As Reid's warm tongue flicked across her length, Audrey cried out. Reid explored every inch of her, and when she plunged her tongue inside Audrey's wetness, she moaned loudly. Reid gripped her thighs as if using them as a railing while tasting and savoring Audrey like a new wine.

She slipped her fingers inside Audrey with ease. The pressure inside her climbed as Reid slid two fingers into her, filling her completely. Audrey gasped and clenched the comforter while her other hand searched for Reid's, who grabbed ahold of her fingers and gave an assuring squeeze.

"Fuck, Reid," Audrey said through ragged breaths. "You feel so fucking good inside me."

Reid's moan turned the quiet hum of pleasure deep inside Audrey into deep throb.

"You taste and sound better than I imagined when I got myself off in the cabin," Reid said, her words humming against Audrey's clit.

Imagining Reid fucking herself to the thought of Audrey pushed her over the edge. She cried out as the orgasm rippled through every inch of her body. Her limbs felt molten, her nipples hard and heavy, and her clit pulsating. Reid squeezed her clasped hand throughout the entirety, as if the pressure from her interlocked hands helped coax the orgasm out of her. Audrey tossed her free hand over her eyes while trying to piece together her fragmented breaths. Reid tasted her one more time, sending an aftershock through Audrey, before punctuating soft pecks on both thighs.

"You're so fucking sexy," Reid said, her confidence wrapping around her name this time. "I could do that all night."

Audrey sat up and reached her hand between them until she felt Reid's wetness, and fuck, she was dripping.

Reid pressed her forehead against Audrey's and groaned. "You turn me on so much."

"I know," Audrey said, parting Reid's folds and slipping her fingertips inside her. Feeling her depths sent a curl of pleasure low inside her. "And, fuck, you feel as good as you taste."

Reid exhaled a quiet purr of contentment.

"Lie on your back," Audrey demanded.

Reid's eyes flashed as she did what she was told. Audrey moved her fingers deep inside her. Her back arched, begging for more.

"God, you're so wet," Audrey said, her voice low and ragged.

"You…affect…me," Reid said in between each moan.

Audrey pulled Reid's swollen clit into her mouth and lightly sucked on it while her fingers continued to move in and out. Reid's hips rocked as she fully unraveled. Her lips parted as soft moans escaped, the movement of her breasts mirroring each thrust Audrey made inside her. Her breath quickened, urging Audrey to keep doing exactly what she was with her mouth and fingers. She loved how Reid combed her fingers through Audrey's hair, collected a fistful, and gently tugged, securing Audrey in place as if worried she would stray.

"Fuck, Audrey, I'm so close."

Reid tasted and sounded like Audrey had imagined when she'd fucked herself right after their hot tub make out. She nibbled, sucked, and put her tongue to work until Reid's hips desperately rocked against her.

"I'm coming," she cried out as her walls started to clench around Audrey's fingers.

Audrey groaned into her wetness and savored her. She could feel Reid tightening around her fingers as each whimper grew stronger and louder.

Reid's orgasm was slow and long, gradually building until she arched her hips, grabbed and bit into a pillow, and moaned loudly. After her body shuddered with residual pleasure, she collapsed and breathed out a fragmented exhale.

Audrey kissed her way up to Reid's hip bones, sucked and twirled her tongue against her favorite spot. A few inches above from Reid's hip bones was the little pink scar from the fire coral, and Audrey planted a tender kiss on it. A hum of pleasure seeped out of Reid, her eyes still closed, but one side of her mouth turned into a smile as if she was very content from the passionate fucking.

Audrey hovered over Reid's breasts and stared at her nipples, hardened into tall peaks. She couldn't help herself. She sucked one into her mouth. Reid grunted and gripped the back of her hair, holding her right there until Audrey's kiss punctuated it like an end of a sentence. She moved to the other nipple and twirled her tongue around it enough to feel it rise in her mouth.

"That was even sexier than I imagined," Audrey said, a whisper away from Reid earlobes. "And I imagined it several times."

Reid opened her eyes. "*Several* times?"

Audrey nodded and combed her fingers through Reid's waves, mirroring one of Reid's nervous habits that she was quickly growing to enjoy. "Oh yes. Several times. Not just at the cabin."

"This is news to me."

"You're not the only one who keeps some things for herself."

Reid wrapped her legs around Audrey's waist and flipped her on her back. The move was completely unexpected…and fucking sexy. She lay on her back, gladly at Reid's mercy. "You should tell me more about it. After I make you come again."

CHAPTER SEVENTEEN

Reid didn't consider herself a fantastic cook by any means. Her busy schedule and the fact that she spent most of her day out on a boat meant the simpler, the better, like her beloved pizza Lunchables. She did pride herself on her sandwich-making skills, the perfect on-the-go meal. Mr. and Mrs. Lin might have been wine sommeliers, but she was definitely a sandwich sommelier.

Except her skills didn't quite cut it when she had a beautiful naked woman sleeping in her bed and not just any woman, Audrey McCann. Reid's body was still tingling from the night before, and she wanted to properly woo Audrey and thank her for all the orgasms with an impressive breakfast. Well, she wanted to try, at the very least.

She snuck out of the apartment and walked to the grocery store to pick up all the necessary ingredients. Even with her limited cooking skills, she was going to give Audrey her very best.

She whipped up a stack of chocolate chip pancakes, hash browns, scrambled eggs, a plate of crispy bacon, and two steaming cups of coffee. She wished that she had a tray that she could use to deliver the breakfast but settled for her wooden cutting board. As she carefully walked up the stairs to her bedroom, she found Audrey in bed, half wrapped in her duvet with her hair spread across the pillow. The sound of Reid approaching seemed to cause her to slowly drift awake, and as she blinked at what Reid had in her hands, she sat up.

"Did you make breakfast?" she said, rubbing her eyes.

"Can you not smell the immaculate scents wafting from my kitchen right now?" She positioned the cutting board on Audrey's lap.

"*This* looks immaculate. Wow. I had no idea you could cook."

"I'm a woman of many talents," she said as she left to retrieve her own breakfast and join Audrey in bed.

When she came back with another cutting board holding her plate, she positioned herself back in bed.

Audrey leaned and kissed her on the cheek. "Thank you. This is really kind of you."

"And it was really kind of you to do all those things to me last night," she said and planted kisses along the column of Audrey's neck.

Audrey laughed through a soft whimper. "I was trying to be sweet, Reid."

"I was too."

Audrey looked at her skeptically. "Do you do this for all the girls who sleep over?"

"I couldn't tell you the last time I had a woman spend the night, so, no." She ate her first bite of pancakes, and she was pretty impressed with how they turned out. After she'd burned the first two, the rest of the stack had turned out perfectly. "I'm pretty selective on who I make breakfast for. You should feel honored."

Audrey put a hand over her heart. "I'm so incredibly honored." She bit into a slice of crispy bacon. After taking a moment to eat, she asked, "What are we going to tell Emma?"

Reid lowered her fork. She hadn't even thought about Emma. She had been so focused on breakfast—and the fact that Audrey was naked under the duvet—that nothing else had crossed her mind. "Do we have to tell her?"

"No, but she's going to figure it out eventually."

"Well, we can cross that bridge when we get there. I want to enjoy this just between us a little more," she said, before planting a kiss on Audrey's temple.

"How do you think she will react?"

Reid thought for a moment. "She'll probably collapse from shock."

"How do you think Sadie would have reacted?"

"She would have probably shipped us so hard, it would have gotten mildly annoying but in an adorable, Sadie way. I imagine every time we all hung out, she would ask a bunch of questions and need to be constantly updated."

Audrey laughed. "That sounds about right."

Once they finished breakfast, Reid was quick to discard the empty plates in the kitchen before running back to bed. Flashes of Audrey's hands and mouth all over her ignited a new wave of need. She needed to satisfy her craving for Audrey a few more times before she left.

They got lost in the sheets and the other's limbs as they sunk into another round. Reid touched and kissed every inch of Audrey and reveled in the intoxicating sounds of her soft moans. She felt starved for Audrey's taste; clearly, breakfast hadn't fully satisfied her hunger. When Audrey's tongue applied pressure where Reid needed it the most, she wished she didn't share a wall with neighbors and could scream out the pleasure reverberating through her instead of burying her face in a pillow. They would definitely need to do this in a secluded cabin at some point.

As they got to know each other again, Reid discovered a nascent glow—a radiance she doubted Audrey herself knew—that had started to form inside her. Even amidst her own grief and heartbreak, Audrey's positivity and warmth shone through the darkness. It was a rare quality Reid wanted to capture in a bottle and hold on to forever.

As she watched Audrey slip into her jean shorts, Reid let out a huff of fake frustration. *How dare she put her clothes back on after I so thoughtfully freed her from them last night?* She reached a hand out to the empty space in her bed that was still warm from Audrey's body. "Do you have to leave?"

Audrey smiled. "I'm going on a winery trolley tour with some of my teacher friends."

"Is Magnolia Springs on the route?"

"It's not."

Reid feigned shock. "Are you cheating on Magnolia Springs?"

Audrey hooked her bra in place, ruining the most stunning view of her perfect breasts. Reid wanted to pull her back into bed, throw off the bra, and suck on them. "Am I?"

"How are you going to break the news to Emma?"

"I'll buy her a bottle of Lambrusco. I'm sure that will fix everything."

Reid ran through her mental calendar for the week, trying to figure out when she could see Audrey again. She really wanted to take her on a proper date. Reid might not have had a great track record with choosing the best women, but she was very confident in her ability to put together a fantastic date. She wasn't quite sure where this skill came from since she could only recall her parents ever going on one date.

Once in middle school, they'd asked the Russos if they wouldn't mind watching her and Cameron for the evening. She, Sadie, and Cameron had sat in Sadie's bedroom talking about how odd it was:

"Your parents don't go on dates?" Sadie had asked. She and Cameron had exchanged a glance as if they were just finding out that was abnormal.

"No," Reid had said. "Do yours?"

Sadie had nodded casually. "Yeah, like once a month, and I'm stuck with Bryan." She'd made a disgusted grunt.

Little did thirteen-year-old Reid know that she and Cameron would grow up to be hopeless romantics. Cameron wore his heart on his sleeve, and God, he was going to make the best husband. Reid, on the other hand, wanted love and romance but was afraid of getting her heart crushed again. She wasn't as proactive about dating and finding love as her brother, but that didn't mean she didn't know how to be romantic.

And she really wanted to treat Audrey the way she deserved. It had become clear during their road trip that Audrey's ex-girlfriend had fallen short of doing that once their honeymoon stage was over, and things had started getting real. Audrey deserved to see not every woman out there was like Becca.

And maybe Reid needed a reminder that not every kiss, date, or fluttering in her stomach led to heartbreak.

She fought her rising panic, knowing that taking the step of asking Audrey out on a date would throw them onto a tightrope. One wrong move could permanently fracture the fragile friendship they'd only recently pieced back together.

The insufferable week in between the flight home and now showed Reid it didn't take long for her to miss Audrey. Her heart wanted to leap out and hop into Audrey's purse. She didn't have time to think about all the pros and cons of dating. She just wanted that date. She wanted more time.

She sat up and moved to the end of the bed. "I have a question."

"What's that?" Audrey said, slipping her feet into her tennis shoes. Once she had them secured, she walked over to Reid and positioned herself between her legs.

Just being near her had Reid's body begging for another release. She placed her hands on Audrey's hips and pulled her closer. She loved how Audrey's stare raked over her mouth before looking her in the eyes. It sent a zing down to her clit, as if she hadn't already been thoroughly satisfied over the last twelve hours.

She attempted to clear the dryness in her throat to no avail. "Would you maybe want to get dinner sometime?"

Audrey straightened as her eyebrows rose in a silent question. "Are you asking me out?"

"Yes, yes, I am."

"On a date?"

"Why do you sound so surprised?" Reid said playfully. "I was literally just inside you."

She thought it was cute how the pink quickly filled Audrey's cheeks. "I just…I wasn't expecting it. But I'd love to go on a date."

"Since I'll be in town on Friday for the tattoo appointment and the time capsule, can I take you out on Saturday?"

"Only if you spend the night with me on Friday," Audrey said.

Reid raised a curious brow. "What about Emma? Don't you think she would notice us leaving together?"

"I don't think so. She'll be too focused on the tattoo and opening the time capsule."

"You're right," Reid said. "Pencil me in for Friday night…and Saturday."

❖

Audrey really needed this summer vacation. As much as she loved her job, the two and a half months off were well deserved. Teachers also assumed the role of babysitter, parent, role model, and depending on what state you lived in, school security. It was overwhelming wearing all those different hats on top of losing her best friend.

Before the trip, she'd worried that dealing with Reid would be too much, and she'd expected to lose her mind and patience somewhere in Middle America. She didn't expect the road trip to be the easy part. Adjusting to her new life without Sadie and without a girlfriend was the biggest hurdle, one she wasn't sure if she knew how to get over.

She tried to busy herself. She made plans with her teacher friends, took long walks, and purged her closet of clothes she'd forgotten she even owned. A few days after her night with Reid, she went to her old home to help her dad repaint the kitchen.

When they'd moved to Temecula, Audrey had been very underwhelmed with the house her dad had bought. She couldn't understand why they would leave their beautiful two-story Colonial home in Shaker Heights, Ohio for a ranch home that had barely been updated since the 1980s. However, that was exactly what her father had wanted: the distraction of completely renovating the home. He'd dedicated so much time, effort, and money into creating a peaceful and beautiful space for them, and it felt as much like a home could be without her mother's warm smile and radiant energy filling the rooms. She knew her mom would have loved it just as much as their home in Shaker.

They spent the day drinking beers, blasting her dad's favorite music from the seventies, and painting over the warm caramel color he'd painted their first summer in California with a bright white paint. After the second coat, they sat at the kitchen table and admired their work.

"It's very…white in here," Audrey said, taking in the walls, white granite marble countertops, and white cabinets. She needed to remember to pack sunglasses next time she came over.

"It's going to look much better when I paint the cabinets navy," he said and took a swig of Corona. "Just wait. That's next week's project."

"You know, for being recently retired, you sure are busying yourself."

"For being on summer vacation, you're doing the same thing," he said with a smirk.

"Fair point. It's better to busy myself than to feel all my feels. If you need a painting buddy next week, I'm your gal."

"I might hold you to that. I'm just ready to get this kitchen updated. It's feels too much like 2010. Also, it's okay to feel your feels. You've been through a lot the past few months."

"I'm really feeling it now that we're back. The downside to having summers off is that Emma and Reid work during the week, so I have to find ways to entertain myself during the day."

"I just have to say, I think it's great you and Reid reconnected on the trip."

She'd filled him in on the entire road trip while they'd painted the kitchen. She'd left out the spicier details of their "reconnection." It took a long chug of Corona to hide the heat seeping through her cheeks.

"Yeah, it was a nice surprise," Audrey said. "She was really helpful with the entire Becca situation."

"I'm glad, hon. That has to mean something, don't you think?"

"Yeah. Even though she's been through something similar, I never imagined that Reid would be someone who would help me through it all."

"You know, I was cheated on once," he said casually.

Audrey perked up. This was a brand-new story. "What? Really? I had no idea."

"Yup, in college. That one hurt."

"How come this is the first I'm hearing about this?"

"It's old news. Plus, if she hadn't cheated on me, I would never have met your mother."

"All I knew was you and Mom met at your cousin's wedding."

"Well, I can tell you that going to that wedding was the last thing I wanted to do. I didn't want to be surrounded by love when I had just gotten my heart broken, but I was a groomsman. I remember standing up during the ceremony and seeing your mom in the crowd, and the rest is history." He rested a nurturing hand on her shoulder. "I know it can feel like you'll never recover from being betrayed by a person you loved. But the right person will always try to show up for you and work to build real trust and commitment. I have no doubt you will find that person."

"Thanks Dad," Audrey said, giving him a side hug.

"Anyway, I hope it continues, you and Reid being friendly. I'm sure it's nice to have her and Emma around right now."

"I'm seeing them tomorrow. We're filling in Sadie's triangle on our matching tattoos with purple and meeting Jeremy to go through the time capsule we made the summer after high school graduation."

"That sounds like a nice tribute," he said, "and I am sure that time capsule is going to bring up plenty of wonderful memories."

Spending a day with her dad was just as fun as spending it with her friends. Time flowed so easily with him; they always got so lost in their conversations that she barely checked her phone. It wasn't until later that evening that she finally got to reading her unread texts.

Right above a text from Reid was an unread message from Becca. She blinked a couple of times, trying to snap herself out of the panic that swept through her. She couldn't believe she had a text from Becca. Just as she was still trying to stabilize herself in her new life without Sadie, Becca came plowing back in with another plot twist.

Hey. Are you back from your trip? If so, I was wondering if you would like to meet up for coffee or a drink tomorrow? I understand if you don't want to, but if there's a chance you're interested, it would be nice to clear the air and apologize. Just let me know.

Seeing a text from Becca felt like running full force into a cement wall. Of course, she'd fantasized about the opportunity to confront Becca and get some closure, but she never expected it to actually happen. The confusion and shock over the suddenness of the breakup rushed through her all over again. She knew that in order to completely move on and open her heart fully to Reid, she needed closure, ideally as soon as possible.

She hoped Reid would understand if she canceled one of their nights together so she could get the answers she needed. She just had no idea how to tell her.

After typing, deleting, and typing again, she sent a text to Reid: *Hey, something came up, will explain in person, but I have to cancel our post-time capsule sleepover tomorrow. I'm still really looking forward to our date Saturday.*

And then, she finally responded to Becca: *Sure, I'll let you know when I am free this weekend.*

She seriously hoped she was doing the right thing.

CHAPTER EIGHTEEN

Reid admired the fresh orchid purple ink filling in the last triangle on her tattoo. "This was a really great idea, Auds," she said, glancing at Audrey, who sat on the opposite end of Jeremy's living room couch.

She hoped the compliment would coax a smile from Audrey, who had seemed distant all day. She assumed it was because of whatever had come up that had made Audrey cancel their night together. She'd have been lying if she'd said she didn't feel disappointed when she'd read Audrey's text. She'd been looking forward to holding Audrey in her arms all week.

She hoped they could talk about what was going on, but between getting the tattoos and driving to Jeremy's, they hadn't had a moment alone.

Just as they sat at the kitchen table, Jeremy brought in pizza boxes and set them down. Reid slid a hand onto Audrey's thigh under the table and gave her a reassuring squeeze. Something was definitely off with her. The hint of a smile she flashed at Reid looked forced, a thousand thoughts swimming behind her eyes.

Reid just wished she knew what was going on so she could help.

Right as she was about to say something, Emma came into the kitchen with the time capsule. She placed the sky blue and white Toms shoebox right next to the two pizza boxes. A wave of nostalgia hit Reid. She'd forgotten how obsessed Sadie had been with those shoes. At one point, she'd had about ten pairs and would incessantly remind all of them that the company would deliver a pair of shoes to a child in need for each pair someone bought, so really, her obsession was for a good cause.

Without even opening the box, it already felt like 2013.

As everyone helped themselves to pizza, Sadie's pride and joy—her border collie mix, Charlie—wagged his tail more enthusiastically as he sat right next to Jeremy.

"You know, I haven't seen Charlie this energetic since...well... Sadie died," Jeremy said as he grabbed two slices of pizza.

"That's because he smells pepperoni," Emma said teasingly and looked back down at Charlie. "I'm so sorry your parents are vets. I'd give you a pepperoni because you're just the bestest boy."

"Sorry, Charlie, we have a time capsule to open," Jeremy said and patted his head. "Reid, will you do the honors?"

She wiped her hands on a paper towel before opening the box. Inside, a white envelope rested on top written in Sadie's purple handwriting: *Please open the time capsule with Jeremy. He won't shut up about it.*

Reid laughed as she read that part out loud. She glanced at Audrey to see if it had elicited even a smile. She sighed when Audrey's face remained blank.

"I just really want to know what's in the box," Jeremy said. "It holds a part of Sadie's life that I've never seen before."

"You should do the honors and read the letter," Reid said. "That's what we did on the trip. We all took turns, and now it's yours."

His eyes widened. "Really?"

"Go for it," Emma said.

A soft smile landed as he opened up the envelope and unfolded the letter. "Wow, she even wrote this in purple pen?"

"Jer, she wrote *every* letter in purple pen," Emma said. "Your wife had a serious obsession."

His smile grew wistful. "I know."

Hi friends...plus Jeremy, give Charlie a kiss for me please.

Welcome to the summer of 2013, the last summer of our youth. I can't believe it's been eleven years since that night we created the bucket list and started our time capsule. I did have the pleasure of opening and going through it, and wow, I totally forgot about Emma's quest to get a six-pack so she could impress the Berkeley boys. Now that was a different time.

But in all seriousness, going through this box was another reminder of how much I truly love you. I'd give anything to go back to that summer and experience it again. Cheering on Emma during her early morning runs, the rest of us blasting Audrey's iPod from the comfort of Reid's really crappy AC-less Buick. We were so committed to this bucket list and to our friendship, which I guess was easy to do before life started happening and slowed our momentum.

I hope that when you go through the time capsule, you remember that last summer we had at home, the last summer of our youth. You three were truly the best friends I could have ever asked for. Love you more than I can put into words.

XOXO Sadie

Jeremy let out a deep exhale. "I'm probably going to cry, aren't I?"

"You won't be the only one," Emma said.

Reid pushed down a swell of guilt remembering her role in the end of their friend group. She took a deep breath and leaned in, trying to remember what they put in their time capsule all those years ago.

Jeremy pulled out a handful of pictures, his gaze steady on them. "These are some old photos," he said, looking up and waving them.

The first picture was of the four of them in Sadie's bedroom, posing for the selfie on her bed. They'd joked how the picture would probably turn out like crap, and even though Sadie's forehead was cut off and the photo was blurry, it looked perfect.

There were pictures from graduation day—the four of them in their awful brown gowns—pictures of them with classmates they hadn't spoken to since high school, and various pictures from that summer.

"Oh, look, it's a picture of you guys getting your tattoos," Jeremy said, pointing to a picture of Reid getting inked.

They pulled out and examined each item afterward: Sadie's gold graduation cap tassel with a 2013 chain dangling off it, Emma's maroon

Fitbit she'd donated at the end of the summer because she was done "getting fit for her freshman year," Audrey's iPod touch that she'd had all throughout high school and added to the box once she switched to an iPhone, and a ticket stub from when the four of them saw Taylor Swift's Red tour just days before they'd left for college.

As he passed the items around, Reid kept a close eye on Audrey. Jeremy and Emma seemed too excited to notice her subdued demeanor, but Reid certainly wasn't. She realized this was probably what it felt like to see someone's emotional walls and not be able to break them. Usually, she was the one doing the hiding.

She didn't like the feeling one bit. "Is everything okay?" she whispered.

Audrey shrugged. "I just have a lot on my mind. I'll fill you in when we get a chance to chat alone. I promise, it's not related to us."

Emma handed Audrey the stack of pictures. "It's hard to believe this is all from eleven years ago." When she passed Audrey the ticket stub, she narrowed her eyes. "Hey, Auds, you all right? You've been really quiet."

Audrey tacked on the fakest smile Reid had ever seen. "I'm fine. It's just been a long week." She looked at her half-eaten slice of pizza that she hadn't touched since they'd opened the time capsule. Jeremy got up and started collecting the paper plates, giving them space to talk.

Reid combed through her brain for any reason Audrey might be upset. She thought back to their casual and flirty texts throughout the week, and nothing seemed obvious. Maybe she was worried about Emma noticing them leave together and wanted to play it safe? Maybe it was a work issue that had popped up or something with her dad. Whatever it was, Reid felt frustrated that Audrey hadn't even told her the basic details before they'd all gotten together.

Reid met Emma's concerned stare, and she looked as confused as Reid felt. She raised her eyebrows at Emma expectantly, attempting to telepathically say, "You are the therapist here, say something."

Emma looked back at Audrey. "Did something happen?"

Audrey hesitated for a moment before letting out a heavy exhale.

"Something happened," Reid said. Her muscles tensed.

"Becca texted me last night," Audrey said, her voice dropping.

Emma's mouth dropped, and Reid's stomach coiled like she was punched in her pizza-filled stomach. She felt stupid that she hadn't even considered that Audrey's mood could be Becca related. A mix of hurt and confusion bubbled to the surface as she realized that Becca must have been why Audrey had canceled their plans.

"Oh, okay," Emma said with surprise in her voice. "That's a bit of a plot twist."

"It absolutely is."

"What did she say?"

Audrey gave Reid an apologetic look, pulled out her phone, and read Becca's text out loud. Each sentence added to Reid's anxiety. Her nerves bubbled in her throat and left a sour taste in her mouth. Or maybe that sour taste was the snarky comments that quickly rose to the surface of her mind. She wasn't quite sure, but for the time being, she swallowed the snark.

"Wow, okay," Emma said. "Did you respond?"

"Yeah, I just said I'd meet up with her later tonight."

The room started to spin. Why the hell hadn't Audrey told her about this before they'd met up today? Was she hoping to get back together with Becca? How could she cancel their plans for someone who had treated her so terribly? Reid knew if she asked these questions, her shaking voice would give them away to Emma, so she tightened her jaw and stared at Audrey in shock.

"How are you feeling about it?" Emma said.

"I'm, I don't know, I have a lot of thoughts."

"Like what?"

"I have a lot of conflicting emotions."

"Conflicting emotions?" Reid couldn't help herself, and the question came out much sharper than she intended.

Audrey's possibly cheating ex-girlfriend wanting to get back with her shouldn't have warranted "conflicting emotions."

"Let her explain, Reid," Emma said through a sigh.

"What? I didn't know there would be conflicting emotions."

"Well, there are," Audrey snapped.

Why was she sniping back? Her defensiveness must have been because she hadn't gotten over Becca…or whatever idea of Becca that lived in her head. Reid knew the pain of an unexpected breakup, but she had been so focused on whatever was happening between them that she hadn't considered Becca's lingering impact on Audrey. She liked what she and Audrey had and didn't want it to end, especially for a woman who hadn't appreciate Audrey when she'd had her.

Reid internally kicked herself for opening up. She should have trusted her instincts, the ones that had grown with each devastating setback in her dating life.

"What are your emotions?" Emma said.

Audrey chewed her lip. "I don't know. I'm angry and confused and disoriented, and I want answers. I want to know when she started thinking about breaking up with me, why it came out of left field, why the hell she was flirting with Maya, if she's with Maya."

"And what happens if she's not with Maya, and she says it all was a mistake, then what?" Reid said.

"Her text says she wants to apologize and give me answers, not that she wants to get back together," Audrey said. But the fact that she couldn't look Reid in the eyes didn't make her very convincing.

Reid felt like an absolute idiot. Of course Audrey was still a mess over her first dramatic lesbian breakup. How could Reid let herself feel safe with someone who was in no position to actually date?

But the fact that she'd gotten pushed aside to cater to Becca was a punch to the stomach. Even if their hookup was nothing more than a fling to Audrey, Reid still deserved to hear this without other people around. Emma's presence made it so she couldn't ask the questions she really needed to.

"I think it's fair that you feel confused," Emma said to Audrey. "Your breakup was really devastating, and you have the chance to get the answers you've been wanting. Are you upset she texted you? Sad? Relieved?"

Audrey paused yet again. Reid was getting really sick of this conversation. The discomfort of hearing Audrey conflicted over her shitty girlfriend made her skin burn and crawl. "I think, all of the above."

Reid's entire stomach bottomed out.

"It's okay to miss her, " Emma said. "It's okay to want to reconcile, and it's okay to be confused, but your decision shouldn't be based on feelings."

She wanted to yell at Emma. This was a time for her to take off her therapist hat and actually be real with Audrey. Giving Becca any time of day wasn't worth her time, and it would be detrimental. She could already picture Audrey being a mess over Becca's answers. Why couldn't Emma just say that?

"I just want some clarity," Audrey said. "I still feel the whiplash."

"I bet," Emma said. "Hopefully, you two talking about it will give you that. But be cautious if she tries to get back together."

"I doubt that will happen," Audrey said.

Reid let out a humorless laugh. "Why not? Your ex-girlfriend is after a feeling, and it's called external validation."

Audrey let out a grunt, ran both her hands through her hair, and stood, saying, "I need some air."

"And I need to go," Reid said, standing too.

Emma and Audrey both shot her a surprised look.

"Really?" Emma said, confused.

"I'm tired, and I have an early class tomorrow."

Audrey's features contorted at the lie. Reid didn't understand why she looked so perplexed and hurt, as if she was still thinking Reid would want to spend another second engulfed in this ridiculous conversation.

"Oh, okay," Emma said. She stood and gave her a hug. "Are you sure you're all right?"

The softness in her voice made Reid's eyes sting. She willed away the threatening tears and forced a smile. "I'm fine."

Emma frowned, but Reid couldn't worry about Emma believing her. She just needed to get out of the house. She called her good-byes to Jeremy and went straight to her car. Right as she opened up the driver's door, she heard Audrey calling her name.

"Reid, wait. I need to talk to you—"

She turned and found Audrey scampering down the driveway in her socks. "You had all day to tell me, but instead, you drop that bomb in front of Emma? What happened to telling me in person? Like, privately?"

"I'm…I'm sorry. That was my plan, but then Emma asked—"

"And you could have told her you didn't want to talk about it. You could have told me over text, but instead, I'm blindsided in front of her, and I just have to play it cool as if we didn't just sleep together last weekend?"

"That was never my intention, Reid."

"And here I thought this was something work related or that your dad needed you. I didn't think I'd get pushed aside for Becca."

"You didn't get pushed aside. I don't want to go on the date and be distracted by all the possible things she could want to talk about. I thought it would be better if I got it out of the way so I could enjoy our time together."

"So I get the short end of the stick? The woman who discarded you gets priority?"

"That's not what I'm trying to do. I just want to get this over with and move on."

"And what if she wants to get back together?"

Audrey frowned. "I never said I was considering getting back together with her."

"You didn't have to." She got in the car and buckled her seat belt. "It's written all over your face."

"That's very presumptuous. Becca and I have a history, and I deserve to know what the hell is going on so I can move on with my life."

"Okay, well, good luck exploring that history."

"Reid, stop. You know how hard this has been for me," Audrey said defensively.

She laughed. "Oh, I do. I spent the entire road trip listening to it and was dumb enough to think you were ready to actually date me."

"You aren't dumb. I'm still processing everything—"

"You're setting yourself up to get your heart destroyed again. You're not going to change her, Audrey. Trust me, I know." She turned on the car.

"Are you seriously going to just leave? Without talking about this? Just like last time?"

"Wow," Reid said in utter disbelief. She didn't think Audrey still had it in her for cheap jabs. "Clearly, you need some time and space to *process* everything, and so do I. I hope you get everything you want from her."

When Audrey's mouth opened, Reid shut the door and backed out of the driveway. As she drove away, tears rolled down her cheeks. Audrey acting evasive and not clueing her into what was going on felt like a betrayal of their budding trust. The reasons their friendship originally ended came flooding back.

She had been naive to think that lightning couldn't strike twice.

Chapter Nineteen

Audrey's head hadn't stopped spinning since she'd read Becca's text, and her heart hadn't stopped hurting since Reid had looked absolutely shattered and driven away. She was so mad at herself for not telling Reid about her plan before they'd all gotten together.

She had been so excited for their weekend together, especially their date Saturday. She'd thought about it all week, staring at her closet, trying to figure out what to wear. Had she made the right choice canceling tonight? Instead of getting lost right now in Reid's beautiful eyes, she was sitting on her patio love seat, waiting for Becca to pull up in her driveway. Hopefully, it would be worth it, and Becca would answer all the questions that had piled like bricks on her sternum for the past month.

If she could redo yesterday, she would have done it in a heartbeat. She would have pulled Reid aside and told her before their tattoos and explained why she needed to talk to Becca before they could go on their first real date. She'd butchered it so easily and quickly, and her stomach churned as she wondered if she'd just ruined everything she had with Reid, the unexpected person who'd helped her through her worst days.

When Becca's dark gray Honda Civic pulled into her driveway, an uncomfortable sensation slithered throughout her body, suffusing her limbs with heaviness. She hated how her chest lurched when Becca got out of the car. Unlike the majority of the time they'd spent together, Becca was clad in lounging attire: a black tank top that offered a modest yet enticing view of her cleavage and jean shorts that flaunted her muscular athletic legs. Audrey felt a surge of hurt as she pictured Becca and Maya training for the marathon….and other things that would have helped tone her legs.

As Becca stepped up on the patio, Audrey noticed she was wearing makeup. Either she had just come from somewhere or she was dressing up to impress Audrey. Whatever the reason, she looked beautiful. Audrey chastised herself for the involuntary stomach flip when Becca approached. That wasn't supposed to happen after the past month of pain, anger, and a newfound connection with Reid. She wasn't supposed to feel any lingering spark of attraction to a woman who broke her heart, and yet, here she was with a traitorous body.

"Hey," Becca said in a soft tone. She extended her arms just a bit, but Audrey wasn't going to fall for her deliberately sexy outfit or the civil, sympathetic hug. She knew if she accepted her hug, the feelings she was trying to tame would erupt all over her, and she couldn't let her feelings get in the way of the facts.

Becca had blindsided her at her lowest. She had to keep reminding herself that every time the spark flickered in her.

"Hey," she said flatly and remained in her seat.

Becca's arms fell to her sides as her smile dwindled. She took a seat on the patio swing, leaving a safe distance between them. "How are you?" she said, seemingly struggling to look her in the eye. "How was the trip?"

No part of Audrey had the urge to share any part of her life now. Becca had made it clear by the way she'd left that she genuinely didn't care that much. "It was fine. We don't have to do this, you know. The small talk. You said you wanted to talk, so let's just get into it."

"Okay, if that's what you really want."

"I think I deserve some answers. I thought what we had was worth more than being blindsided with a breakup right before I went on a trip…and right in the middle of grieving my best friend." She was thankful that the anger started rising in her and killed off the remaining desire for things to go back to how they were before.

"I know the timing was really bad, and I'm sorry about that, I really am. It's just that things had been off for a while and—"

"Things were off because Sadie was dying, Becca. I don't know what you were expecting from me."

"I wanted to feel wanted. We went from being inseparable and all over each other to having barely any physical or emotional connection. I know how much losing Sadie destroyed you. I know because I was there. I watched it all. I don't regret taking care of you or being there for you when you needed someone, but it was really hard for me too. You hardly asked me how I was doing, you made no effort to try to do anything with me, and for a while, I could let it go because you were struggling."

"And instead of, I don't know, talking to me about it, your immediate go-to was to break up with me?"

"I didn't feel like I had the space to say anything."

Audrey held in her eye roll at Becca's cop-out answer. "So you broke up with me instead, bailing when things got tough instead of talking?"

Becca looked at her hands. "I'm sorry, Audrey. I didn't want to put any more pressure on you. It felt wrong to advocate for myself."

"It's not wrong to advocate for yourself, Becca. But we both know that's not the whole story."

"What do you mean?"

"I think there was someone else."

Becca froze.

"Well, was there?"

"Audrey—"

"It's a yes or no. Did you really not think I would see your pictures of you and Maya at the You Hall? You really think I didn't see those flirty comments just days after we broke up?"

"You saw those?"

Audrey laughed. "Seriously? Of course I did. They were right in front of my face on your Instagram. You could have at least had the decency to block me or hide the posts from me."

"I didn't even think about that."

"Were you cheating on me?" The hurt rose in her so high, she was close to yelling. "I don't know what's so difficult about the question."

"Nothing actually happened while you and I were together—"

Audrey's eyes widened. "Wow. Fuck you, Becca."

"It took me by surprise, it took us both by surprise. I never once lied to you."

Even though Audrey desperately tried to swallow back her tears, they seeped out of her like a broken dam.

"It was a mistake, Audrey. All of it was a mistake." Becca shook her head as her voice cracked.

Audrey swatted at the pesky tears continuing to free fall. "Why was it a mistake?"

"Long story short, she's not you."

Don't you dare let this get to you. She doesn't get to drop you for Maya and then play the victim. She took a deep breath. "Then, why did you break up with me?"

"Because." She finally looked up. "I was being selfish. The last couple of months have been extremely hard on both of us for different reasons, and I felt so lost."

"Lost?"

"I just…you pulled away and rightfully so. You were going through a lot, but…I just….I missed you. I missed the spark, our connection, what we had when we started dating. It was clear Maya liked me, and it felt so good and enticing."

"So now that you dipped your finger in someone else, and it didn't fulfill your fantasy, you want me back?" Audrey said, still lost in Becca's tornado of confessions.

"I've always wanted you, Audrey. I just wanted how things were before—"

"Before Sadie died?"

Becca shook her head. "Before life got in the way. I know I lost your trust. I get that. I know trust takes time, and I'm committed to earning that trust back if you're willing to give me some time."

"Becca," Audrey said, low and stern.

Her eyebrows rose. "What?"

Audrey could hear the panic in Becca's voice, as if she'd been swimming in a pool of regret and guilt since they'd broken up. She might not have had any trust for Becca anymore, but hearing the crack in her voice and seeing the pain in her eyes was a clear indication that she wasn't bullshitting. "This is a lot, Becca. The breakup gave me whiplash. This is giving me whiplash—"

"I know," she said sympathetically. "I know I hurt you. I know that I ruined us, but I don't feel lost anymore. I want what I had with you. More than anything. I love you, Audrey. That never stopped."

"Don't say that," Audrey said, and another round of tears stung her eyes. "Don't say it if you don't mean it."

"Of course I mean it. You know that."

"I don't, though." Her voice cracked. "You broke up with me when I really needed you just to chase a fantasy instead of doing the work to maintain a relationship. How is that love? How could I ever trust that it won't happen again?"

"If you give me the time, I'll show you the kind of girlfriend that I know I can be, one who you absolutely deserve."

In all of the scenarios Audrey had played in her head in the last twenty-four hours, she'd never imagined this would happen. Reid was completely right about Becca's intentions, and Audrey felt unprepared. Becca got off the swing and walked over to sit next to her on the love seat. Audrey's body vibrated at being so close, smelling the familiar perfume that had once comforted her, seeing the watery eyes that used to stare lovingly into hers.

Becca reached for her hand and held it, and even though Audrey wanted to pull away, she couldn't. Her hand lay limp, Becca's thumb gently caressing her knuckles.

"Audrey," Becca said, low, soft, and convincing. She used her free hand to wipe away Audrey's tears, and Audrey's face naturally fell into her tender, consoling touch. Becca's hand stopped wiping and palmed her face. Telling her to stop danced on Audrey's tongue but didn't waltz through her lips like she wanted it too. Her brain and heart fought, yet again, for dominance.

She met Becca's gaze and searched for the truth behind those brown eyes.

Becca's stare fell to her mouth, and she leaned in. Audrey didn't move, knowing she had the power to stop all of it. That she needed to stop it. Becca's soft lips met hers with extreme hesitancy. The kiss felt full of promises, as if Becca was trying to convince her how sorry she was. Audrey searched inwardly for some indication that their pieces were falling back into place or that familiar spark that lit up her limbs and made her body beg for more. Instead, her entire body tensed, and she flinched away. Becca's eyes shot open, rounded in one last plea for Audrey to forgive her.

Kissing Becca wasn't the same as before. It didn't feel safe, and she didn't feel protected. All of it felt forced, fitting a round peg into a square hole.

It didn't feel anything like kissing Reid.

"I can't do this," Audrey said, barely above a whisper. "I'm sorry, Becca, but it's too late."

"Audrey—"

She peeled Becca's hand off hers and stood. "We can't go back to what we had before. I don't know how I could ever feel safe with you after you ended things like you did. I'm sorry, but I…I think you should go."

Becca hung her head for a second, wiped her face, and stood. "I'm really sorry, Audrey," she said, waiting a second as if giving Audrey one last chance to take it all back.

"Please go."

Becca nodded in acceptance, and without saying anything else, she walked back to her car.

Becca's touch had felt like a hug from a cactus, her lips a bitter taste that Audrey wanted to scrub off. If Becca kissing her had a positive side, it was that Audrey now wanted nothing more than to be in Reid's warm, gentle arms. Feeling her embrace had become the safety net she needed. She wanted Reid even more than she did before her conversation with Becca.

When Audrey went inside, she wiped the last taste of Becca from her mouth.

CHAPTER TWENTY

Cameron's mouth hung open. "Are you fucking kidding me?"

"No, I'm not," Reid said, wishing she was.

"Well, that's a fucking plot twist. My God." He washed his surprise back with a long sip from his glass of Magnolia Springs red blend.

Reid needed a drink, or rather, an entire bottle to nurse the ache still lodged in her chest from Friday. She hadn't had the energy to drive back to Oceanside last night, so she'd driven from Jeremy's to her Mom's house. She'd spent the entire night and day wallowing in her old childhood room, keeping her phone on *do not disturb*, and dodging prodding questions from her mom. Out of concern, her mom had called Cameron for backup, and he'd driven out to Temecula to grill her with questions.

It was now Saturday evening, and they were on the outdoor patio of Magnolia Springs. A gorgeous sunset, the view of the rolling vineyards, and lots of wine were just what the doctor ordered to get her talking. The doctor, of course, being Cameron. He'd insisted Reid get out of the house, and Magnolia Springs was practically their home away from home.

Plus, she couldn't beat the family discount the Lins always gave them when they visited.

"I can't believe you hooked up with Audrey."

"Yeah, neither can I, and it's seeming like a giant mistake."

"Have you heard from her at all?"

She shrugged. "I put my phone on *do not disturb* after I left Jeremy's yesterday. I don't care about whatever she has to say."

Cameron gave her a side-eye. "Reid."

"What? Clearly, it was a one time, meaningless thing. If that wasn't the case, she wouldn't have canceled on me for her shitty ex. Or she would have at least told me about it before we were with Emma and Jeremy. She acted so surprised when I was upset. She knows all about Natalie and Shelby. She knows I take dating seriously, and she acted like all of this was so…trivial. If she wants to give Becca another chance, she can have at it."

He thinned his lips into a disapproving scowl. "Don't wall yourself off again."

"Why not? It prevents people from hurting me. I shouldn't even care so much. We've only slept together once."

"Because maybe it wasn't trivial for you."

"I have no idea how I feel. I thought I did, but I don't anymore."

"I think your reaction means you have real feelings and are afraid of losing her."

Her eyes stung. Natalie and Shelby had crinkled her up like a useless piece of paper. She's worked hard to smooth out those wrinkles, and she refused to let anyone else treat her like she was discardable. God, she was so tired of feeling broken. She wanted nothing more than to be whole, and Audrey was the first person in a long time who had made her feel that.

Of course she was absolutely afraid of losing her.

"I really am," Reid admitted, barely above a whisper.

"Reid." Cameron's voice softened as he placed a hand on her shoulder. "Don't you think you need to talk to her?"

Instead of responding, she diverted the conversation. "Since when did you turn into a hopeless romantic?"

"When are you going to become one?"

She did consider herself the occasional hopeless romantic but usually kept it boxed up. Like how her mom cared for her grandma's china set. Those porcelain plates only saw the light of day on Thanksgiving and Christmas and remained in the kitchen hutch for the other three hundred and sixty-three days of the year.

"When I meet the right woman," she said, filling her glass.

"You're only going to meet her if you let people in, and you don't. Sometimes it takes a few bumps to find the right person."

She raised a skeptical brow. "And you've been there?"

"You might be five years older than me, but I can confidently say I'm in love. Has it always been easy with Wendy? Absolutely not. But I knew what we had was worth the hard work and commitment. And most of the time? Smooth sailing."

"That's because you're more patient than me."

He rolled his eyes and finished his glass before pouring himself another. "It takes patience to be in a relationship, Reid. Stop acting like Mom and Dad. You think you've mastered this facade that you don't need anyone, but I *know* you. I see right through it."

She leaned into the table, deciding to entertain him in whatever moral lesson he wanted to instill in her. "Okay, Cameron," she said doubtfully. "What do you see?"

He flashed a confident smirk, as if he knew he would win her challenge. "You want love. You want a real connection. You want a partner who adds value to your life. But you're fucking terrified of them letting you down...or you letting them down. So you retreat and hide because it's much easier than the potential heartbreak that comes from opening up to another person. You can open up to me because we're family. We tell each other everything. Always have. But you could have so much more. You could have love, passion, connection, a partner who loves you inside and out, and who knows exactly how to help you mend all those broken pieces. I know you want that, and if you let that special person in, you'll see that it's worth the potential for hurt. Whatever you had with Audrey made you start to open up to that possibility. That alone is worth noting."

"I know you're right. That's why this hurts so much."

He creased his eyebrows. "Do you really think Audrey viewed this as trivial? She doesn't seem like the type of person to just, I don't know, sleep with people."

"She isn't, but on the road trip, she said maybe she needed to try it, and apparently, I was the one she decided to try with. I thought last weekend meant something more, which is why I opened up and asked her out. Now I just feel like an idiot."

Right as Cameron opened his mouth to say something, someone yelled, "You!"

Both of them turned. Emma headed toward them in a determined walk. Her boyfriend, Matt, trailed behind her, his lips pressed together as if in warning. Emma aimed a finger at Reid. Without her saying more, Reid knew she was in trouble. Emma had texted her on Friday night asking if she was okay, but Reid had never texted her back. She was too wrapped up in her wallowing.

"I know I owe you a text," Reid said.

"You owe me a text *and* an explanation," Emma said, pulling a chair out to sit. She faced Cameron. "Hi," she said before snapping back at Reid.

Reid looked over her shoulder and waved to Matt. "Hi, Matt."

"I think we're all going to need another bottle of wine," he said. "You might need something stronger. Just a warning. I'll go order it."

Reid frowned and looked back at Emma. "What's going on?"

Matt excused himself to go back inside. Emma's glare bore right into her. "Spill."

"Spill what?"

"Don't act dumb."

Reid let out an uncomfortable laugh. "Ems, I have no idea what you're talking about."

She crossed her arms. "Oh really? There's nothing you want to tell me? At all?"

Of course there was something, but she wasn't going to hand that information over so easily. "Uh, no?"

"What about you, Cameron," Emma said, turning to him, "will you tell me?"

"You know what?" he said, backing his chair up and standing. "I think Matt is going to need help with the wine. I don't think he knows about the seasonal specials."

"Cameron," Reid said sternly.

"How will he know the specials? I *have* to tell him." He quickly left the table, leaving her on her own with Emma who looked directly at her, unblinking.

She imagined this was what Emma did with her clients when they wouldn't open up during sessions. She just zeroed in on them and had an excruciating awkward stare down until they fessed up.

"Do you think I'm dumb?" Emma said. She placed her elbow on the table and rested her knuckles against her temple. "I have a master's degree in psychology. I get paid to read people. Do you really want to play this game?"

"I have no idea what game we're playing."

"Oh, okay, we're playing it. What's going on between you and Audrey?"

Reid's entire body flushed. Prickly bumps popped up her spine and on the back of her neck. "What…what are you talking about?"

"I thought something was up on our trip. By the end, you were a bit flirty, but I mostly assumed that was just friendly banter. I even noticed you using your special, 'I'm into you' voice with her after you removed her tick. But Friday night solidified everything. You looked so hurt about Becca texting her, and it's not like you were particularly quiet as you argued on the driveway. Plus, now you are ignoring all my texts."

"Because I've been dealing with stuff."

"Yeah? With what?" she asked pointedly.

"How did you even know I was here?"

"Reid, you share your location with me. I checked to make sure you weren't dead and found your little minion face at the winery. Now stop deflecting, and answer the question."

Reid grunted and drank a few large gulps of wine, searching for liquid courage.

"Fine. There was something going on. *Was* is the key word in this."

Emma tossed her hands in the air before they fell back on the table. "I fucking knew it. When the hell did it happen?"

Reid rolled her eyes. "Gatlinburg. We made out in the hot tub. After you had gone to bed."

Emma laughed. "You're welcome, then. Is that it?"

"We also made out after the moonshine tasting."

Emma's mouth fell. "Oh my God." She pulled out her phone and sent a text. "Matt needs to hurry up with the wine. Jesus." She set her phone down and looked at Reid with anticipation. "Have you two… slept together?"

A pain lodged itself in Reid's chest. She thought about how exciting and thrilling their one night together was. She'd started the road trip living in a world of gray, and for a while, Audrey had added streaks of color she hadn't seen in months. But the color had vanished just as unexpectedly as it had arrived. Without Audrey, the familiar grays seemed so much darker now.

"Yeah," Reid said softly, full of regret. She hung her head and stared at her wineglass. "Last weekend. She spent the night, and it felt so right, for me at least. I thought she felt the same. I was supposed to spend the night with her on Friday, and I had this entire date planned for her tonight. Obviously, that's not happening."

Emma's features softened with sympathy. "Reid, I'm so sorry."

She shrugged. "It is what it is. Just like Audrey said, they have history. We had two days together. I can't compete with that."

"Reid, I think it's very important to understand Audrey was hurting and confused by the text. She wasn't necessarily wanting to get back together with Becca."

She considered Emma's observation. When she took emotions out of the equation, she could see how getting a text from Becca, alongside what she and Reid were starting, could have thrown Audrey off and made her confused.

She noticed Emma's phone flashing with a text. Emma read it and then turned her phone face down on the table. "Matt said they ran into my mom and got swept up in the tasting room. I guess she's pushing the pinot noir on them and bringing out a bunch of food. Typical Marian."

"That sounds way more fun than this conversation."

Emma shook her head. "No. We're talking first, and then we join the guys. Have you and Audrey talked since Friday night?"

Reid laughed. "No. I'm sure she has been texting, but I haven't wanted to check my phone. Has she talked to you?"

Emma shook her head. "I haven't heard from her since Friday. She left in a hurry and said she needed some space."

"You'd get more out of her than I would."

"I think when you feel ready, you should read her messages and give her a chance to explain."

She wanted her phone to light up with Audrey's name. She wanted to take Audrey on a nice date. She wanted Audrey's arms around her. She wanted to sit close to Audrey and exist in a world that was only theirs, supporting each other through the chaos they'd spent ten days driving away from. Now that they were back home, she wanted Audrey to fill her space with joy, friendship, and care.

She wanted Audrey.

"Remember Sadie's firefly letter?" Reid said, her mind placing her right in the middle of Sadie's words.

"Yeah. What about it?"

"She's my speck of light in darkness."

"Reid," Emma said soothingly and placed a gentle hand on her wrist.

The nurturing touch prompted her eyes to well with hot tears. She gave a one-arm shrug and swallowed back the pulling in her throat. She couldn't break down in the middle of the Magnolia Springs patio with dozens of people surrounding them. "Maybe this is just a sign that it's a mistake. We have a whole past, and we're friends, well, we're supposed to be friends. It could get messy again. Look at it now, it's already messy."

Reid's thoughts swam through her mind like an unruly school of fish. What had happened when Audrey talked to Becca? Were they back together? If not, did Audrey even want to date Reid? Should they even pursue something more than a friendship? If they did—and it didn't work—would they lose each other forever? It would be easy to agree they'd hooked up because they had gotten carried away in their grief. But the thought of fully letting this connection with Audrey go settled like sour milk in her stomach.

"I know this is a complicated situation," Emma said, "but if Audrey is your spark of light, don't you think you need to at least be honest with her?"

Reid shook her head and blinked back tears. "All of my past instincts are telling me to run, but I don't think I can."

"There you go. Listen to your body and follow that light."

The spiraling in her head danced with the wine to create a pounding headache. She needed to go back to her mom's and sleep it off. Everyone tried to convince her to stay to drink the wine that Matt and Cameron came back with, but she knew she wouldn't be good company.

When she got back to her mom's, she locked herself in her room, chugged some water, and popped some ibuprofen. She finally checked her phone and saw multiple missed texts from Audrey. She decided to deal with it in the morning with a clear head.

She really needed Sadie right now, and the fact that she couldn't text her broke Reid's heart. When giving advice, Emma always tried to remain neutral and diplomatic. Sometimes, Reid just needed Sadie's unfiltered and brutally honest opinions. Both friend roles were necessary, but at the present moment, she wanted Sadie. She needed to hear the tough love that Sadie had never been shy about giving.

She imagined what Sadie would have thought of all of this. She'd loved gossip. She'd always called it "tea time" and insisted on drinking a glass of wine because it was "so much better than crappy tea." Reid missed their tea time. If Sadie was still alive, Reid would have texted her the teapot emoji. She knew Sadie would have driven over with a bottle and her undivided attention.

Reid was so desperate for a semblance of her old life that she grabbed her phone and texted Sadie the teapot emoji. The message turned green right after it was sent, and Reid's entire body numbed.

Jeremy must have canceled her phone plan, which meant soon, some stranger would be assigned Sadie's number, if they hadn't been already.

She flipped her phone over on the nightstand, clutched a pillow to her chest, and cried all of her pain into the fabric that smelled like home.

Chapter Twenty-one

Reid had clearly said something to Emma because Saturday night, Audrey's phone blew up with messages. Not feeling up for texting, she called Emma and filled her in on, well, everything.

"And now Reid won't respond to my texts or calls," Audrey said, finishing her story.

"She's hurting and confused," Emma said. "You need to keep trying."

If only Audrey knew how to keep trying. After they hung up and before going to sleep, she sent one last message. *Hey, I am so sorry for what happened. Can we please get together and talk soon?*

As she waited for a text, she tossed and turned all night, checking for a response. It terrified her how much she missed Reid. Going one day without talking to her since their night together felt more painful than the six years of not being friends. Losing Sadie and going through a breakup had pushed her off a cliff, and yet, there had come an expected parachute saving her in the form of Reid.

The next morning, she eagerly checked her phone. Her stomach tightened at the sight of Reid's name.

I'm off work Wednesday. We can talk in person then.

Cold, but better than no response. Now she just had to plan a seriously good apology. Because God, did she want to fix this.

❖

Audrey barely made it to Wednesday. She tried distracting herself over the last few days by helping her dad paint his kitchen cabinets, but she spent most of her time ruminating on her impending conversation with Reid.

As she opened her door, her first instinct was to give Reid a hug, but her wounded and hurt expression kept Audrey's arms at her sides. "Hey," Audrey said, trying to sound as calm as her anxiety would allow.

"Hi."

Those beautiful eyes that only a week and a half ago looked at her with equal parts vulnerability and desire now held contempt and pain.

Audrey opened the door. A stifling breeze of awkward tension trailed behind Reid and settled into the living room. Reid perched on the side of the couch closest to the door as if ready to make a mad dash out at any moment. Audrey got the memo; she needed space.

Audrey sat on the opposite end and faced her. "Reid, I'm so sorry about Friday. I was just blindsided by Becca's text, and I wasn't thinking clearly. You were in the forefront of my mind the entire time. I wanted to get the conversation with her out of the way as soon as possible so I could focus completely on whatever is happening with us. I should have found time to tell you before our tattoos. It was unfair to tell you about it in front of Emma when we couldn't have a real conversation. The last thing I wanted was for it to ruin our date. I was really looking forward to it."

"Yeah, me too," she said just as flatly. Her hardened stare felt as blinding as the sun, and looking directly at her started to become too intense.

Audrey pulled her eyes away and focused on the remote lying between them. "I did talk to Becca," she said as the confession grated against her throat.

"Yeah, and did she want you back?"

Audrey thinned her lips. She braced for Reid's response after she told her the truth. "Yeah."

Reid let out a hollow laugh. "Wow."

"And you were right, she'd hooked up with Maya. And then she kissed me and—"

"Whoa, what? She kissed you?"

Audrey swallowed hard at the anger surfacing in Reid's tone. "Yes, but it didn't—"

"And what did you do? Did you stop her?"

"I did, and you want to know why?" When Reid didn't respond, Audrey finally looked up. "Because I felt nothing. If anything, it gave me the ick. I told her to leave. I got the answers I wanted, and now that I have them, no part of me wants her back. At all."

"Why did this have to ruin our weekend?"

"I'm so sorry it did. I needed that closure, Reid. She pulled the rug out from underneath me. You know that more than anyone."

"I do, but seeing her didn't change how she treated you."

"I wanted to talk to you about it, but you ran away. If you just gave me the chance to explain—"

"We talked about her the entire trip. I didn't want to hear any more about how you were confused. Plus, we had plans, and when you canceled them for Becca, it made me feel like I didn't matter to you at all."

"Being with you has made me feel so much joy and comfort during a time when I felt so incredibly sad and numb. That means something to me. *You* matter to me."

Audrey watched her words pierce through Reid's stubborn walls, her posture relaxing and her features softening. As the anger seemed to dissolve, Audrey realized that at Reid's core was fear. The way her eyebrows rose and her eyes rounded, she could easily see Reid was frightened about something.

"I have a feeling that I might mean something to you to," Audrey said delicately, the admission hammered in her ribcage.

"You do," Reid barely muttered above a whisper. "And that scares me."

"Why?"

"Because *you* scare me."

Audrey swallowed. "Why?"

Reid looked back at her lap and faltered. "Because you make me feel a lot of things I haven't felt in a long time. Actually, I don't think I've ever felt like this. It's terrifying because I don't want to lose you."

"You haven't lost me."

Reid picked at her thumb cuticle while chewing her lip.

Audrey scooted over to her side of the couch and placed a hand on her fidgeting hand and gave it a comforting squeeze.

"I thought I was going to," Reid said, staring at their connected hands. At least she wasn't pulling away, a sign that they were getting somewhere. "And what I feel now…I know it's risky. We just reconciled, and if we keep doing what we're doing, and it fails again, I'm going to lose you all over again. The first time was hard, but this time? It will be so much harder because of how you make me feel. The last time I came close to feeling like this about someone, I was crushed entirely."

"But I'm not Natalie or Shelby, Reid. I would never treat you like that…and you know that."

Reid pressed her lips together, still focused on their hands. "But I got a glimpse of that hurt on Friday. I know this thing is new, but it really hurt to not know why you canceled, find out in front of Emma, and then feel pushed aside for Becca after everything she put you through…after everything *we've* been through."

"I didn't mean to hurt you, Reid."

She looked up. "I know, but that's what's scary. We don't try to hurt people, and it still happens. We're still recovering from six years ago."

"But we're not those versions of ourselves anymore. We're older, more mature—"

"Yeah, but we're also friends. What happens if we explore this, and it fails? I feel like that would really solidify the end of our friendship forever. We wouldn't come back from that, two heartbreaks? We would resent each other."

"And what if it actually works out? What if we explore this, and it lasts? Have you ever asked yourself that?"

She knew Reid hadn't. One thing she'd really learned about Reid on their trip was just how scared she was about anything remotely risky or anything that could end in real feelings. For Audrey, taking that huge risk with Reid was worth it. She didn't have to think twice. She would always choose getting her heart broken for trying rather than always wondering what could have been.

She could feel Reid shutting down and rebuilding her walls. As frustrating as that was, she knew Reid needed patience and compassion.

"I know you're scared," Audrey said, clasping her hands tighter. She figured a nurturing touch would help ease her. "I'm scared too, but the feelings are mutual, you know. This feels different, and the last couple of days of not being able to text you have sucked. I don't want to go back to that."

"So I'm not out of my mind for feeling this way about you?"

Audrey shook her head. "If you're out of your mind, then I'm out of my mind, but I really don't care because I'm really confident in what I want, and that's you, Reid." Audrey's heart thrummed so hard waiting for Reid to say something, she worried that it would fall right out of her chest. Reid seemed deep in thought, and Audrey couldn't read the expression on her face. "What are you thinking?" she said through her shaky voice.

Reid pressed her lips together again as if swallowing the truths Audrey desperately wanted to hear. "I'm thinking about you kissing her."

Audrey grabbed her free hand and rubbed her thumb over Reid's knuckles. "The kiss didn't mean anything, Reid. I literally went inside and wiped my mouth."

She didn't mean for it, but Reid let out a chuckle. "You didn't."

Audrey nodded. "I promise you that I did. I don't regret the kiss, but that's only because it gave me clarity. When I kiss you, I feel it everywhere. All over my body, in my chest, in my stomach, and I can confidently say that never happened with Becca. I didn't know kissing someone could make me feel *that* much. I feel it in my bones with you."

Reid rapidly blinked back tears with no success. They fell down her cheeks. She attempted to wipe them away as if hoping Audrey hadn't seen them. Audrey leaned in to dry her cheek and held her hand there. Her stomach flipped. That touch alone sparked a fire low inside her that was ignited by tenderness and comfort. All she wanted to do was hold Reid, anything to tell her that she didn't have to be this afraid.

"Please tell me what you're thinking," Audrey said, placing her palm over her chest to steady her chaotic heartbeat.

"I really want to kiss you again," Reid said, meeting her gaze. The desire in her voice sent a flash of arousal through Audrey.

"Then kiss me."

Once Reid's stare zeroed in on Audrey's mouth, she leaned, and finally, those lips Audrey had been desperately craving latched on to hers. Every nerve ending flickered with every movement Reid made against her lips. The baby hairs on her arms rose, the top of her head tingled and radiated down to her toes, and her pulse found a way to thrum in her throat.

How was this feeling not worth the risk? How could she turn away from this? Reid had the ability to kiss her inside and out; the steady grip her palms had on Audrey's face hinted that she didn't want to lose this either, that this feeling of a firework sparking to take off and explode was just as rare for her as it was for Audrey.

If there was any morsel of a doubt living inside Audrey, kissing Reid again and washing the last taste of Becca from her mouth was enough for her to be fully confident. She was all in. A mountain of poker chips pushed to the middle as she collected her prize, a needy whimper that slipped from Reid and landed on Audrey's tongue.

This was absolutely worth risking their friendship, the glue still drying between their broken piece.

Who was she kidding? Their friendship had ended six years ago. This was new territory, and Audrey was desperate to explore it. So she did just that. She teased Reid's lips with her tongue, and Reid's mouth fell open. Each kiss and swipe of the tongue made Audrey starved for more. She slipped her hand behind Reid's head and grabbed a fistful of hair.

Reid moaned into her mouth, and need overtook Audrey. She was desperate for more. She slid her hands up under the hem of Reid's shirt, grazing her skin, and a trail of goose bumps sprouted under her fingertips. She loved feeling and hearing how much her touch and her kissing affected Reid.

They peeled each other's clothes off and got lost in each other's limbs and warm, soft skin. Audrey thanked her former self for buying such a comfortable wide couch as Reid straddled her, and she felt the evidence of her arousal gliding along her bare thigh with each rock of Reid's hips. That alone caused a soft murmur to escape her. She raked her nails up Reid's back and held on to her like a railing, bracing herself for how every rock and ragged breath unraveled her. Reid was slick against Audrey's skin, a low panting of moans accompanied her movements. Audrey loved the feeling of Reid's naked body molded against hers. She could have Reid draped all over her for the entire night and still find new parts she had to touch, taste, and explore.

Reid attempted to maintain control. Audrey had a feeling that she had always been the one leading, guiding, and giving during sex. Even though Audrey was desperate for release, she needed to show Reid how sorry she was and how much she appreciated her.

Audrey pulled away and sucked on the soft part of Reid's neck. Reid's head fell back as she let out another groan, granting Audrey full access to whatever parts of her body Audrey wanted. She swirled her tongue on Reid's warm skin, sucked another moan from her, and trailed her tongue down her collarbone and the swell of her breasts. She brought one of her perfect nipples into her mouth and sucked until it hardened against her tongue. God, Reid had the most perfect, reactive nipples. It was hard to pry her mouth away, and Reid's sounds and undulating hips didn't help. She buried her face in the crook of Audrey's neck, sighing and breathing heavily as Audrey licked and teased. Audrey slipped a hand in between them to feel just how wet Reid was for her and almost melted into the soft fabric of the couch with pleasure.

She hooked her hands around Reid's thighs and looked up at her. "Sit on my face," Audrey said. "I need to taste you."

Reid's mouth parted, but she didn't hesitate. She moved up and positioned herself on the back of the couch, and when Audrey sucked her into her mouth, Reid cried out. She ran her tongue deep into Reid, and fuck, she tasted incredible. She gripped Reid's thighs tighter.

"Fuck, Audrey," Reid moaned as if she had no control over what came out of her. She moved herself all over Audrey's mouth. "You feel so good."

Audrey sank her tongue inside her and savored how the wetness collected on her face. She devoured her, lapping along her. Audrey knew she was close by the way her legs squeezed around her head. She moved her hands up to Reid's ass and gripped her. Reid's hips bucked at the touch, another cry escaped and filled the living room.

"I'm so close."

Audrey pried her mouth away to say, "Come for me, baby." She flicked, licked, and sucked on Reid's clit as Reid rode her face, faster, harder, and determined.

"Fuck, I'm coming," Reid said through labored breaths.

Her body tensed around Audrey's head as she cried out the earth-shattering orgasm. Audrey's moans wrapped around Reid's, her sounds enough to completely undo Audrey. As Reid slowed, Audrey slid her hands from her ass to her waist and pressed her thumbs gently along her sexy hip bones.

Finally, Reid sank back down to lie on top of Audrey, who nuzzled her damp face in her neck. Audrey grazed her fingertips along Reid's back, feeling her heart pounding against her.

Reid placed a hand on Audrey's cheek and lifted her head just a bit for her lips to press against Audrey's earlobe. "You're so fucking sexy, Audrey," she said softly. She pulled away and her stare darkened on her, determination saturating her pupils. "I need you to spread your legs now."

Audrey listened to that gentle yet authoritative tone. Once she spread her legs, Reid crawled on top of her, positioning her wet pussy over Audrey's. At the touch, Audrey whimpered. Reid's stare never wavered. She cupped Audrey's face and slowly started to rock herself. Their sweat-slicked bodies molded them together. Audrey's body had never felt so alive or cherished before. They moved in rhythm, riding, holding, and gasping for breath. She clasped Reid's back as another curl of heat ignited in her, pushing her toward the precipice.

"Not yet, baby," Reid said and kissed her tenderly before pressing her forehead against Audreys. "I want to come with you."

Audrey locked her stare on Reid's, waiting for Reid to tell her when she could come. Both their hips rocked and searched for release, and as Reid's eyebrows rose, her sounds becoming louder, she said through a ragged breath, "Now."

She didn't have to tell her twice. Audrey wrapped her arms around Reid, nuzzled into her neck, and cried out her orgasm. She bit Reid's shoulder, and Reid let out the most delicious sounds she'd ever heard.

It was easily the most intimate experience of her life.

When Reid collected her breath, she planted soft kisses all over Audrey's forehead, down her cheek to her neck, and across her collarbone before pulling back to look at her.

Audrey opened her eyes, finally feeling her lungs fill up. Pink blossomed on Reid's cheeks as she collected her breath. Her eyes blazed a trail across Audrey's naked body, sending a shiver through her.

"Fuck, Reid," Audrey said as she collected her breath. She tucked a loose wavy strand behind Reid's air and held her cheek. "That was…"

"I know," Reid said.

"Wow."

Reid plopped to the side and cozied up against Audrey, slinging an arm over her stomach. They lay there for a few moments, steadying their breath. The air-conditioning provided a wave of coolness over their warm bodies.

Audrey had never expected to have the most passionate sex she'd ever had with Reid Haley on her couch, but my God, now that she had, she could make love to her all night and never get bored.

She traced invisible lines along Reid's arm as her other hand held Reid's. She loved how tightly Reid held her, as if how they were lying now, with Reid's head on her shoulder and arm securing her close, wasn't enough contact for her.

"Audrey?"

"Hm?" She still couldn't form words. All she had the strength to do was play with Reid's interlocking fingers, loving the way their hands looked meshed together.

"I have pretty big feelings for you."

Audrey glanced up and found Reid's smile blossoming like the sun poking through after a summer thunderstorm. "I know. I have big feelings for you. It's weird how right this feels," Audrey said. "Isn't it?"

Reid kissed her cheek. She loved how affectionate Reid was after sex. It was a completely different side to her, one that Audrey had a feeling she needed more of in the regular day-to-day.

"Maybe we should have been doing this the entire time," Reid said.

Audrey laughed. "Sleeping together?"

Reid nodded. "Imagine if we just stopped yelling at each other in Springfield and kissed instead. All our problems would have been solved."

"I don't know if your twenty-three year old self was thinking about that in the moment."

"No, maybe not, but my fourteen year old self did in your cute gym shorts."

"So you've mentioned."

"But guess what?" Her voice softened as she skimmed her fingers along Audrey's arm.

"What?" Audrey said, goose bumps breaking out on her skin.

"The crush has come back, and I really, *really* would love to take you out on that date. Just promise you won't cancel this time."

"I won't, I swear." She leaned in and sealed her promise with a long, tender kiss.

Epilogue

January 29, 2026

“I can’t believe we did it,” Reid said, staring at the bucket list that sat on Jeremy’s coffee table. “We really finished the list.”

Audrey sat next to her on the couch, holding her hand. Emma and Matt sat on the opposite end, and Jeremy and Cameron were cross-legged on the floor, directly in front of the table. Charlie, wearing a birthday hat, stared intently at Jeremy’s plate of pepperoni pizza, panting eagerly.

“Did we ever think it would happen?” Audrey said.

“I had major doubts,” Reid answered.

Audrey squeezed her hand. “We know, babe. You were a big grouch about it when we read the first letter.”

“Because of you,” Reid said and planted a kiss on her cheek.

“Aw,” Cameron sang, “And now you two are living together and so in love.”

Reid caught Audrey’s soft smile. One of the greatest honors of her life had been watching the sparkle revive in Audrey’s eyes again over the last year and a half. It was even more special because she was the reason for it, as Audrey had said countless times over their relationship. The last year and a half had been the hardest, saddest, and most challenging time but also the most rewarding. She’d learned how to experience joy alongside grief, something she’d had no idea was possible. Her love for Audrey had tucked between the spaces of her heartbeats, settled carefully inside her guarded heart, and blossomed in between the cracks. She made Reid feel whole again.

That summer, Audrey had accepted a seventh grade language arts position at one of the Oceanside middle schools. The driving back and forth from Oceanside and Temecula had been too much for how often they'd wanted to spend time with each other. The weekdays apart had dragged like the endless expanse of the ocean.

After Sadie died, Reid had dreaded the mornings, waking up with cement blocks of grief and dread stacked on her diaphragm. Then, Audrey had slipped back into her life like a warm breeze, and now, she looked forward to them. Cooking breakfast for Audrey in bed before they spent a few hours at the beach, or even better, when she brought Audrey to the boat to scuba dive with her classes.

She wasn't sure how she got so damn lucky.

Audrey's smile grew. "I do love you," she said. "Very much."

"*Et tu, Bruté*?" Audrey flashed her a playful side-eye. Reid laughed and planted a soft kiss on her lips. "And I love you," Reid whispered in her ear. "Very much."

"If Sadie were here, she would definitely be taking credit for this," Jeremy said.

"She'd probably want to officiate the wedding," Cameron added.

"Which is happening when, by the way?" Matt asked, leaning over Emma to catch a glance at them.

"When all of you shut up about it," Reid said. "The more you ask, the more I want to wait out of spite."

"Why are you so stubborn?" Audrey said.

Reid grinned. "You seem to like it."

"I do. Just a little," Audrey said, holding up an inch with her fingers.

"I just have to say," Emma chimed in. "We always said we wanted to find someone who looked at us the way Jeremy and Sadie looked at each other—"

Jeremy raised an eyebrow. "Wait. Seriously?"

"Seriously," Emma replied.

Jeremy's smile consumed his face, as if he'd gotten lost in the happy memories with Sadie. "I'm so glad you two found that with each other. I'm even more honored that my relationship with Sadie was the bar. She would totally be gloating right now."

"As always," Reid added.

"As much as I am here for this lovefest, we have something important to do," Emma said and pulled a purple pen from her purse.

"Who wants to do the honors?" Audrey said.

Reid looked over at Jeremy. "I think you should do it."

"Are you sure?" he said, his voice softening.

"Absolutely. We couldn't have finished this list without you."

Emma stood and walked over to him, bestowing the pen like a knight would a sword. "I present you with this purple pen. May the force be with you."

Jeremy bowed his head and accepted it.

"You'll reference *Star Wars* but refuse to watch it with me?" Matt said.

"Babe, I'm not going to watch seventeen *Star Wars* movies," Emma said as she took her spot back on the couch.

"There aren't seventeen. There are eleven."

"It's the same thing: too many."

Jeremy directed the pen at Emma. "There's no *Star Wars* slander in this house." He hovered the pen over the final bucket list item, *Start a tradition*, took a deep breath and drew a purple line through it.

Sadie would have loved that their tradition was celebrating her birthday.

Just like last year, the first January 29th without Sadie, they kept it simple, feasting on pizza and cake and playing a bunch of games. It might not have sounded special to outsiders, but it was the perfect way to honor and remember her, and they knew Sadie wouldn't have wanted it any other way.

Reid stole a few glances while Audrey listened to everyone talk about Sadie. She honestly had no idea what she would have done without her. Audrey had encouraged her to open up and talk and face her grief head on.

As if she could feel Reid's stare, Audrey looked over and gave her a loving smile. "You okay?" she said softly enough that no one else heard.

Reid loved how often Audrey checked in. She was more than okay, but having someone so attentive and ready to pull her from the depths of despair was exactly why Audrey had felt like a life preserver for the last year and a half.

Reid loved how Audrey's eyes softened when they landed on her, and she knew that right after she told Audrey she was okay, Audrey would insert herself back into the conversation, letting go of that sparkle that only seemed to come out whenever she was looking at Reid.

She hadn't thought it was possible to love someone this much, but as she came to realize, Audrey McCann was in no way ordinary. All the best and happiest memories had Audrey in them.

"Yeah, I'm okay," Reid whispered through a smile. "I love you."

"And you know I love you just as much?"

Reid nodded. "I do. I feel it too." She kissed the back of Audrey's hand before mentally stepping back into reality. She faced the rest of the group. "Now, none of us have to be alone every January twenty-ninth."

"And it's now a day we don't have to dread," Audrey added. "I was actually really excited about seeing all of you, eating Sadie's favorite pizza, and playing all her favorite games."

Charlie licked his lips, and since the last time Reid had looked, he had inched closer to Jeremy's plate, and the birthday hat started tilting to the side. Jeremy patted his head, picked a pepperoni off his pizza, and held it up. Charlie swallowed it whole.

"Well, if Charlie is getting his treat," Emma said. She hopped off the couch once again and scampered into the kitchen where she grabbed the bottle of sparkling wine and flutes for everyone. Once she filled everyone's glass, she held hers up. "To Sadie and to finishing the bucket list."

"To Sadie and the bucket list," they echoed, clinking glasses.

After taking a sip, they turned their attention to the list on the table. Seeing all the items crossed off caused a small wave of emotion to wash over Reid. She couldn't believe they'd actually done it. Completing the list of eighteen promises they'd made thirteen years ago and a nineteenth from Sadie before she died.

"Happy thirty-first birthday, Sadie," Jeremy said with a smile that brimmed with tears. "Because of you, we're all here today, celebrating you, and we will continue to celebrate you every January twenty-ninth."

"And because of you, we finished the bucket list I honestly thought we wouldn't ever finish," Emma added.

"And you're the reason why the friend group is back together," Audrey said.

"And the reason why Audrey and I are together," Reid said, gazing at her.

"Get a room," Cameron said.

Reid shot him a glare. "Stop ruining my moments."

"Now that we have officially crossed off the last item, we have one more letter to read," Jeremy said, holding up the last envelope.

Reid couldn't believe it. It had been a year and a half since they'd read the letter for the time capsule. She'd had a feeling that when they finally decided on a tradition, it would probably include a letter, but she didn't know how listening to Sadie's words again would inflate the happiness in her lungs. The letters that used to feel like crushing pain now felt like the sunshine hitting her face after a cold dark winter.

"Are we ready?"

Reid looked at Audrey, then caught Emma's glance at them. They exchanged a smile, as if the same memories all swiped through their minds at the same time.

"I'm ready," Emma said.

"Me too," Audrey replied.

Reid smiled. "Me three. I miss those letters. Who should read it?"

Emma and Audrey responded at the same time, "You should, Reid."

She took the envelope from Jeremy and unfolded the letter. She inhaled a deep breath, cleared her throat, and read.

Hi friends!

I'M BACK! Did you miss me? I'm sure you did. I actually have no idea if or when you're going to read this, but I have faith that, at some point, you'll all be friends again and have started a tradition. I'm assuming you chose something absolutely wonderful. I wish I knew what it was, but I guess I'll know when I'm hooked up to the Afterlife Wi-Fi. You can run, but you can't hide. I'll always know.

"But this new bucket list item wasn't part of the original! It wasn't part of the blood oath," I'm sure Reid has already complained. As a

ghost, I get absolute immunity. I added this because, ideally, going on the road trip—and you know, me dying—mended the friend group. We created the bucket list because we wanted to stay close to each other throughout college. If you're reading this, I'm assuming that Rome didn't fall again, and I thought the three of you could use something to keep the friend group intact throughout adulthood.

Whatever that tradition is, my hope is that it continues to bring you together and help you create new memories. I might not have made it to thirty—silver lining is that I entered the pearly gates of Heaven with fabulous, winkle-free skin—but I still got a little taste of how fast life moves and pulls us away from loved ones. We can get so wrapped up in our life between jobs, family, relationships, and simply trying to stay afloat, and the last thing I want is for the chaos of life to once again sever the special friendship we have. How many people can say they're still best friends with the people they met at fourteen? We watched each other grow up, make mistakes, fall in love, and start families, all while standing right next to each other. And sure, there was a little hiccup, and the group broke apart, but if you're reading this now, you found a way to come back together, and still, not many people get to say that they're still friends with those they met when they were kids. That alone is something special and worth holding onto. I'm so proud of us, so proud of you.

I hope that whatever tradition you start grounds you and reminds you of the truly special bond we formed as kids. It's not something we should take for granted. Hold on to it, even during the times you inevitably annoy one another.

Well, my hand is officially cramping, so I guess I need to wrap it up. Thank you for giving me the best fifteen years of my life. I love you all to the edge of the universe and back. This is me officially signing off.

XOXO forever,

Sadie

About the Author

Morgan Lee Miller is a Goldie Award-winning author of contemporary romance novels packed with all the feelings. She's a Northeast Ohio transplant living in Washington, DC, with her two feline children, Milo and Elsa. She loves all things animals, spicy food that makes her cry, and the thing she loves the most: procrastinating on writing her next novel.

Books Available from Bold Strokes Books

Behold My Heart by Ronica Black. Alora Anders is a highly successful artist who's losing her vision. Devastated, she hires Bodie Banks, a young struggling sculptor as a live-in assistant. Can Alora open her mind and her heart to accept Bodie into her life? (978-1-63679-810-3)

Fearless Hearts by Radclyffe. One wounded woman, one determined to protect her—and a summertime of risk, danger, and desire. (978-1-63679-837-0)

Forever Family by L.M. Rose. Two friends come together after tragedy to raise a baby, finding love along the way. (978-1-63679-868-4)

Stranger in the Sand by Renee Roman. Grace Langley is haunted by guilt. Fagan Shaw wishes she could remember her past. Will finding each other bring the closure they're looking for in order to have a brighter future? (978-1-63679-802-8)

The Nursing Home Hoax by Shelley Thrasher and Ann Faulkner. In this fresh take for grown-ups on the classic Nancy Drew series, crime-solving duo Taylor and Marilee investigate suspicious activity at a small East Texas nursing home. (978-1-63679-806-6)

The Rise and Fall of Conner Cody by Chelsey Lynford. A successful yet lonely Hollywood starlet must decide if she can let go of old wounds and accept a chance at family, friendship, and the love of a lifetime. (978-1-63679-739-7)

A Conflict of Interest by Morgan Adams. Tensions rise when a one-night stand becomes a major conflict of interest between an up-and-coming senior associate and a dedicated cardiac surgeon. (978-1-63679-870-7)

A Magnificent Disturbance by Lee Lynch. These everyday dykes and their friends will stop at nothing to see the women's clinic thrive and, in the process, their ideals, their wounds, and a steadfast allegiance to one another make them heroes. (978-1-63679-031-2)

A Marvelous Murder by David S. Pederson. When a hated director is found dead in his locked study, movie star Victor Marvel, his boyfriend Griff, and friend Eve seek to uncover what really happened to Orland Orcott. (978-1-63679-798-4)

Big Corpse on Campus by Karis Walsh. When University Police Officer Cappy Flannery investigates what looks like a clear-cut suicide, she discovers that the case—and her feelings for librarian Jazz—are more complicated than she expected. (978-1-63679-852-3)

Charity Case by Jean Copeland. Bad girl Lindsay Chase came home to Connecticut for a fresh start, but an old, risky habit provides the chance to save the day for her new love, Ellie. (978-1-63679-593-5)

Moments to Treasure by Ali Vali. Levi Montbard and Yasmine Hassani have found a vast Templar treasure, but there is much more to the story—and what is left to be found. (978-1-63679-473-0)

The Stolen Girl by Cari Hunter. Detective Inspector Jo Shaw is determined to prove she's fit for work after an injury that almost killed her, but a new case brings her up against people who will do anything to preserve their own interests, putting Jo—and those closest to her—directly in the line of fire. (978-1-63679-822-6)

Discovering Gold by Sam Ledel. In 1920s Colorado, a single mother and a rowdy cowgirl must set aside their fears and initial reservations about one another if they want to find love in the mining town each of them calls home. (978-1-63679-786-1)

Dream a Little Dream by Melissa Brayden. Savanna can't believe it when Dr. Kyle Remington, the woman who left her feeling like a fool, shows up in Dreamer's Bay. Life is too complicated for second chances. Or is it? (978-1-63679-839-4)

Emma by the Sea by Sarah G. Levine. A delightful modern-day romance inspired by Emma, one of Jane Austen's most beloved novels. (978-1-63679-879-0)

Goodbye, Hello by Heather K O'Malley. With so much time apart and the challenges of a long-distance relationship, Kelly and Teresa's second chance at love may end just as awkwardly as the first. (978-1-63679-790-8)

One Measure of Love by Annie McDonald. Vancouver's hit competitive cooking show Recipe for Success has begun filming its second season and two talented young chefs are desperate for more than a winning dish. (978-1-63679-827-1)

The Smallest Day by J.M. Redmann. The first bullet missed—can Micky Knight stop the second bullet from finding its target? (978-1-63679-854-7)

To Please Her by Elena Abbott. A spilled coffee leads Sabrina into a world of erotic BDSM that may just land her the love of her life. (978-1-63679-849-3)

Two Weddings and a Funeral by Claudia Parr. Stella and Theo have spent the last thirteen years pretending they can be just friends, but surely "just friends" don't make out every chance they get. (978-1-63679-820-2)

Coming Up Clutch by Anna Gram. College softball star Kelly "Razor" Mitchell hung up her cleats early, but when former crush, now coach Ashton Sharpe shows up on her doorstep seven years later, beautiful as ever, Razor hopes the longing in her gaze has nothing to do with softball. (978-1-63679-817-2)

Firecamp by Jaycie Morrison. Going their separate ways seemed inevitable for two people as different as Fallon and Nora, while meeting up again is strictly coincidental. (978-1-63679-753-3)

Fixed Up by Aurora Rey. When electrician Jack Barrow and artist Ellie Lancaster get stuck on a job site during a blizzard, close quarters send all sorts of sparks flying. (978-1-63679-788-5)

Stranded by Ronica Black. Can Abigail and Whitley overcome their personal hang-ups and stubbornness to survive not only Alaska, but a dangerous stalker as well? (978-1-63679-761-8)

Whisk Me Away by Georgia Beers. Regan's a gorgeous flake. Ava, a beautiful untouchable ice queen. When they meet again at a retreat for up-and-coming pastry chefs, the competition, and the ovens, heat up. (978-1-63679-796-0)